"And the Bathroom Must Have a Large Tub"

GET-RICH-QUICK
WALLINGFORD

A cheerful account of the rise and fall of
an American Business Buccaneer

By GEORGE RANDOLPH CHESTER

Author of
" The Making of Bobby Burnit," " The Cash Intrigue,"
Etc.

WITH FOUR ILLUSTRATIONS

Fredonia Books
Amsterdam, The Netherlands

Get-Rich-Quick Wallingford:

A Cheerful Account of the Rise and Fall of an
American Business Buccaneer

by

George Randolph Chester

ISBN: 1-58963-619-8

Reprinted from the 1908 edition

Fredonia Books
Amsterdam, The Netherlands
http://www.fredoniabooks.com

In order to make original editions of historical works
available to scholars at an economical price, this
facsimile of the original edition of 1908 is
reproduced from the best available copy and has
been digitally enhanced to improve legibility, but the
text remains unaltered to retain historical
authenticity.

TO THE LIVE BUSINESS MEN OF AMERICA—THOSE
WHO HAVE BEEN "STUNG" AND THOSE WHO
HAVE YET TO UNDERGO THAT PAINFUL
EXPERIENCE—THIS LITTLE TALE IS
SYMPATHETICALLY DEDICATED

Contents

CONTENTS

CONTENTS

7

CONTENTS

GET-RICH-QUICK WALLINGFORD

CHAPTER I

IN WHICH J. RUFUS WALLINGFORD CONCEIVES A BRILLIANT INVENTION

THE mud was black and oily where it spread thinly at the edges of the asphalt, and wherever it touched it left a stain; it was upon the leather of every pedestrian, even the most fastidious, and it bordered with almost laughable conspicuousness the higher marking of yellow clay upon the heavy shoes of David Jasper, where he stood at the curb in front of the big hotel with his young friend, Edward Lamb. Absorbed in "lodge," talk, neither of the oddly assorted cronies cared much for drizzle overhead or mire underfoot; but a splash of black mud in the face must necessarily command some attention. This surprise came suddenly to both from the circumstance of a cab having dashed

9

up just beside them. Their resentment, bubbling hot for a moment, was quickly chilled, however, as the cab door opened and out of it stepped one of those impressive beings for whom the best things of this world have been especially made and provided. He was a large gentleman, a suave gentleman, a gentleman whose clothes not merely fit him but distinguished him, a gentleman of rare good living, even though one of the sort whose faces turn red when they eat; and the dignity of his worldly prosperousness surrounded him like a blessed aura. Without a glance at the two plain citizens who stood mopping the mud from their faces, he strode majestically into the hotel, leaving Mr. David Jasper and Mr. Edward Lamb out in the rain.

The clerk kowtowed to the signature, though he had never seen nor heard of it before—"J. Rufus Wallingford, Boston." His eyes, however, had noted a few things: traveling suit, scarf pin, watch guard, ring, hatbox, suit case, bag, all expensive and of the finest grade.

"Sitting room and bedroom; outside!" directed Mr. Wallingford. "And the bathroom must have a large tub."

The clerk ventured a comprehending smile as he noted the bulk before him.

WALLINGFORD

"Certainly, Mr. Wallingford. Boy, key for 44-A. Anything else, Mr. Wallingford?"

"Send up a waiter and a valet."

Once more the clerk permitted himself a slight smile, but this time it was as his large guest turned away. He had not the slightest doubt that Mr. Wallingford's bill would be princely, he was positive that it would be paid; but a vague wonder had crossed his mind as to who would regrettingly pay it. His penetration was excellent, for at this very moment the new arrival's entire capitalized worth was represented by the less than one hundred dollars he carried in his pocket, nor had Mr. Wallingford the slightest idea of where he was to get more. This latter circumstance did not distress him, however; he knew that there was still plenty of money in the world and that none of it was soldered on, and a reflection of this comfortable philosophy was in his whole bearing. As he strode in pomp across the lobby, a score of bellboys, with a carefully trained scent for tips, envied the cheerfully grinning servitor who followed him to the elevator with his luggage.

Just as the bellboy was inserting the key in the lock of 44-A, a tall, slightly built man in a glove-fitting black frock suit, a quite

11

ministerial-looking man, indeed, had it not
been for the startling effect of his extravagantly curled black mustache and his pierc-
ing black eyes, came down the hallway, so
abstracted that he had almost passed Mr.
Wallingford. The latter, however, had eyes
for everything.

"What's the hurry, Blackie?" he inquired
affably.

The other wheeled instantly, with the snappy
alertness of a man who has grown of habit to
hold himself in readiness against sudden sur-
prises from any quarter.

"Hello, J. Rufus!" he exclaimed, and shook
hands. "Boston squeezed dry?"

Mr. Wallingford chuckled with a cumbrous
heaving of his shoulders.

"Just threw the rind away," he confessed.
"Come in."

Mr. Daw, known as "Blackie" to a small but
select circle of gentlemen who make it their
business to rescue and put carefully hoarded
money back into rapid circulation, dropped
moodily into a chair and sat considering his
well-manicured finger-nails in glum silence,
while his masterful host disposed of the bellboy and the valet.

"Had your dinner?" inquired Mr. Wallingford as he donned the last few garments of a fresh suit.

"Not yet," growled the other. "I've got such a grouch against myself I won't even feed right, for fear I'd enjoy it. On the cheaps for the last day, too."

Mr. Wallingford laughed and shook his head. "I'm clean myself," he hastened to inform his friend. "If I have a hundred I'm a millionaire, but I'm coming and you're going, and we don't look at that settle-up ceremony the same way. What's the matter?"

"I'm the goat!" responded Blackie moodily. "The original goat! Came clear out here to trim a sucker that looked good by mail, and have swallowed so much of that citric fruit that if I scrape myself my skin spurts lemon juice. Say, do I look like a come-on?"

"If you only had the shaving-brush goatee, Blackie, I'd try to make you bet on the location of the little pea," gravely responded his friend.

"That's right; rub it in!" exclaimed the disgruntled one. "Massage me with it! Jimmy, if I could take off my legs, I'd kick myself with them from here to Boston and never lose a stroke. And me wise!"

"But where's the fire?" asked J. Rufus,

bringing the end of his collar to place with a dexterous jerk.

"This lamb I came out to shear—rot him and burn him and scatter his ashes! Before I went dippy over two letter-heads and a nice round signature, I ordered an extra safety-deposit vault back home and came on to take his bank roll and house and lot, and make him a present of his clothes if he behaved. But not so! *Not*—so! Jimmy, this whole town blew right over from out of the middle of Missouri in the last cyclone. You've got to show everybody, and then turn it over and let 'em see the other side, and I haven't met the man yet that you could separate from a dollar without chloroform and an ax. Let me tell you what to do with that hundred, J. Rufe. Just get on the train and give it to the conductor, and tell him to take you as far ay-way from here as the money will reach!"

Mr. Wallingford settled his cravat tastefully and smiled at himself in the glass.

"I like the place," he observed. "They have tall buildings here, and I smell soft money. This town will listen to a legitimate business proposition. What?"

"Like the milk-stopper industry?" inquired

Mr. Daw, grinning appreciatively. "How is your Boston corporation coming on, anyhow?"

"It has even quit holding the bag," responded the other, "because there isn't anything left of the bag. The last I saw of them, the thin and feeble stockholders were chasing themselves around in circles, so I faded away."

"You're a wonder," complimented the black-haired man with genuine admiration. "You never take a chance, yet get away with everything in sight, and you never leave 'em an opening to put the funny clothes on you."

"I deal in nothing but straight commercial propositions that are strictly within the pale of the law," said J. Rufus without a wink; "and even at that they can't say I took anything away from Boston."

"Don't blame Boston. You never cleaned up a cent less than five thousand a month while you were there, and if you spent it, that was your lookout."

"I had to live."

"So do the suckers," sagely observed Mr. Daw, "but they manage it on four cents' worth of prunes a day, and save up their money for good people. How is Mrs. Wallingford?"

"All others are base imitations," boasted the large man, pausing to critically consider the flavor of his champagne. "Just now, Fanny's in New York, eating up her diamonds. She was swallowing the last of the brooch when I left her, and this morning she was to begin on the necklace. That ought to last her quite some days, and by that time J. Rufus expects to be on earth again."

A waiter came to the door with a menu card, and Mr. Wallingford ordered, to be ready to serve in three quarters of an hour, at a choice table near the music, a dinner for two that would gladden the heart of any tip-hunter.

"How soon are you going back to Boston, Blackie?"

"To-night!" snapped the other. "I was going to take a train that makes it in nineteen hours, but I found there is one that makes it in eighteen and a half, so I'm going to take that; and when I get back where the police are satisfied with half, I'm not going out after the emerald paper any more. I'm going to make them bring it to me. It's always the best way. I never went after money yet that they didn't ask me why I wanted it."

The large man laughed with his eyes closed.

"Honestly, Blackie, you ought to go into legitimate business enterprises. That's the only game. You can get anybody to buy stock when

you make them print it themselves, if you'll
only bait up with some little staple article that
people use and throw away every day, like ice-
cream pails, or corks, or cigar bands, or—or—
or carpet tacks.'' Having sought about the
room for this last illustration, Mr. Wallingford became suddenly inspired, and, arising,
went over to the edge of the carpet, where he
gazed down meditatively for a moment. ''Now,
look at this, for instance!'' he said with final
enthusiasm. ''See this swell red carpet fas-
tened down with rusty tacks? There's the
chance. Suppose those tacks were covered
with red cloth to match the carpet. Blackie,
that's my next invention.''

''Maybe there are covered carpet tacks,'' observed his friend, with but languid interest.

''What do I care?'' rejoined Mr. Wallingford. ''A man can always get a patent, and
that's all I need, even if it's one you can throw
a cat through. The company can fight the patent after I'm out of it. You wouldn't expect
me to fasten myself down to the grease-cov-
ered details of an actual manufacturing business, would you?''

''Not any!'' rejoined the dark one emphatically. ''You're all right, J. Rufus. I'd go
into your business myself if I wasn't honest.

But, on the level, what do you expect to do here?''

"Organize the Universal Covered Carpet Tack Company. I'll begin to-morrow morning. Give me the list you couldn't use.''

"Don't get in bad from the start," warned Mr. Daw. "Tackle fresh ones. The particular piece of Roquefort, though, that fooled me into a Pullman compartment and kept me grinning like a drunken hyena all the way here, was a pinhead by the name of Edward Lamb. When Eddy fell for an inquiry about Billion Strike gold stock, he wrote on the firm's stationery, all printed in seventeen colors and embossed so it made holes in the envelopes when the cancellation stamp came down. From the tone of Eddy's letter I thought he was about ready to mortgage father's business to buy Billion Strike, and I came on to help him do it. Honest, J. Rufus, wouldn't it strike you that Lamb was a good name? Couldn't you hear it bleat?''

Mr. Wallingford shook silently, the more so that there was no answering gleam of mirth in Mr. Daw's savage visage.

"Say, do you know what I found when I got here?" went on Blackie still more ferociously. "I found he was a piker bookkeeper, but with five thousand dollars that he'd wrenched out

18

of his own pay envelope, a pinch at a clip; and every time he takes a dollar out of his pocket his fingers creak. His whole push is like him, too, but I never got any further than Eddy. He's not merely Johnny Wise—he's the whole Wise family, and it's only due to my Christian bringing up that I didn't swat him with a brick during our last little chatter when I saw it all fade away. Do you know what he wanted me to do? He wanted me to prove to him that there actually was a Billion Strike mine, and that gold had been found in it!"

Mr. Wallingford had ceased to laugh. He was soberly contemplating.

"Your Lamb is my mutton," he finally concluded, pressing his finger tips together. "He'll listen to a legitimate business proposition."

"Don't make me fuss with you, J. Rufus," admonished Mr. Daw. "Remember, I'm going away to-night," and he arose.

Mr. Wallingford arose with him. "By the way, of course I'll want to refer to you; how many addresses have you besides the Billion Strike? A mention of that would probably get me arrested."

"Four: the Mexican and Rio Grande Rubber Company, Tremont Building; the St. John's

GET-RICH-QUICK

Blood Orange Plantation Company, 643 Third Street; the Los Pocos Lead Development Company, 868 Schuttle Avenue, and the Sierra Cinnabar Grant, Schuttle Square, all of which addresses will reach me at my little old desk-room corner in 1126 Tremont Building, Third and Schuttle Avenues; and I'll answer letters of inquiry on four different letter-heads, If you need more I'll post Billy Riggs over in the Cloud Block and fix it for another four or five.''

"I'll write Billy a letter myself," observed J. Rufus. "I'll need all the references I can get when I come to organize the Universal Covered Carpet Tack Company."

"Quit kidding," retorted Mr. Daw.

"It's on the level," insisted J. Rufus seriously. "Let's go down to dinner."

CHAPTER II

THERE were twenty-four applicants for the position before Edward Lamb appeared, the second day after the initial insertion of the advertisement which had been designed to meet his eye alone. David Jasper, who read his paper advertisements and all, in order to get the full worth of his money out of it, telephoned to his friend Edward about the glittering chance.

Yes, Mr. Wallingford was in his suite. Would the gentleman give his name? Mr. Lamb produced a card, printed in careful imitation of engraving, and it gained him admission to the august presence, where he created some surprise by a sudden burst of laughter.

"Ex-cuse me!" he exclaimed. "But you're the man that splashed mud on me the other night!"

When the circumstance was related, Mr. Wallingford laughed with great gusto and shook hands for the second time with his visitor. The incident helped them to get upon a most cordial footing at once. It did not occur to either of them, at the time, how appropriate it was that Mr. Wallingford should splash mud upon Mr. Lamb at their very first meeting.

"What can I do for you, Mr. Lamb?" inquired the large man.

"You advertised ——" began the caller.

"Oh, you came about that position," deprecated Mr. Wallingford, with a nicely shaded tone of courteous disappointment in his voice. "I am afraid that I am already fairly well suited, although I have made no final choice as yet. What are your qualifications?"

"There will be no trouble about that," returned Mr. Lamb, straightening visibly. "I can satisfy anybody." And Mr. Wallingford had the keynote for which he was seeking.

He knew at once that Mr. Lamb prided himself upon his independence, upon his local standing, upon his efficiency, upon his business astuteness. The observer had also the experience of Mr. Daw to guide him, and, moreover, better than all, here was Mr. Lamb himself. He was a broad-shouldered young man, who stood well upon his two feet; he dressed with a proper and decent pride in his prosperity, and wore looped upon his vest a watch chain that by its very weight bespoke the wearer's solid worth. The young man was an open book, whereof the pages were embossed in large type.

"Now you're talking like the right man," said the prospective employer. "Sit down. You'll understand, Mr. Lamb, that my question was only a natural one, for I am quite particular about this position, which is the most important one I have to fill. Our business is to be a large one. We are to conduct an immense plant in this city, and I want the office work organized with a thorough system from the beginning. The duties, consequently, would begin at once. The man who would become secretary of the Universal Covered Carpet Tack Company, would need to know all about the concern from its very inception, and until I have secured that exact man I shall take no steps toward organization."

Word by word, Mr. Wallingford watched the face of Edward Lamb and could see that he was succumbing to the mental chloroform. However, a man who at thirty has accumulated five thousand is not apt to be numbed without struggling.

"Before we go any further," interposed the patient, with deep, deep shrewdness, "it must be understood that I have no money to invest."

"Exactly," agreed Mr. Wallingford. "I stated that in my advertisement. To become secretary it will be necessary to hold one share of stock, but that share I shall give to the right applicant. I do not care for him to have any investment in the company. What I want is the services of the best man in the city, and to that end I advertised for one who had been an expert bookkeeper and who knew all the office routine of conducting a large business, agreeing to start such a man with a salary of two hundred dollars a month. That advertisement stated in full all that I expect from the one who secures this position—his expert services. I may say that you are only the second candidate who has had the outward appearance of being able to fulfill the requirements. Actual efficiency would naturally have to be shown."

Mr. Wallingford was now quite coldly insistent. The proper sleep had been induced.

"For fifteen years," Mr. Lamb now hastened to advise him, "I have been employed by the A. J. Dorman Manufacturing Company, and can refer you to them for everything you wish to know. I can give you other references as to reliability if you like."

Mr. Wallingford was instant warmth.

"The A. J. Dorman Company, indeed!" he

exclaimed, though he had never heard of that concern. "The name itself is guarantee enough, at least to defer such matters for a bit while I show you the industry that is to be built in your city." From his dresser Mr. Wallingford produced a handful of tacks, the head of each one covered with a bit of different-colored bright cloth. "You have only to look at these," he continued, holding them forth, and with the thumb and forefinger of the other hand turning one red-topped tack about in front of Mr. Lamb's eyes, "to appreciate to the full what a wonderful business certainty I am preparing to launch. Just hold these tacks a moment," and he turned the handful into Mr. Lamb's outstretched palm. "Now come over to the edge of this carpet. I have selected here a tack which matches this floor covering. You see those rusty heads? Imagine the difference if they were replaced by this!"

Mr. Lamb looked and saw, but it was necessary to display his business acumen.

"Looks like a good thing," he commented; "but the cost?"

"The cost is comparatively nothing over the old steel tack, although we can easily get ten cents a paper as against five for the common ones, leaving us a much wider margin of profit than the manufacturers of the straight tack obtain. There is no family so poor that will use the old, rusty tinned or bronze tack when these are made known to the trade, and you can easily compute for yourself how many millions of packages are used every year. Why, the Eureka Tack Company, which practically has a monopoly of the carpet-tack business, operates a manufacturing plant covering twenty solid acres, and a loaded freight car leaves its warehouse doors on an average of every seven minutes! You cannot buy a share of stock in the Eureka Carpet Tack Company at any price. It yields sixteen per cent. a year dividends, with over eighteen million dollars of undivided surplus—and that business was built on carpet tacks alone! Why, sir, if we wished to do so, within two months after we had started our factory wheels rolling we could sell out to the Eureka Company for two million dollars; or a profit of more than one thousand per cent. on the investment that we are to make."

For once Mr. Lamb was overwhelmed. Only three days before he had been beset by Mr. Daw, but that gentleman had grown hoarsely eloquent over vast possessions that were beyond thousands of miles of circumambient space, across vast barren reaches where desert sands

sent up constant streams of superheated atmosphere, with the "hot air" distinctly to be traced
throughout the conversation; but here was
something to be seen and felt. The points of the
very tacks that he held pricked his palm, and
his eyes were still glued upon the red-topped
one which Mr. Wallingford held hypnotically
before him.

"Who composes your company?" he managed to ask.

"So far, I do," replied Mr. Wallingford with
quiet pride. "I have not organized the company.
That is a minor detail. When I go searching
for capital I shall know where to secure it. I
have chosen this city on account of its manufacturing facilities, and for its splendid geo-
graphical position as a distributing center."

"The stock is not yet placed, then," mused
aloud Mr. Lamb, upon whose vision there already glowed a pleasing picture of immense
profits.

Why, the thing was startling in the magnificence of its opportunity! Simple little trick,
millions and millions used, better than anything
of its kind ever put upon the market, cheaply
manufactured, it was marked for success from
the first!

"Stock placed? Not at all," stated Mr.

Wallingford. "My plans only contemplate in-corporating for a quarter of a million, and I mean to avoid small stockholders. I shall try to divide the stock into, say, about ten holdings of twenty-five thousand each."

Mr. Lamb was visibly disappointed.

"It looks like a fine thing," he declared with a note of regret.

"Fine? My boy, I'm not much older than you are, but I have been connected with several large enterprises in Boston and elsewhere—if any one were to care to inquire about me they might drop a line to the Mexican and Rio Grande Rubber Company, the St. John's Blood Orange Plantation Company, the Los Pocos Lead Development Company, the Sierra Cinna-bar Grant, and a number of others, the addresses of which I could supply—and I never have seen anything so good as this. I am staking my entire business judgment upon it, and, of course, I shall retain the majority of stock myself, inasmuch as the article is my in-vention."

This being the psychological moment, Mr. Wallingford put forth his hand and had Mr. Lamb dump the tacks back into the large palm that had at first held them. He left them open to view, however, and presently Mr. Lamb picked out one of them for examination. This particular tack was of an exquisite apple-green color, the covering for which had been clipped from one of Mr. Wallingford's own expensive ties, glued to its place and carefully trimmed by Mr. Wallingford's own hands. Mr. Lamb took it to the window for closer admiration, and the promoter, left to himself for a moment, stood before the glass to mop his face and head and neck. He had been working until he had perspired; but, looking into the glass at Mr. Lamb's rigid back, he perceived that the work was well done. Mr. Lamb was profoundly convinced that the Universal Covered Carpet Tack Company was an entity to be respected; nay, to be revered! Mr. Lamb could already see the smoke belching from the tall chimneys of its factory, the bright lights gleaming out from its myriad windows where it was working overtime, the thousands of workmen streaming in at its broad gates, the loaded freight cars leaving every seven minutes!

"You're not going home to dinner, are you, Mr. Lamb?" asked Mr. Wallingford suddenly. "I owe you one for the splash, you know."

"Why—I'm expected home."

"Telephone them you're not coming."

"We—we haven't a telephone in the house."

"Telephone to the nearest drug store and send a messenger over."

Mr. Lamb looked down at himself. He was always neatly dressed, but he did not feel equal to the glitter of the big dining room downstairs.

"I am not—cleaned up," he objected.

"Nonsense! However, as far as that goes, we'll have 'em bring a table right here." And, taking the matter into his own hands, Mr. Wallingford telephoned for a waiter.

From that moment Mr. Lamb strove not to show his wonder at the heights to which human comfort and luxury can attain, but it was a vain attempt; for from the time the two uniformed attendants brought in the table with its snowy cloth and began to place upon it the shining silver and cut-glass service, with the center-piece of red carnations, he began to grasp at a new world—and it was about this time that he wished he had on his best black suit. In the bathroom Mr. Wallingford came upon him as he held his collar ruefully in his hand, and needed no explanation.

"I say, old man, we can't keep 'em clean, can we? We'll fix that."

The bellboys were anxious to answer summons from 44-A by this time. Mr. Wallingford never used money in a hotel except for tips. It was scarcely a minute until a boy had that collar, with instructions to get another just like it.

"How are the cuffs? Attached, old man? All right. What size shirt do you wear?"

Mr. Lamb gave up. He was now past the point of protest. He told Mr. Wallingford the number of his shirt. In five minutes more he was completely outfitted with clean linen, and when, washed and refreshed and spotless as to high lights, he stepped forth into what was now a perfectly appointed private dining room, he felt himself gradually rising to Mr. Wallingford's own height and able to be supercilious to the waiters, under whose gaze, while his collar was soiled, he had quailed.

It was said by those who made a business of dining that Mr. Wallingford could order a dinner worth while, except for the one trifling fault of over-plenty; but then, Mr. Wallingford himself was a large man, and it took much food and drink to sustain that largeness. Whatever other critics might have said, Mr. Lamb could have but one opinion as they sipped their champagne, toward the end of the meal, and this opinion was that Mr. Wallingford was a genius, a prince of entertainers, a master of finance, a gentleman to be imitated in every particular, and that a man should especially blush to question his financial standing or integrity.

They went to the theater after dinner—box seats—and after the theater they had a little cold snack, amounting to about eleven dollars, including wine and cigars. Moreover, Mr. Lamb had gratefully accepted the secretaryship of the Universal Covered Carpet Tack Company.

CHAPTER III

MR. WALLINGFORD'S LAMB IS CAREFULLY INSPIRED WITH A FLASH OF CREATIVE GENIUS

THE next morning, in spite of protests and warnings from his employer, Mr. Lamb resigned his position with the A. J. Dorman Company, and, jumping on a car, rode out to the far North Side, where he called at David Jasper's tumble-down frame house. On either side of this were three neat houses that David had built, one at a time, on land he had bought for a song in his younger days; but these were for renting purposes. David lived in the old one for exactly the same reason that he wore the frayed overcoat and slouch hat that had done him duty for many years—they made him as comfortable as new ones, and appearances fed no one nor kept anybody warm.

Wholesome Ella Jasper met the caller at the door with an inward cordiality entirely out of proportion to even a close friend of the family, but her greeting was commonplaceness itself.

"Father's just over to Kriegler's, getting his

glass of beer and his lunch," she observed as he shook hands warmly with her. Sometimes she wished that he were not quite so meaninglessly cordial; that he could be either a bit more shy or a bit more bold in his greeting of her.

"I might have known that," he laughed, looking at his watch. "Half-past ten. I'll hurry right over there," and he was gone.

Ella stood in the doorway and looked after him until he had turned the corner of the house; then she sighed and went back to her baking. A moment later she was singing cheerfully.

It was a sort of morning lunch club of elderly men, all of the one lodge, the one building association, the one manner of life, which met over at Kriegler's, and "Eddy" was compelled to sit with them for nearly an hour of slow beer, while politics, municipal, state and national, was thoroughly thrashed out, before he could get his friend David to himself.

"Well, what brings you out so early, Eddy?" asked the old harness maker on the walk home. "Got a new gold-mining scheme again to put us all in the poorhouse?"

Eddy laughed.

"You don't remember of the kid-glove miner taking anybody's money away, do you?" he

WALLINGFORD

demanded. "I guess your old chum Eddy saw
through the grindstone that time, eh?"

Mr. Jasper laughed and pounded him a
sledge-hammer blow upon the shoulder. It
was intended as a mere pat of approval.

"You're all right, Eddy. The only trouble
with you is that you don't get married. You'll
be an old bachelor before you know it."

"So you've said before," laughed Eddy,
"but I can't find the girl that will have me."

"I'll speak to Ella for you."

The younger man laughed lightly again.

"She's my sister," he said gayly. "I
wouldn't lose my sister for anything."

David frowned a little and shook his head to
himself, but he said nothing more, though the
wish was close to his heart. He thought he
was tactful.

"No, I've got that new job," went on young
Lamb. "Another man from Boston, too. I'm
in charge of the complete office organization of
a brand-new manufacturing business that's to
start up here. Two hundred dollars a month to
begin. How's that?"

"Fine," said David. "Enough to marry on.
But it sounds too good. Is he a sharper, too?"

"He don't need to be. He seems to have
plenty of money, and the article he's going to

35

start manufacturing is so good that it will pay him better to be honest than to be crooked. I don't see where the man could go wrong. Why, look here!'' and from his vest pocket he pulled an orange-headed tack. ''Carpet tack—covered with any color you want—same color as your carpet so the tacks don't show—only cost a little bit more than the cheap ones. Don't you think it's a good thing?''

David stopped in the middle of the sidewalk and put on his spectacles to examine the trifle critically.

''Is that all he's going to make—just tacks?''

''Just tacks!'' exclaimed the younger man. ''Why, Dave, the Eureka Tack Company, that has a practical monopoly now of the tack business in this country, occupies a plant covering twenty acres. It employs thousands of men. It makes sixteen per cent. a year dividends, and has millions of dollars surplus in its treasury—undivided profits! Long freight trains leave its warehouses every day, loaded down with nothing but tacks; and that's all they make — just tacks! Why, think, Dave, of how many millions of tacks are pulled out of carpets and thrown away every spring!''

Mr. Jasper was still examining the tack from

head to point with deep interest. Now he drew a long breath and handed it back.

"It's a big thing, even if it is little," he admitted. "Watch out for the man, though. Does he want any money?"

"Not a cent. Why, any money I've got he'd laugh at. I couldn't give him any. He's a rich man, and able to start his own factory. He's going to organize a quarter of a million stock company and keep the majority of the stock himself."

"It might be pretty good stock to buy, if you could get some of it," decided Dave after some slow pondering.

"I wish I could, but there is no chance. What stock he issues is only to be put out in twenty-five-thousand-dollar lots."

Again David Jasper sighed. Sixteen per cent. a year! He was thinking now of what a small margin of profit his houses left him after repairs and taxes were paid.

"It looks to me like you'd struck it rich, my boy. Well, you deserve it. You have worked hard and saved your money. You know, when I got married I had nothing but a set of harness tools and the girl, and we got along."

"Look here, Dave," laughed his younger friend, whose thirty years were unbelievable in

that he still looked so much like a boy, "some
of these days I will hunt up a girl and get married, just to make you keep still about it, and
if I have any trouble I'll throw it up to you as
long as you live. But what do you think of
this chance of mine? That's what I came out
for—to get your opinion on it."

"Well," drawled Dave, cautious now that
the final judgment was to be pronounced, "you
want to remember that you're giving up a good
job that has got better and better every year
and that will most likely get still better every
year; but, if you can start at two hundred a
month, and are sure you're going to get it, and
the man don't want any money, and he isn't a
sharper, why, it looks like it was too good to
miss."

"That's what I think," rejoined Mr. Lamb
enthusiastically. "Well, I must go now. I
want to see Mr. Lewis and John Nolting and
one or two of the others, and get their advice,"
and he swung jubilantly on a car.

It was a pleasant figment this, Eddy Lamb's
plan of consulting his older friends. He always
went to them most scrupulously to get their advice, and afterward did as he pleased. He was
too near the soil, however—only one generation
away—to make many mistakes in the matter

of caution, and so far he had swung his little
financial ventures with such great success that
he had begun to be conceited.

He found Mr. Wallingford at the hotel, but
not waiting for him by any means. Mr. Wallingford was very busy with correspondence
which, since part of it was to his wife and to
"Blackie" Daw, was entirely too personal to be
trusted to a public stenographer, and he frowningly placed his caller near the window with
some new samples of tacks he had made that
morning; then, for fifteen minutes, he silently
wrote straight on, a course which allowed Mr.
Lamb the opportunity to reflect that he was,
after all, not entitled to have worn that air of
affable familiarity with which he had come into
the room. In closing his letter to Mr. Daw the
writer added a postscript: "The Lamb is here,
and I am now sharpening the shears."

His letters finished and a swift boy called to
despatch them, Mr. Wallingford drew a chair
soberly to the opposite side of the little table
at which he had seated Mr. Lamb. Like every
great captain of finance, he turned his back to
the window so that his features were in shadow,
while the wide-set, open eyes of Mr. Lamb,
under their good, broad brow, blinked into the
full light of day, which revealed for minute

study every wrinkle of expression in his features.

"I forgot to warn you of one thing last night, and I hope you have not talked too much," Mr. Wallingford began with great seriousness. "I reposed such confidence in you that I did not think of caution, a confidence that was justified, for from such inquiries as I have made this morning I am perfectly satisfied with your record—and, by the way, Mr. Lamb, while we are upon this subject, here is a list of references to some of whom I must insist that you write, for my own satisfaction if not for yours. But now to the main point. The thing I omitted to warn you about is this," and here he sank his voice to a quite confidential tone: "I have not yet applied for letters patent upon this device."

"You have not?" exclaimed Mr. Lamb in surprise. The revelation rather altered his estimate of Mr. Wallingford's great business ability.

"No," confessed the latter. "You can see how much I trust you, to tell you this, because, if you did not know, you would naturally suppose that the patent was at least under way, and I would be in no danger whatever; but I am not yet satisfied on one point, and I want the device perfect before I make application. It has worried me quite a bit. You see, the heads of these tacks are too smooth to retain the cloth. It is very difficult to glue cloth to a smooth metal surface, and if we send out our tacks in such condition that a hammer will pound the cloth tops off, it will ruin our business the first season. I have experimented with every sort of glue I can get, and have pounded thousands of tacks into boards, but the cloth covering still comes off in such large percentage that I am afraid to go ahead. Of course, the thing can be solved—it is merely a question of time—but there is no time now to be lost."

From out the drawer of the table he drew a board into which had been driven some dozens of tacks. From at least twenty-five per cent. of them the cloth covering had been knocked off.

"I see," observed the Lamb, and he examined the board thoughtfully; then he looked out of the window at the passing traffic in the street.

Mr. Wallingford tilted back his chair and lit a fat, black cigar, the barest twinkle of a smile playing about his eyes. He laid a mate to the cigar in front of the bookkeeper, but the latter paid no attention whatever to it. He

41

was perfectly absorbed, and the twinkles around the large man's eyes deepened.

"I say!" suddenly exclaimed Mr. Lamb, turning from the window to the capitalist and throwing open his coat impatiently, as if to get away from anything that encumbered his free expression, "why wouldn't it do to roughen the heads of the tacks?"

His eyes fairly gleamed with the enthusiasm of creation. He had found the answer to one of those difficult problems like: "What bright genius can supply the missing letters to make up the name of this great American martyr, who was also a President and freed the slaves? L-NC-LN. $100.00 in GOLD to be divided among the four million successful solvers! *Send no money* until afterwards!"

Mr. Wallingford brought down the legs of his chair with a thump.

"By George!" he ejaculated. "I'm glad I found you. You're a man of remarkable resource, and I must be a dumbhead. Here I have been puzzling and puzzling with this problem, and it never occurred to me to roughen those tacks!"

It was now Mr. Lamb's turn to find the fat, black cigar, to light it, to lean back comfortably and to contemplate Mr. Wallingford with

triumphantly smiling eyes. The latter gentleman, however, was in no contemplative mood.
He was a man all of energy. He had two bellboys at the door in another minute. One he
sent for a quart of wine and the other to the
hardware store with a list of necessities, which
were breathlessly bought and delivered: a
small table-vise, a heavy hammer, two or three
patterns of flat files and several papers of
tacks. Already in one corner of Mr. Wallingford's room stood a rough serving table which
he had been using as a work bench, and Mr.
Lamb could not but reflect how everything
needed came quickly to this man's bidding, as
if he had possessed the magic lamp of Aladdin.
He was forced to admire, too, the dexterity with
which this genius screwed the small vise to the
table, placed in its jaws a row of tacks, and,
pressing upon them the flat side of one of the
files, pounded this vigorously until, upon lifting
it up, the fine, indented pattern was found repeated in the hard heads of the tacks. The
master magician went through this operation
until he had a whole paper of them with roughened heads; then, glowing with fervid enthusiasm which was quickly communicated to
his helper, he set Mr. Lamb to gluing bits of
cloth upon these heads, to be trimmed later

with delicate scissors, an extra pair of which Mr. Wallingford sent out to get. When the tacks were all set aside to dry the coworkers addressed themselves to the contents of the ice pail; but, as the host was pulling the cork from the bottle, and while both of them were perspiring and glowing with anticipated triumph in the experiment, Mr. Wallingford's face grew suddenly troubled.

"By George, Eddy"—and Mr. Lamb beamed over this early adoption of his familiar first name—"if this experiment succeeds it makes you part inventor with me!"

Eddy sat down to gasp.

CHAPTER IV

J. RUFUS ACCEPTS A TEMPORARY ACCOMMODATION
AND BUYS AN AUTOMOBILE

THE experiment was a success. Immediately after lunch they secured a fresh pine board and pounded all the tacks into it. Not one top came off. The fact, however, that Mr. Lamb was part inventor, made a vast difference in the proposition.

"Now, we'll talk cold business on this," said Mr. Wallingford. "Of course, the main idea is mine, but the patent must be applied for by both as joint inventors. Under the circumstances, I should say that about one fourth of the value of the patent, which we shall sell to the company for at least sixty thousand dollars, would be pretty good for your few minutes of thought, eh?"

Mr. Lamb, his head swimming, agreed with him thoroughly.

"Very well, then, we'll go right out to a lawyer and have a contract drawn up; then we'll go to a patent attorney and get the thing

45

under way at once. Do you know of a good lawyer?"

Mr. Lamb did. There was a young one, thoroughly good, who belonged to Mr. Lamb's lodge, and they went over to see him. There is no expressing the angle at which Mr. Lamb held his head as he passed out through the lobby of the best hotel in his city. If his well-to-do townsmen having business there wished to take notice of him, well and good; if they did not, well and good also. He needed nothing of them.

It was with the same shoulder-squared self-gratification that he ushered his affluent friend into Carwin's office. Carwin was in. Unfortunately, he was always in. Practice had not yet begun for him, but Lamb was bringing fortune in his hand and was correspondingly elated. He intended to make Carwin the lawyer for the corporation. Mr. Carwin drew up for them articles of agreement, in which it was set forth, with many a whereas and wherein, that the said party of the first part and the said party of the second part were joint inventors of a herein described new and improved carpet tack, the full and total benefits of which were to accrue to the said parties of the first part and the second part, and to their

46

heirs and assigns forever and ever, in the proportion of one fourth to the said party of the first part and three fourths to the said party of the second part.

Mr. Carwin, as he saw them walk out with the precious agreement, duly signed, attested and sealed, was too timid to hint about his fee, and Mr. Lamb could scarcely be so indelicate as to call attention to the trifle, even though he knew that Mr. Carwin was gasping for it at that present moment. The latter had hidden his shoes carefully under his desk throughout the consultation, and had kept tucking his cuffs back out of sight during the entire time. There were reasons, however, why Mr. Wallingford did not pay the fee. In spite of the fact that everything was charged at his hotel, it did take some cash for the bare necessities of existence, and, in the past three days, he had spent over fifty dollars in mere incidentals, aside from his living expenses.

Mr. Lamb did not know a patent lawyer, but he had seen the sign of one, and he knew where to go right to him. The patent lawyer demanded a preliminary fee of twenty-five dollars. Mr. Lamb was sorry that Mr. Christopher had made such an unfortunate "break," for he felt that the man would get no more of

Mr. Wallingford's business. The latter drew out a roll of bills, however, paid the man on the spot and took his receipt.

"Will a ten-dollar bill help hurry matters any?" he asked.

"It might," admitted the patent lawyer with a cheerful smile.

His office was in a ramshackle old building that had no elevator, and they had been compelled to climb two flights of stairs to reach it. Mr. Wallingford handed him the ten dollars.

"Have the drawings and the application ready by to-morrow. If the thing can be expedited we shall want you to go on to Washington with the papers."

Mr. Christopher glowed within him. Wherever this man Wallingford went he left behind him a trail of high hopes, a glimpse of a better day to dawn. He was a public benefactor, a boon to humanity. His very presence radiated good cheer and golden prospects.

As they entered the hotel, said Mr. Wallingford:

"Just get the key and go right on up to the room, Eddy. You know where it is. Make yourself at home. Take your knife and try the covering on those last tacks we put in. I'll be up in five or ten minutes."

WALLINGFORD

When Mr. Wallingford came in Mr. Lamb
was testing the tack covers with great gratification. They were all solid, and they could
scarcely be dug off with a knife. He looked up
to communicate this fact with glee, and saw a
frowning countenance upon his senior partner.
Mr. J. Rufus Wallingford was distinctly vexed.

"Nice thing!" he growled. "Just got a
notice that there is an overdraft in my bank.
Now, I'll have to order some bonds sold at a
loss, with the market down all around; but
that will take a couple of days and here I am
without cash—without cash! Look at that!
Less than five dollars!"

He threw off his coat and hat in disgust and
loosened his vest. He mopped his face and
brow and neck. Mr. Wallingford was extremely
vexed. He ordered a quart of champagne in a
tone which must have made the telephone clerk
feel that the princely guest was dissatisfied with
the house. "Frappé, too!" he demanded.
"The last I had was as warm as tea!"

Mr. Lamb, within the past day, had himself
begun the rise to dizzy heights; he had breathed
the atmosphere of small birds and cold bottles
into his nostrils until that vapor seemed the
normal air of heaven; the ordinary dollar had
gradually shrunk from its normal dimensions

of a peck measure to the size of a mere dot, and, moreover, he considered how necessary pocket money was to a man of J. Rufus Wallingford's rich relationship with the world.

"I have a little ready cash I could help you out with, if you will let me offer it," he ventured, embarrassed to find slight alternate waves of heat flushing his face. The borrowing and the lending of money were not unknown by any means in Mr. Lamb's set. They asked each other for fifty dollars with perfect nonchalance, got it and paid it back with equal unconcern, and no man among them had been known to forget. Mr. Wallingford accepted quite gracefully.

"Really, if you don't mind," said he, "five hundred or so would be quite an accommodation for a couple of days."

Mr. Lamb gulped, but it was only a sort of growing pain that he had. It was difficult for him to keep up with his own financial expansion.

"Certainly," he stammered. "I'll go right down and get it for you. The bank closes at three. I have only a half hour to make it."

"I'll go right with you," said Mr. Wallingford, asking no questions, but rightly divining that his Lamb kept no open account. "Wait a minute. I'll make you out a note — just so there'll be something to show for it, you know."

He hurriedly drew a blank from his pocket. filled it in and arose from the table.

"I made it out for thirty days, merely as a matter of business form," stated Mr. Wallingford as they walked to the elevator, "but, as soon as I put those bonds on the market, I'll take up the note, of course. I left the interest in at six per cent."

"Oh, that was not necessary at all," protested Mr. Lamb.

The sum had been at first rather a staggering one, but it only took him a moment or two to get his new bearings, and, if possible, he held his head a trifle higher than ever as he walked out through the lobby. On the way to the bank the capitalist passed the note over to his friend.

"I believe that's the right date; the twenty-fifth, isn't it?"

"The twenty-fifth is right," Mr. Lamb replied, and perfunctorily opened the note. Then he stopped walking. "Hello!" he said. "You've made a mistake. This is for a thousand."

"Is that so? I declare! I so seldom draw

less than that. Well, suppose we let it go at a thousand.''

Time for gulping was passed.

"All right," said the younger man, but he could not make the assent as sprightly as he could have wished. In spite of himself the words drawled.

Nevertheless, at his bank he handed in his savings-book and the check, and, thoroughly permeated by the atmosphere in which he was now moving, he had made out the order for eleven hundred dollars.

"I needed a little loose change myself," he explained, as he put a hundred into his own pocket and passed the thousand over to Mr. Wallingford.

Events moved rapidly now. Mr. Wallingford that night sent off one hundred and fifty dollars to his wife.

"Cheer up, little girl," he wrote her. "Blackie came here and reported that this was a grouch town. I've been here three days and dug up a thousand, and there's more in sight. I've been inquiring around this morning. There is a swell little ten-thousand-dollar house out in the rich end of the burg that I'm going to buy to put up a front, and you know how I'll buy it. Also I'm going over to-morrow and pick out an automobile. I need it in my business. You ought to see what long, silky wool the sheep grow here."

The next morning was devoted entirely to pleasure. They visited three automobile firms and took spins in four machines, and at last Mr. Wallingford picked out a five-thousand-dollar car that about suited him.

"I shall try this for two weeks," he told the proprietor of the establishment. "Keep it here in your garage at my call, and, by that time, if I decide to buy it, I shall have my own garage under way. I have my eye on a very nice little place out in Gildendale, and if they don't want too much for it I'll bring on Mrs. Wallingford from Boston."

"With pleasure, Mr. Wallingford," said the proprietor.

Mr. Lamb walked away with a new valuation of things. Not a penny of deposit had been asked, for the mere appearance of Mr. Wallingford and his air of owning the entire garage were sufficient. In the room at the hotel that afternoon they made some further experiments on tacks, and Mr. Wallingford gave his young partner some further statistics concerning the Eureka Company: its output, the number of men it employed, the number of machines it had in operation, the small start it had, the immense profits it made.

"We've got them all beat," Mr. Lamb enthusiastically summed up for him. "We're starting much better than they did, and with, I believe, the best manufacturing proposition that was ever put before the public."

It was not necessary to supply him with any further enthusiasm. He had been inoculated with the yeast of it, and from that point onward would be self-raising.

"The only thing I am afraid of," worried Mr. Wallingford, "is that the Eureka Company will want to buy us out before we get fairly started, and, if they offer us a good price, the stockholders will want to stampede. Now, you and I must vote down any proposition the Eureka Company make us, no matter what the other stockholders want, because, if they buy us out before we have actually begun to encroach upon their business, they will not give us one fifth of the price we could get after giving them a good scare. Between us, Eddy, we'll hold six tenths of the stock and we must stand firm."

Eddy stuck his thumbs in his vest pocket and with great complacency tapped himself alternately upon his recent luncheon with the finger tips of his two hands.

"Certainly we will," he admitted. "But say; I have some friends that I'd like to bring into this thing. They're not able to buy blocks of stock as large as you suggested, but, maybe, we could split up one lot so as to let them in."

"I don't like the idea of small stockholders," Mr. Wallingford objected, frowning. "They are too hard to handle. Your larger investors are business men who understand all the details and are not raising eternal questions about the little things that turn up; but since we have this tack so perfect I've changed my plan of incorporation, and consequently there is a way in which your friends can get in. We don't want to attract any attention to ourselves from the Eureka people just now, so we will only incorporate at first for one thousand dollars, in ten shares of one hundred dollars each—sort of a dummy corporation in which my name will not appear at all. If you can find four friends who will buy one share of stock each you will then subscribe for the other six shares, for which I will pay you, giving you one share, as I promised. These four friends of yours then, if they wish, may take up one block of twenty-five thousand when we make the final corporation, which we will do by increasing our capital stock as soon as we get our corporation papers. These friends of yours would, necessarily, be on our first board of directors, too, which will hold for one year, and it will be an exceptional opportunity for them."

"I don't quite understand," said Mr. Lamb.

"We incorporate for one thousand only," explained Mr. Wallingford, slowly and patiently, "ten shares of one hundred dollars each, all fully paid in. The Eureka Company will pay no attention to a one-thousand-dollar company. As soon as we get our corporation papers, we original incorporators will, of course, form the officers and board of directors, and we will immediately vote to increase our capitalization to one hundred thousand dollars, in one thousand shares of one hundred dollars each. We will vote to pay you and I as inventors sixty thousand dollars or six hundred shares of stock for our patents—applied for and to be applied for during a period of five years to come—in carpet-tack improvements and machinery for making the same. We will offer the balance of the forty thousand dollars stock for sale, to carry us through the experimental stage—that is, until we get our machinery all in working order. Then we will need one hundred thousand dollars to start our factory. To get that, we will reincorporate for a three-hundred-thousand capital, taking up all the outstanding stock and giving to each stockholder two shares at par for each share he then holds. That will take up two hundred thousand dollars of the stock and leave one hundred thousand for sale at par. You, in place of fifteen thousand dollars' worth of stock as your share for the patent rights, will have thirty thousand dollars' worth, or three hundred shares, and if, after we have started operating, the Eureka Company should buy us out at only a million, you would have a hundred thousand dollars net profit.''

A long, long sigh was the answer. Mr Lamb saw. Here was real financiering.

"Let's get outside," he said, needing fresh air in his lungs after this. "Let's go up and see my friend, Mr. Jasper."

In ten minutes the automobile had reported. Each man, before he left the room, slipped a handful of covered carpet tacks into his coat pocket.

CHAPTER V

THE UNIVERSAL COVERED CARPET TACK COMPANY
FORMS AMID GREAT ENTHUSIASM

THE intense democracy of J. Rufus Wallingford could not but charm David Jasper, even though he disapproved of diamond stick-pins and red-leather-padded automobiles as a matter of principle. The manner in which the gentleman from Boston acknowledged the introduction, the fine mixture of deference due Mr. Jasper's age and of cordiality due his easily discernible qualities of good fellowship, would have charmed the heart out of a cabbage.

"Get in, Dave; we want to take you a ride," demanded Mr. Lamb.

David shook his head at the big machine, and laughed.

"I don't carry enough insurance," he objected.

Mr. Wallingford had caught sight of a little bronze button in the lapel of Mr. Jasper's faded and threadbare coat.

"A man who went through the battle of

Bull Run ought to face anything," he laughed back.

The shot went home. Mr. Jasper *had* acquitted himself with honor in the battle of Bull Run, and without further ado he got into the invitingly open door of the tonneau, to sink back among the padded cushions with his friend Lamb. As the door slammed shut, Ella Jasper waved them adieu, and it was fully three minutes after the machine drove away before she began humming about her work. Somehow or other, she did not like to see her father's friend so intimately associated with rich people.

They had gone but a couple of blocks, and Mr. Lamb was in the early stages of the enthusiasm attendant upon describing the wonderful events of the past two days — especially his own share in the invention, and the hundred thousand dollars that it was to make him within the year—when Mr. Wallingford suddenly halted the machine.

"You're not going to get home to dinner, you know, Mr. Jasper," he declared.

"Oh, we have to! This is lodge night, and I am a patriarch. I haven't missed a night for twenty years, and Eddy, here, has an office, too—his first one. We've got ten candidates to-night."

"I see," said Mr. Wallingford gravely. "It is more or less in the line of a sacred duty. Nevertheless, we will not go home to dinner. I'll get you at the lodge door at half past eight. Will that be early enough?"

Mr. Jasper put his hands upon his knees and turned to his friend.

"I guess we can work our way in, can't we, Eddy?" he chuckled, and Eddy, with equally simple pleasure, replied that they could.

"Very well. Back to the house, chauffeur." And, in a moment more, they were sailing back to the decrepit little cottage, where Lamb jumped out to carry the news to Ella. She was just coming out of the kitchen door in her sunbonnet to run over to the grocery store as Edward came up the steps. He grabbed her by both shoulders and dragged her out.

"Come on; we're going to take you along!" he threatened, and she did not know why, but, at the touch of his hands, she paled slightly. Her eyes never faltered, however, as she laughed and jerked herself away.

"Not much, you don't! I'm worried enough as it is with father in there — and you, of course."

He told her that they would not be home to

supper, and, for a second time, she wistfully
saw them driving away in the big red machine.

Mr. Wallingford talked with the chauffeur
for a few moments, and then the machine leaped
forward with definiteness. Once or twice Mr.
Wallingford looked back. The two in the tonneau were examining the cloth-topped tacks,
and both were talking volubly. Mile after mile
they were still at it, and the rich man felt relieved of all responsibility. The less he said in
the matter the better; he had learned the invaluable lesson of when not to talk. So far
as he was concerned, the Universal Covered
Carpet Tack Company was launched, and he
was able to turn his attention to the science
of running the car, a matter which, by the time
they had reached their stopping point, he had
picked up to the great admiration of the expert
driver. For the last five miles the big man ran
the machine himself, with the help of a guiding
word or two, and when they finally stopped in
front of the one pretentious hotel in the small
town they had reached, he was so completely
absorbed in the new toy that he was actually
as nonchalant about the new company as he
would have wished to appear. His passengers
were surprised when they found that they had
come twenty miles, and Mr. Wallingford

showed them what a man who knows how to dine can do in a minor hotel. He had everybody busy, from the proprietor down. The snap of his fingers was as potent here as the clarion call of the trumpet in battle, and David Jasper, though he strove to disapprove, after sixty years of somnolence woke up and actually enjoyed pretentious luxury.

There were but five minutes of real business conversation following the meal, but five minutes were enough. David Jasper had called his friend Eddy aside for one brief moment.

"Did he give you any references?" he asked, the habit of caution asserting itself.

"Sure; more than half a dozen of them."

"Have you written to them?"

"I wrote this morning."

"I guess he wouldn't give them to you if he wasn't all right."

"We don't need the references," urged Lamb. "The man himself is reference enough. You see that automobile? He bought it this morning and didn't pay a cent on it. They didn't ask him to."

It was a greater recommendation than if the man had paid cash down for the machine; for credit is mightier than cash, everywhere.

"I think we'll go in," said Dave.

'Think he would go in! It was only his conservative way of expressing himself, for he was already in with his whole heart and soul. In the five minutes of conversation between the three that ensued, David Jasper agreed to be one of the original incorporators, to go on the first board of directors, and to provide three other solid men to serve in a like capacity, the preliminary meeting being arranged for the next morning. Mr. Wallingford passed around his black cigars and lit one in huge content as he climbed into the front seat with the chauffeur, to begin his task of urging driver and machine back through the night in the time that he had promised.

That was a wonderful ride to the novices. Nothing but darkness ahead, with a single stream of white light spreading out upon the roadway, which, like a fast descending curtain, lowered always before them; a rut here, a rock there, angle and curve and dip and rise all springing out of the night with startling swiftness, to disappear behind them before they had given even a gasp of comprehension for the possible danger they had confronted but that was now past. Unconsciously they found themselves gripping tightly the sides of the car, and yet, even to the old man, there was a strange sense of exhilaration, aided perhaps by wine, that made them, after the first breathless five miles, begin to jest in voices loud enough to carry against the wind, to laugh boisterously, and even to sing, by-and-by, a nonsensical song started by Lamb and caught up by Wallingford and joined by the still firm voice of David Jasper. The chauffeur, the while bent grimly over his wheel, peered with iron-nerved intensity out into that mysterious way where the fatal snag might rise up at any second and smite them into lifeless clay, for they were going at a terrific pace. The hoarse horn kept constantly hooting, and every now and then they flashed by trembling horses drawn up at the side of the road and attached to "rigs," the occupants of which appeared only as one or two or three fish-white faces in the one instant that the glow of the headlight gleamed upon them. Once there was a quick swerve out of the road and back into it again, where the rear wheel hovered for a fraction of a second over a steep gully, and not until they had passed on did the realization come to them that there had been one horse that had refused, either through stubbornness or fright, to get out of the road fast enough. But what is a danger past when a myriad lie before, and what are dangers ahead when a myriad have been passed safely by? The exhilaration became almost an intoxication, for, in spite of those few moments when mirth and gayety were checked by that sudden throb of what might have been, the songs burst forth again as soon as a level track stretched ahead once more.

"Five minutes before the time I promised you!" exclaimed Mr. Wallingford in jovial triumph, jumping from his seat and opening the door of the tonneau for his passengers just in front of the stairway that led to their lodge-rooms.

They climbed out, stiff and breathless and still tingling with the inexplicable thrill of it all.

"Eleven o'clock in the morning, remember, at Carwin's," he reminded them as they left him, and afterward they wondered why such a simple exertion as the climbing of one flight of stairs should make their hearts beat so high and their breath come so deep and harsh. It would have been curious, later that night, to see Edward Lamb buying a quart of champagne for his friends, and protesting that it was not cold enough!

Mr. Wallingford stepped back to the chauffeur.

"What's your first name?" he inquired.

"Frank, sir."

"Well, Frank, when you go back to the shop you tell them that you're to drive my machine hereafter when I call for it, and when I get settled down here I want you to work for me. Drive to the hotel now and wait."

Before climbing into the luxury of the tonneau he handed the chauffeur a five-dollar bill.

"All right, sir," said Frank.

At the hotel, the man of means walked up to the clerk and opened his pocketbook.

"I have a little more cash than I care to carry around. Just put this to my credit, will you?" and he counted out six one-hundred-dollar bills.

As he turned away the clerk permitted himself that faint trace of a smile once more. His confidence was justified. He had known that somebody would pay Mr. Wallingford's acrobatic bill. His interesting guest strode out to the big red automobile. The chauffeur was out in a second and had the tonneau open before the stately but earnestly willing doorman of the hotel could perform the duty.

"Now, show us the town," said Wallingford as the door closed upon him, and when he came in late that night his eyes were red and his

66

speech was thick; but there were plenty of
eager hands to see safely to bed the prince who
had landed in their midst with less than a
hundred dollars in his possession.

He was up bright and vigorous the next
morning, however. A cold bath, a hearty
breakfast in his room, a half hour with the
barber and a spin in the automobile made him
elastic and bounding again, so that at eleven
o'clock he was easily the freshest man among
the six who gathered in Mr. Carwin's office.
The incorporators noted with admiration, which
with wiser men might have turned to suspicion,
that Mr. Wallingford was better posted on corporation law than Mr. Carwin himself, and that
he engineered the preliminary proceedings
through in a jiffy. With the exception of
Lamb, they were all men past forty, and not
one of them had known experience of this
nature. They had been engaged in minor oc-
cupations or in minor business throughout their
lives, and had gathered their few thousands
together dollar by dollar. To them this new
realm that was opened up was a fairyland, and
the simple trick of watering stock that had
been carefully explained to them, one by one,
pleased them as no toy ever pleased a child.
They had heard of such things as being vague

and mysterious operations in the realms of finance and had condemned them, taking their tone from the columns of editorials they had read upon such practices; but, now that they were themselves to reap the fruits of it, they looked through different spectacles. It was a just proceeding which this genius of commerce proposed; for they who stood the first brunt of launching the ship were entitled to greater rewards than they who came in upon an assured certainty of profits, having waited only for the golden cargo to be in the harbor.

As a sort of sealing of their compact and to show that this was to be a corporation upon a friendly basis, rather than a cold, grasping business proposition, Mr. Wallingford took them all over to a simple lunch in a private dining room at his hotel. He was careful not to make it too elaborate, but careful, too, that the luncheon should be notable, and they all went away talking about him: what a wonderful man he was, what a wonderful business proposition he had permitted them to enter upon, what wonderful resources he must have at his command, what wonderful genius was his in manipulation, in invention, in every way.

There was a week now in which to act, and Mr. Wallingford wasted no time. He picked out his house in the exclusive part of Gildendale, and when it came to paying the thousand dollars down, Mr. Wallingford quietly made out a sixty-day note for the amount.

"I beg your pardon," hesitated the agent, "the first payment is supposed to be in cash."

"Oh, I know that it is supposed to be," laughed Mr. Wallingford, "but we understand how these things are. I guess the house itself will secure the note for that length of time. I am going to be under pretty heavy expense in fitting up the place, and a man with any regard for the earning power of money does not keep much cash lying loose. Do you want this note or not?" and his final tone was peremptory.

"Oh, why, certainly; that's all right," said the agent, and took it.

Upon the court records appeared the sale, but even before it was so entered a firm of decorators and furnishers had been given *carte blanche*, following, however, certain artistic requirements of Mr. Wallingford himself. The result that they produced within the three days that he gave them was marvelous; somewhat too garish, perhaps, for people of good taste, but impressive in every detail; and for all this he paid not one penny in cash. He was accredited with being the owner of a house in the exclusive suburb, Gildendale. On that accrediting the furnishing was done, on that accrediting he stocked his pantry shelves, his refrigerator, his wine cellar, his coal bins, his humidors, and had started a tailor to work upon half a dozen suits, among them an automobile costume. He had a modest establishment of two servants and a chauffeur by the time his wife arrived, and on the day the final organization of the one-thousand-dollar company was effected, he gave a housewarming for his associates of the Universal Covered Carpet Tack Company. Where Mr. Wallingford had charmed, Mrs. Wallingford fascinated, and the five men went home that night richer than they had ever dreamed of being; than they would ever be again.

CHAPTER VI

THE first stockholders' meeting of the Tack Company was a cheerful affair, held around a table that was within an hour or so to have a cloth; for whenever J. Rufus Wallingford did business, he must, perforce, eat and drink, and all who did business with him must do the same. The stockholders, being all present, elected their officers and their board of directors: Mr. Wallingford, president; Mr. Lamb, secretary; Mr. Jasper, treasurer; and Mr. Lewis, David Jasper's nearest friend, vice president, these four and Mr. Nolting also constituting the board of directors. Immediately after, they adopted a stock, printed form of constitution, voted an increase of capitalization to one hundred thousand dollars, and then adjourned.

The president, during the luncheon, made them a little speech in which he held before them constantly a tack with a crimson top glued upon a roughened surface, and alluded to the invaluable services their young friend, Edward Lamb, had rendered to the completion of the company's now perfect and flawless article of manufacture. He explained to them in detail the bigness of the Eureka Tack Manufacturing Company, its enormous undivided profits, its tremendous yearly dividends, the fabulous price at which its stock was quoted, with none for sale; and all this gigantic business built upon a simple tack!—Gentlemen, not nearly, not *nearly* so attractive and so profitable an article of commerce as this per-fect little convenience held before them. The gentlemen were to be congratulated upon a bigger and brighter and better fortune than had ever come to them; they were all to be congratulated upon having met each other, and since they had been kind enough, since they had been trusting enough, to give him their confidence with but little question, Mr. Wallingford felt it his duty to reassure them, even though they needed no reassurance, that he was what he was; and he called upon his friend and their secretary, Mr. Lamb, to read to them the few letters that he understood had been received from the Mexican and Rio Grande Rubber Company, the St. John's Blood Orange Plantation Company, the Los Pocos Lead Development

Company, the Sierra Cinnabar Grant, and others.

Mr. Lamb—Secretary Lamb, if you please— arose in self-conscious dignity, which he strove to taper off into graceful ease.

"It is hardly worth while reading more than one, for they're all alike," he stated jovially, "and if anybody questions our president, send him to his friend Eddy!" Whereupon he read the letters.

According to them, Mr. Wallingford was a gentleman of the highest integrity; he was a man of unimpeachable character, morally and financially; he was a genius of commerce; he had been sought, for his advice and for the tower of strength that his name had become, by all the money kings of Boston; he was, in a word, the greatest boon that had ever descended upon any city, and all of the gentlemen who were lucky enough to be associated with him in any business enterprise that he might back or vouch for, could count themselves indeed most fortunate. The letters were passed around. Some of them had embossed heads; most of them were, at least, engraved; some of them were printed in two or three rich colors; some had beautifully tinted pictures of vast Mexican estates, and Florida plantations, and Nevada mining ranges.

They were impressive, those letter-heads, and when, after passing the round of the table, they were returned to Mr. Lamb, four pairs of eyes followed them as greedily as if those eyes had been resting upon actual money.

In the ensuing week the committee on factories, consisting of Mr. Wallingford, Mr. Lamb and Mr. Jasper, honked and inspected and lunched until they found a small place which would "do for the first year's business," and within two days the factory was cleaned and the office most sumptuously furnished; then Mr. Wallingford, having provided work for the secretary, began to attend to his purely personal affairs, one of which was the private consulting of the patent attorney. Upon his first visit Mr. Christopher met him with a dejected air.

"I find four interferences against your application," he dolefully stated, "and they cover the ground very completely."

"Get me a patent," directed Mr. Wallingford shortly.

Mr. Christopher hesitated. Not only was his working jacket out at the elbows, but his street coat was shiny at the seams.

"I am bound to tell you," he confessed, after quite a struggle, "that, while I *might*

74

get you some sort of a patent, it would not hold water.''

"I don't care if it wouldn't hold pebbles or even brickbats," retorted Mr. Wallingford. "I'm not particular about the mesh of it. Just you get me a patent—any sort of a patent, so it has a seal and a ribbon on it. I believe it is part of your professional ethics, Mr. Christopher, to do no particular amount of talking except to your clients.

"Well, yes, sir," admitted Mr. Christopher.

"Very well, then; I am the only client you know in this case, and I say—get a patent! After all, a patent isn't worth as much as a dollar at the Waldorf, except to form the basis of a lawsuit," whereat Mr. Christopher saw a great white light and his conscience ceased to bother him.

Meanwhile the majestic wheels of state revolved, and at the second meeting of the board of directors the secretary was able to lay before them the august permission of the Commonwealth to issue one hundred thousand dollars of stock in the new corporation. In fact, the secretary was able to show them a book of especially printed stock certificates, and a corporate seal had been made. Their own seal! Each man tried it with awe and pride. This also was a cheerful board meeting, wherein the directors, as one man, knowing beforehand what they were to do, voted to Mr. Wallingford and Mr. Lamb sixty thousand dollars in stock, for all patents relating to covered carpet tacks or devices for making the same that should be obtained by them for a period of five years to come. The three remaining members of the board of directors and the one stockholder who was allowed to be present by courtesy then took up five thousand dollars' worth of stock each and guaranteed to bring in, by the end of the week, four more like subscriptions, two of which they secured; and, thirty thousand dollars of cash having been put into the treasury, a special stockholders' meeting was immediately called. When this met it was agreed that they should incorporate another company under the name of the Universal Covered Tack Company, dropping the word "Carpet," with an authorized capital of three hundred thousand dollars, two hundred thousand of which was already subscribed.

It took but a little over a month to organize this new company, which bought out the old company for the consideration of two hundred thousand dollars, payable in stock of the new company. With great glee the new stockhold-

WALLINGFORD

ers bought from themselves, as old stock-holders, the old company at this valuation, each man receiving two shares of one hundred dollars face value for each one hundred dollars' worth of stock that he had held before. It was their very first transaction in water, and the delight that it gave them one and all knew no bounds; they had doubled their money in one day! But their elation was not half the elation of J. Rufus Wallingford, for in his possession he had ninety thousand dollars' worth, par value, of stock, the legitimacy of which no one could question, and the market price of which could be to himself whatever his glib tongue had the opportunity to make it. In addition to the nine hundred shares of stock, he had a ten-thousand-dollar house, a five-thousand-dollar automobile and unlimited credit; and this was the man who had landed in the city but two brief months before, with no credit in any known spot upon the globe, and with less than one hundred dollars in his pocket!

It is a singular commentary upon the honesty of American business methods that so much is done on pure faith. The standing of J. Rufus Wallingford was established beyond question. Aside from the perfunctory inquiries that

77

Edward Lamb had made, no one ever took the trouble to question into the promoter's past record. So far as local merchants were concerned, these did not care; for did not J. Rufus own a finely appointed new house in Gildendale, and did he not appear before them daily in a fine new automobile? This, added to the fact that he established credit with one merchant and referred the next one to him, referred the third to the second, and the fourth to the third, was ample. If merchant number four took the trouble to inquire of merchant number three, he was told: "Yes, we have Mr. Wallingford on our books, and consider him good." Consequently, Mrs. Wallingford was able to go to any establishment, in her own little runabout that J. Rufus got her presently, and order what she would; and she took ample advantage of the opportunity. She, like J. Rufus, was one of those rare beings of earth for whom earth's most prized treasures are delved, and wrought, and woven, and sewed; for transcendent beauty demands ever more beauty for its adornment. In all the city there was nothing too good for either of them, and they got it without money and without price. The provider of all this made no move toward paying even a retainer upon his automobile, for in-

stance; but, when the subtle intuition within
him warned that the dealer would presently
make a demand, he calmly went in and selected
the neat little runabout for his wife, and had
it added to his bill. After he had seen the runabout glide away, the dealer was a little aghast
at himself. He had firmly intended, the next
time he saw Mr. Wallingford, to insist upon a
payment. In place of that, he had only jeopard-
ized two thousand dollars more, and all that
he had to show for it were half a dozen covered
tacks which J. Rufus had left him to ponder
upon. In the meantime, Lamb's loan of one
thousand had been increased, upon plausible
pretext, to two thousand.

There began, now, busy days at the factory.
In the third floor of their building a machine
shop was installed. Three thousand dollars
went there. Outside, in a large experimental
shop, work was being rapidly pushed on machinery which would make tacks with cross-
corrugated heads. Genius Wallingford had
secretly secured drawings of tack machinery,
and devised slight changes which would evade
the patents, adding dies that would make the
roughened tops. A final day came when, set
up in their shop, the first faulty machine
pounded out tacks ready for later covering, and

every stockholder who had been called in to witness the working of the miracle went away profoundly convinced that fortune was just within his reach. They had their first patent granted now, and the sight of it, on stiff parchment with its bit of bright ribbon, was like a glimpse at dividends. It was right at this time, however, that one cat was let out of the bag. The information came first to Edward Lamb, through the inquiries of a commercial rating company, that their Boston capitalist was a whited sepulcher, so far as capital went. He had not a cent. The secretary, in the privacy of their office, put the matter to him squarely, and he admitted it cheerfully. He was glad that the *exposé* had come—it suited his present course, and he would have brought it about himself before long.

"Who said I had money?" he demanded. "I never said so."

"Well, but the way you live," objected Lamb.

"I have always lived that way, and I always shall. Not only is it a fact that I have no money, but I must have some right away."

"I haven't any more to lend."

"No, Eddy; I'm not saying that you have. I am merely stating that I have to have some.

WALLINGFORD

I am being bothered by people who want it, and I cannot work on the covering machine until I get it," and Mr. Wallingford coolly telephoned for his big automobile to be brought around.

They sat silently in the office for the next five minutes, while Lamb slowly appreciated the position they were in. If J. Rufus should "lay down on them" before the covering machine was perfected, they were in a bad case. They had already spent over twenty thousand dollars in equipping their office, their machine shop, and perfecting their stamping machine, and time was flying.

"You might sell a little of your stock," suggested Lamb.

"We have an agreement between us to hold control."

"But you can still sell a little of yours, and stay within that amount. I'm not selling any of mine."

Mr. Wallingford drew from his pocket a hundred-share stock certificate.

"I have already sold some. Make out fifty shares of this to L. W. Ramsay, twenty-five to E. H. Wyman, and the other twenty-five to C. D. Wyman."

Ramsay and the Wyman Brothers! Ramsay

was the automobile dealer; Wyman Brothers were Wallingford's tailors.

"So much? Why didn't you sell them at least part from our extra treasury stock? There is twenty thousand there, replacing the ten thousand of the old company."

"Why didn't I? I needed the money. I got twenty-five hundred cash from Ramsay, and let him put twenty-five on account. I agreed to take one thousand in trade from Wyman Brothers, and got four thousand cash there."

The younger man looked at him angrily.

"Look here, Wallingford; you're hitting it up rather strong, ain't you? This makes six thousand five hundred, besides two thousand you borrowed from me, that you have spent in three months. You have squandered money since you came here at the rate of three thousand a month, besides all the bills I know you owe, and still you are broke. How is it possible?"

"That's my business," retorted Wallingford, and his face reddened with assumed anger. "We are not going to discuss it. The point is that I need money and must have it."

The automobile drew up at the door, and J. Rufus, who was in his automobile suit, put on his cap and riding coat.

"Where are you going?"

"Over to Rayling."

Lamb frowned. Rayling was sixty miles away.

"And you will not be back until midnight, I suppose."

"Hardly."

"Why, confound it, man, you can't go!" exclaimed Lamb. "They're waiting for you now over at the machine shop, for further instructions on the covering device."

"They'll have to wait!" announced J. Rufus, and stalked out of the door.

The thing had been deliberately followed up. Mr. Wallingford had come to the point where he wished his flock to know that he had no financial resources whatever, and that they would have to support him. It was the first time that he had departed from his suavity, and he left Lamb in a panic. He had been gone scarcely more than an hour when David Jasper came in.

"Where is Wallingford?" he asked.

"Gone out for an automobile trip."

"When will he be back?"

"Not to-day."

Jasper's face was white, but the flush of slow anger was creeping upon his cheeks.

"Well, he ought to be; his note is due."

"What note?" inquired Lamb, startled.

"His note for a thousand dollars that I went security on."

"You might just as well renew it, or pay it. I had to renew mine," said Lamb. "Dave, the man is a four-flusher, without a cent to fall back on. I just found it out this morning. Why didn't you tell me that he was borrowing money of you?"

"Why didn't you tell me he was borrowing money of you?" retorted his friend.

They looked at each other hotly for a moment, and then both laughed. The big man was too much for them to comprehend.

"We are both cutting our eye teeth," Lamb decided. "I wonder how many more he's borrowed money from."

"Lewis, for one. He got fifteen hundred from him. Lewis told me this morning, up at Kriegler's."

Lamb began figuring. To the eight thousand five hundred of which he already knew, here was twenty-five hundred more to be added—eleven thousand dollars that the man had spent in three months! Some bills, of course, he had paid, but the rest of it had gone as the wind blew. It seemed impossible that a man could spend money at the rate of one hundred and twenty-five dollars a day, but this one had done it, and that at first was the point which held them aghast, to the forgetting of their own share in it. They could not begin to understand it until Lamb recalled one incident that had impressed him. Wallingford had taken his wife and two friends to the opera one night. They had engaged a private dining room at the hotel, indulging in a dinner that, with flowers and wines, had cost over a hundred dollars. Their seats had cost fifty. There had been a supper afterward where the wine flowed until long past midnight. Altogether, that evening alone had cost not less than three hundred dollars—and the man lived at that gait all the time! In his home, even when himself and wife were alone, seven-course dinners were served. Huge fowls were carved for but the choicest slices, were sent away from the table and never came back again in any form. Expensive wines were opened and left uncorked after two glasses, because some whim had led the man to prefer some other brand.

Lamb looked up from his figuring with an expression so troubled that his older friend, groping as men will do for cheering words, hit upon the idea that restored them both to their equilibrium.

"After all," suggested Jasper, "it's none of our business. The company is all right."

"That's so," agreed Lamb, recovering his enthusiasm in a bound. "The tack itself can't be beat, and we are making progress toward getting on the market. Suppose the man were to sell all his stock. It wouldn't make any difference, so long as he finishes that one machine for covering the tack."

"He's a liar!" suddenly burst out David Jasper. "I wish he had his machinery done and was away from us. I can't sleep well when I do business with a liar."

"We don't want to get rid of him yet," Lamb reminded him, "and, in the meantime, I suppose he will have to have money in order to keep him at work. You'd better get him to give you stock to cover your note and tell Lewis to do the same. We'll all go after him on that point, and get protected."

David looked troubled in his turn.

"I can't afford it. When I took up that five thousand dollars' worth of stock I only had fifteen hundred in the building loan, and I put a mortgage on one of my houses to make up the amount. If I have to stand this thousand I'll have to give another mortgage, and I swore I'd never put a plaster on my property."

"The tack's good for it," urged Lamb, with conviction.

"Yes, the tack's good," admitted Jasper.

That was the thing which held them all in line—the tack! Wallingford himself might be a spendthrift and a ne'er-do-well, but their faith in the tack that was to make them all rich was supreme. Lamb picked up one from his desk and handed it to his friend. The very sight of it, with its silken covered top, imagination carrying it to its place in a carpet where it would not show, was most reassuring, and behind it, looming up like the immense open cornucopia of Fortune herself, was the Eureka Company, the concern that would buy them out at any time for a million dollars if they were foolish enough to sell. After all, they had nothing to worry them.

David Jasper went up to the bank and had them hold the note until the next day, which they did without comment. David was "good" for anything he wanted. The next day he got hold of Wallingford to get him to renew the note and to give him stock as security for it. When J. Rufus came out of that transaction, in which David had intended to be severe with him, he had four thousand dollars in his pocket, for he had transferred to his indorser five thousand dollars of his stock and Jasper had placed another mortgage on his property. The single tack in his vest pocket had assumed proportions far larger than his six cottages and his home. It was the same with Lewis and one of the others, and, for a week, the inventor struggled with the covering machine.

No one seemed to appreciate the fact that here their genius was confronting a problem that was most difficult of solution. To them it meant a mere bit of mechanical juggling, as certain to be accomplished as the simple process of multiplication; but to glue a piece of cloth to so minute and irregular a thing as the head of a tack, to put it on firmly and leave it trimmed properly at the edges, to do this trick by machinery and at a rate rapid enough to insure profitable operation, was a Herculean task, and the stockholders would have been aghast had they known that J. Rufus was in no hurry to solve this last perplexity. He knew better than to begin actual manufacture. The interference report on the first patent led him to make secret inquiries, the result of which convinced him that the day they went on the market would be the day that they would be disrupted by vigorous suits, backed by millions of capital. He had been right in stating that a patent is of no value except as a basis for lawsuits.

There was only one thing which offset his shrewdness in realizing these conditions, and that was his own folly. Had he been content to devote himself earnestly to the accomplishment even of his own ends, the many difficulties into which he had floundered would never have existed. Always there was the pressing need for money. He was a colossal example of the fact that easily gotten pelf is of no value. His wife was shrewder than he. She had no social aspirations whatever at this time. They were both of them too bohemian of taste and habit to conform to the strict rules which society imposes in certain directions, even had they been able to enter the charmed circle. She cared only to dress as well as the best and to go to such places of public entertainment as the best frequented, to show herself in jewels that would attract attention and in gowns that would excite envy; but she did tire of continuous suspense—and she was not without keenness of perception.

GET-RICH-QUICK

"Jim," she asked, one night, "how is your business going?"

"You see me have money every day, don't you? There's nothing you want, is there?" was the evasive reply.

"Not a thing, except this: I want a vacation. I don't want to be wondering all my life when the crash is to come. So far as I have seen, this looks like a clean business arrangement that you are in now; but, even if it is, it can't stand the bleeding that you are giving it. If you are going to get out of this thing, as you have left everything else you were ever in, get out right away. Realize every dollar you can at once, and let us take a trip abroad."

"I can't let go just yet," he replied.

She looked up, startled.

"Nothing wrong in this, is there, Jim?"

"Wrong!" he exclaimed. "Fanny, I never did anything in my life that the law could get me for. The law is a friend of mine. It was framed up especially for the protection of J. Rufus Wallingford. I can shove ordinary policemen off the sidewalk and make the chief stand up and salute when I go past. The only way I could break into a jail would be to buy one."

She shook her head.

"You're too smart a man to stay out of jail Jim. The penitentiary is full of men who were too clever to go there. You're a queer case, anyhow. If you had buckled down to straight business, with your ability you'd be worth ten million dollars to-day."

He chuckled.

"Look at the fun I'd have missed, though."

But for once she would not joke about their position.

"No," she insisted, "you're looking at it wrong, Jim. You had to leave Boston; you had to leave Baltimore; you had to leave Philadelphia and Washington; you will have to leave this town."

"Never mind, Fanny," he admonished her. "There are fifty towns in the United States as good as this, and they've got coin in every one of them. They're waiting for me to come and get it, and when I have been clear through the list I'll start all over again. There's always a fresh crop of bait-nibblers, and money is being turned out at the mint every day."

"Have it your own way," responded Mrs. Wallingford; "but you will be wise if you take my advice to accumulate some money while you can this time, so that we do not have to take a night train out in the suburbs, as we did when we left Boston.''

Mr. Wallingford returned no answer. He opened the cellar door and touched the button that flooded his wine cellar with light, going down himself to hunt among his bottles for the one that would tempt him most. Nevertheless, he did some serious thinking, and, at the next board-of-directors' meeting, he announced that the covering machine was well under way, showing them drawings of a patent application he was about to send off.

It was a hopeful sign—one that restored confidence. He must now organize a selling department and must have a Chicago branch. They listened with respect, even with elation. After all, while this man had deceived them as to his financial standing when he first came among them, he was well posted, for their benefit, upon matters about which they knew nothing. Moreover, there was the great tack! He went to Chicago and appointed a Western sales agent. When he came back he had sold fifteen thousand dollars' worth of his stock through the introductions gained him by this man.

J. Rufus Wallingford was ''cleaning up.''

CHAPTER VII

WHEREIN THE GREAT TACK INVENTOR SUDDENLY
DECIDES TO CHANGE HIS LOCATION

"IN two weeks we will be ready for the market," Wallingford told inquiring members of the company every two weeks, and, in the meantime, the model for the covering device, in which change after change was made, went on very slowly, while the money went very rapidly. A half dozen of the expensive stamping machines had already been installed, and the treasury was exhausted. The directors began to look worried.

One morning, while Ella Jasper was at her sweeping in the front room, the big red automobile chugged up to the gate and J. Rufus Wallingford got out. He seemed gigantic as he loomed up on the little front porch and filled the doorway.

"Where is your father?" he asked her.

"He is over at Kriegler's," she told him, and directed him how to find the little German saloon where the morning "lunch club" gathered.

Instead of turning, he stood still for a moment and looked her slowly from head to foot. There was that in his look which made her tremble, which made her flush with shame, and when at last he turned away she sat down in a chair and wept.

At Kriegler's, Wallingford found Jasper and two other stockholders, and he drew them aside to a corner table. For a quarter of an hour he was jovial with them, and once more they felt the magnetic charm of his personality, though each one secretly feared that he had come again for money. He had, but not for himself.

"The treasury is empty," he calmly informed them, during a convenient pause, "and the Corley Machine Company insist on having their bill paid. We owe them two thousand dollars, and it will take five thousand more to complete the covering machine."

"You've been wasting money in the company as you do at home," charged David, flaring up at once with long-suppressed grievances. "You had thirty thousand cash to begin with. I was down to the Corley Machine Company myself, day before yesterday, and I saw a pile of things you had them make and throw away that they told me cost nearly five thousand dollars."

"They didn't show you all of it," returned Wallingford coolly. "There's more. You don't expect to perfect a machine without experimenting, do you? Now you let me alone in this. I know my business, and no man can say that I am not going after the best results in the best way. You fellows figure on expense as if we were conducting a harness shop or a grocery store," he continued, whereat Jasper and Lewis reddened with resentment of the sort for which they could not find voice. "Rent, light, power, and wages eat up money every day," he reminded them, "and every day's delay means that much more waste. We *must* have money to complete this covering machine, and we must have it at once. There is twenty thousand dollars' worth of treasury stock for sale, aside from the hundred thousand held in reserve until we are ready to manufacture. That extra stock must be sold right away! I leave it to you," he concluded, rising. "I'm not a stock salesman," and with that brazen statement he left them.

The statement was particularly brazen because that very morning, after he left these men, he disposed of a five-thousand-dollar block of his own stock and turned the money over to his wife before he returned to the office in the afternoon. Lamb received him in a torrent of impatience.

"I feel like a cheat," he declared. "The Corley people were over here again, and say that they do not know us. They only know our money, and they want some at once or they will not proceed with the machinery."

"I have been doing what I could," replied Wallingford. "I put the matter up to Jasper and Lewis and Nolting this morning. I told them they would have to sell the extra treasury stock."

"You did!" exclaimed Lamb. "Why did you go to them? Why didn't you go out and sell the stock yourself?"

"I am not a stock salesman, my boy."

"You have been active enough in selling your private stock," charged Lamb.

"That's my business," retorted Mr. Wallingford. "I am strictly within my legal rights in disposing of my own stock. It is my property, to do with as I please."

"It is obtaining money under false pretenses, for until you have completed this machinery and made a market for our goods, the stock you have sold is not worth the paper it is printed on. It represents no value whatever."

"It represents as much value as treasury stock or any other stock," retorted Mr. Wallingford. "By the way, make a transfer of this fifty-share certificate to Thomas D. Caldwell."

"Caldwell!" exclaimed Lamb. "Why, he is one of the very men we have been trying to interest in some of this treasury stock. He is of our lodge. Last week we had him almost in the notion, but he backed out."

"When the right man came along he bought," said Wallingford, and laughed.

"This money should have gone into our depleted treasury," Lamb declared hotly. "I refuse to make the transfer."

"I don't care; it's nothing to me. I have the money and I shall turn over this certificate to Mr. Caldwell. When he demands the transfer you will have to make it."

"There ought to be some legal way to compel this sale to be made of treasury stock."

"Possibly," admitted Mr. Wallingford; "but there isn't. You will find, my boy, that everything I do is strictly within the pale of the law. I can go into any court and prove that I am an honest man."

Lamb sprang angrily from his chair.

"You're a thief," he charged, his eyes flashing.

"I'm not drawing any salary for it," replied Wallingford, and Lamb halted his anger with a sickened feeling. The two hundred dollars a month that he had been drawing lay heavily upon his conscience.

"I'm going to ask for a reduction in my pay at the next meeting," he declared. "I cannot take the money with a clear conscience."

"That's up to you," replied Wallingford; "but I want to remind you that unless money is put into this treasury within a day or so the works are stopped," and he went out to climb into his auto, leaving the secretary to some very sober thought.

Well, Lamb reflected, what was there to do? But one thing: raise the money by the sale of treasury stock to replenish their coffers and carry on the work. He wished he could see his friend Jasper. The wish was like sorcery, for no more was it uttered than David and Mr. Lewis came in. They were deeply worried over the condition into which affairs had been allowed to drift, but Lamb had cooled down by this time. He allowed them to hold an indignation meeting for a time, but presently he reminded them that, after all, no matter what else was right or wrong, it would be necessary to raise money—that the machine must be finished. They went over to the shop to look at it. The workmen were testing it by hand when they arrived, and it was working with at least a fair degree of accuracy. The inspection committee did not know that the device was entirely impractical. All that they saw was that it produced the result of a finished tack with a cover of colored cloth glued tightly to its head, and to them its operation was a silent tribute to the genius of the man they had been execrating. They came away encouraged. It was Mr. Lewis who expressed the opinion which was gaining ground with all of them.

"After all," he declared, "we're bound to admit that he's a big man."

The result was precisely what Wallingford had foreseen. These men, to save their company, to save the money they had already invested, raised ten thousand dollars among them. David Jasper put another five-thousand-dollar mortgage on his property; Mr. Lewis raised two thousand, and Edward Lamb three thousand, and with this money they bought of the extra treasury stock to that amount. J. Rufus Wallingford returned in the morning. The stock lay open for him to sign; there was ten thousand dollars in the treasury, and a check to the Corley Machine Company, already signed by the treasurer, was also awaiting his signature.

The eight thousand dollars that was left went at a surprisingly rapid rate, for, with a love for polished detail, Wallingford had ordered large quantities of shipping cases, stamps to burn the company's device upon them, japanned steel signs in half a dozen colors to go with each shipment, and many other expensive incidentals, besides the experimental work. There were patent applications and a host of other accumulating bills that gave Lamb more worry and perplexity than he had known in all his fifteen years of service with the Dorman Company. The next replenishment was harder. To get the remaining ten thousand dollars in the treasury, the already committed stockholders scraped around among their friends to the remotest acquaintance, and placed scrip no longer in blocks of five thousand, but of ten shares, of five shares, even in driblets of one and two hundred dollars, until they had absorbed all the extra treasury stock; and in that time Wal-

lingford, by appointing a St. Louis agent, had
managed to dispose of twenty thousand dollars' worth of his own holdings. He was still
"cleaning up," and he brought in his transfer
certificates with as much nonchalance as if he
were turning in orders for tacks.

Rapid as he now was, however, he did not
work quite fast enough. He had still some
fifteen thousand dollars' worth of personal
stock when, early one morning, a businesslike
gentleman stepped into the office where Lamb
sat alone at work, and presented his card. It
told nothing beyond the mere fact that he was
an attorney.

"Well, Mr. Rook, what can I do for you?"
asked Lamb pleasantly, though not without
apprehension. He wondered what J. Rufus had
been doing.

"Are you an officer of the Universal Covered
Tack Company?" inquired Mr. Rook.

"The secretary; Edward Lamb."

"Quite so. Mr. Lamb, I represent the Invisible Carpet Tack Company, and I bring you
their formal notification to cease using their
device;" whereupon he delivered to Edward a
document. "The company assumes that you
are not thoroughly posted as to its article of
manufacture, nor as to its patents covering it,"

GET-RICH-QUICK

he resumed. "They have been on the market three years with this product."

From his pocket he took a fancifully embellished package, and, opening it, he poured two or three tacks into Edward's hand. With dismay the secretary examined one of them. It was an ordinary carpet tack, such as they were about to make, but with a crimson-covered top. Dazed, scarcely knowing what he was doing, he mechanically took his knife from his pocket and cut the cloth from it. The head was roughened for gluing precisely as had been planned for their own!

"Assuming, as I say, that you are not aware of the encroachment," the attorney went on, "the Invisible Company does not desire to let you invite prosecution, but wishes merely to warn you against attempting to put an infringement of their goods on the market. They have plenty of surplus capital, and are prepared to defend their rights with all of it, if necessary. Should you wish to communicate with me or have your counsel do so, my address is on that card," and, leaving the paper of tacks behind him, Mr. Rook left the office.

Without taking the trouble to investigate, Lamb knew instinctively that the lawyer was right, an opinion which later inquiry all too

102

thoroughly corroborated. For three years the Invisible Carpet Tack Company had been supplying precisely the article the Universal Company was then striving to perfect. What there was of that trade they had and would keep, and a sickening realization came to the secretary that it meant a total loss to himself and his friends of practically everything they possessed. The machinery in which their money was invested was special machinery that could be used for no other purpose, and was worth but little more than the price of scrap iron. Every cent that they had invested was gone!

His first thought was for David Jasper. As for himself, he was young yet. He could stand the loss of five thousand. He could go back to Dorman's, take his old position and be the more valuable for his ripened experience, and there was always a chance that a minor partnership might await him there after a few more years; but as for Jasper, his day was run, his sun had set. It was a hard task that confronted the secretary, but he must do it. He called up Kriegler's and asked for David Jasper, and when David came to the telephone he told him what had happened. Over and over, carefully and point by point, he had to explain it, for his friend could not believe, since he could not even comprehend, the blow that had fallen upon him. Suddenly, Lamb found there was no answer to a question that he asked. He called anxiously again and again. He could hear only a confused murmur in the 'phone. There were tramping feet and excited voices, and he gathered that the receiver was left dangling, that no one held it, that no one listened to what he said. Hastily putting on his coat and hat, he locked the office and took a car for the North Side.

J. Rufus Wallingford himself was busy that morning, and in the North Side, too. His huge car whirled past the little frame houses that were covered with mortgages which would never be lifted, and stopped before the home of David Jasper. His jaw was hanging loosely, his big, red face was bloated and splotched, and his small eyes were bloodshot, though they glowed with a somber fire. He had been out all night, and this was one of the few times he had been indiscreet enough to carry his excesses over into the morning; usually he was alcohol proof. At first, blinking and blearing in the sunlight, he had been numb; but an hour's swift ride in the fresh air of the country had revived him, while the ascending sun had started into life again the fumes of the wine that he had drunk, so that all of the evil within him had come uppermost without the restraining caution that belonged to his sober hours. In his abnormal condition the thought had struck him that now was the time for the final coup—that he would dispose of his remaining shares of stock at a reduced valuation and get away, at last, from the irksome tasks that confronted him, from the dilemma that was slowly but surely encompassing him. In pursuance of this idea it had occurred to him, as it never would have done in his sober moments, that David Jasper could still raise money and that he could still be made to do so. Lumbering back to the kitchen door, he knocked upon it, and Ella Jasper opened it. Ella had finished her morning's work hurriedly, for she intended to go downtown shopping, and was already preparing to dress. Her white, rounded arms were bared to the elbow, and her collar was turned in with a "V" at the throat.

The somber glow in Wallingford's eyes leaped into flame, and, without stopping to question her, he pushed his way into the kitchen, closing the door behind him. He lurched suddenly toward her, and, screaming, she flew through the rooms toward the front door. She would have gained the door easily

enough, and, in fact, had just reached it, when
it opened from the outside, and her father, accompanied by his friend Lewis, came suddenly
in. For half an hour, up at Kriegler's, they had
been restoring David from the numb half-
trance in which he had dropped the receiver
of the telephone, and even now he swayed as
he walked, so that his condition could scarcely
have been told from that of Wallingford when
the latter had come through the gate. But
there was this difference between them: the
strength of Wallingford had been dissipated;
that of Jasper had been merely suspended. It
was a mental wrench that had rendered him
for the moment physically incapable. Now,
however, when he saw the author of all his
miseries, a hoarse cry of rage burst from him,
and before his eyes there suddenly seemed to
surge a red mist. Hale and sturdy still, a
young man in physique, despite his sixty years,
he sprang like a tiger at the adventurer who
had wrecked his prosperity and who now had
held his home in contempt.

There was no impact of strained bodies, as
when two warriors meet in mortal combat; as
when attacker and defender prepare to measure
prowess. Instead, the big man, twice the size
and possibly twice the lifting and striking

strength of David Jasper, having on his side, too, the advantage of being in what should have been the summit of life, shrank back, pale to the lips, suddenly whimpering and crying for mercy. It was only a limp, resistless man of blubber that David Jasper had hurled himself upon, and about whose throat his lean, strong fingers had clutched, the craven gurgling still his appeals for grace. Ordinarily this would have disarmed a man like David Jasper, for disgust alone would have stayed his hand, have turned his wrath to loathing, his righteous vengefulness to nausea; but now he was blind, blood-mad, and he bore the huge spineless lump of moral putty to the floor by the force of his resistless onrush.

"Man!" Lewis shouted in his ear. "Man, there's a law against that sort of thing!"

"Law!" screamed David Jasper. "Law! Did it save me my savings? Let me alone!"

The only result of the interference was to alter the direction of his fury, and now, with his left hand still gripping the throat of his despoiler, his stalwart fist rained down blow after blow upon the hated, fat-jowled face that lay beneath him. It was a brutal thing, and, even as she strove to coax and pull her father away, Ella was compelled to avert her face.

The smacking impact of those blows made her turn faint; but, even so, she had wit enough to close the front door, so that morbid curiosity should not look in upon them nor divine her father's madness. Just as she returned to him, however, and even while his fist was upraised for another stroke at that sobbing coward, a spasmodic twitch crossed his face as he gasped deeply for air, and he toppled to the floor, inert by the side of his enemy. Age had told at last. In spite of an abstemious life, the unwonted exertion and the unwonted passion had wreaked their punishment upon him.

It was David's friend Lewis who, with white, set face, helped Wallingford to his feet, and, without a word, scornfully shoved him toward the door, throwing his crumpled hat after him as he passed out. With blood upon his face and two rivulets of tears streaming down across it, J. Rufus Wallingford, the suave, the gentleman for whom all good things of earth were made and provided, ran sobbing, with downstretched quivering lips, to his automobile. The chauffeur jumped out for a moment to get the hat and to dip his kerchief in the stream that he turned on for a moment from the garden hydrant; coming back to the machine, he handed the wet kerchief to his master, then, without instructions, he started home. When his back was thoroughly turned, the chauffeur, despite that he had been well paid and extravagantly tipped during all the months of his fat employment, smiled, and smiled, and kept on smiling, and had all he could do to prevent his shoulders from heaving. He was gratified—was Frank—pleased in his two active senses of justice and of humor.

Just as the automobile turned the corner, Edward Lamb came running down the street from Kriegler's, where he had gone first to find out what had happened, and he met Mr. Lewis going for a doctor. Without stopping to explain, Lewis jerked his thumb in the direction of the house, and Edward, not knocking, dashed in at the door. They had laid David on his bed in the front room, and his daughter bent over him, bathing his brow with camphor. David was speechless, but his eyes were open now, and the gleam of intelligence was in them. As their friend came to the bedside, Ella looked around at him. She tried to gaze up at him unmoved as he stood there so young, so strong, so dependable; she strove to look into his eyes bravely and frankly, but it had been a racking time, in which her strength had been sorely tested, and she swayed slightly toward him. Edward Lamb caught his sister in his arms, but when her head was pillowed for an instant upon his shoulder and the tears burst forth, lo! the miracle happened. The foolish scales fell so that he could see into his own heart, and detect what had lain there unnamed for many a long year—and Ella Jasper was his sister no longer!

"There, there, dear," he soothed her, and smoothed her tresses with his broad, gentle palm.

The touch and the words electrified her. Smiling through her tears, she ventured to look up at him, and he bent and kissed her solemnly and gently upon the lips; then David Jasper, lying there upon his bed, with all his little fortune gone and all his sturdy vigor vanished, saw, and over his wan lips there flickered the trace of a satisfied smile.

Hidden that night in a stateroom on a fast train, J. Rufus Wallingford and his wife, with but such possessions as they could carry in their suit cases and one trunk, whirled eastward.

CHAPTER VIII

MR. WALLINGFORD TAKES A DOSE OF HIS OWN
BITTER MEDICINE

AS the lights of the railroad yard, red and white and green, slid by, so passed out of the ken of these fugitives all those who had contributed to their luxury through the medium of the Universal Covered Carpet Tack Company. Lamb, Jasper, Lewis, Nolting, Ella; what were all these people to them? What were any living creatures except a part of the always moving panorama which composed the background of their lives? Nomads always since their marriage, when Mrs. Wallingford as a girl had run away from home that was no home to join this cheerful knave of fortune, they had known no resting place, no spot on earth that called to them; had formed no new ties and made no new friendships. Where all the world seemed anchored they were ever flitting on, and the faces that they knew belonged but to the more or less vivid episodes by which the man strove after such luxurious ideals as he had. Only a few of the dubious acquaintances which Wallingford had formed in his earlier days of adventure remained for them to greet as they paused before fresh flights afield. "Blackie" Daw, who had recently removed his "office" from Boston to New York, was the most constant of these, and him they entertained in one of the most exclusive hostelries in the metropolis soon after their arrival. Mr. Wallingford's face still bore traces of the recent conflict.

"Fanny's the girl!" he declared with his hand resting affectionately on his wife's shoulder, after he had detailed to Mr. Daw how he had squeezed the covered carpet tack dry of its possibilities. "She's little Mamie Bright, all right. For once we got away with it. I'm a piker, I know, but twenty-eight thousand in yellow, crinkly boys to the good, all sewed up in Fanny's skirt till we ripped it out and soused it in a deposit vault, isn't so bad for four months' work; and now we're on our way to ruin Monte Carlo."

"You're all to the mustard," admired Blackie; "you're the big noise and the blinding flash. As I say, I'd go into some legitimate line myself if I wasn't honest. What bites me, though, is that you got all that out of my little Lamb and his easy friends."

"Easy! Um—m—m—m," commented Mr. Wallingford frowningly, as he unconsciously rubbed the tips of his fingers over the black puff under his right eye. "You've got it wrong. I like to sting the big people best. They take it like a dentist's pet; but when you tap one of these pikers for a couple of mean little thousands he howls like a steam calliope. One old pappy guy started to take it out of my hide, and he tried so hard it gave him paralysis."

Mr. Daw laughed in sympathy.

"You must have had a lively get-away, to judge from the marks the mill left on you; but why this trip across the pond? Are they after you?"

"After me!" scorned J. Rufus. "There's no chance! Why, I never did a thing in my life that stepped outside the law!"

"But you lean way over the fence," charged Blackie with a knowing nod, "and some of these days the palings will break."

"By that time I'll have enough soft money in front of me to ease my fall," announced Wallingford confidently. "I'm for that get-rich-quick game, and you can just bank on me as a winner."

"You'll win all right," agreed Blackie confidently, looking at his watch, "but you're like the rest of us. You'll have to die real sudden if you want to leave anything to your widow. That's the trouble with this quick money. It's lively or you wouldn't catch it on the wing, and it stays so lively after you get it.''

He arose as he concluded this sage observation and buttoned his coat.

"But you're going to stay to dinner with us?" insisted Mrs. Wallingford.

"No," he returned regretfully. "I'd like to, but business is business. I have an engagement to trim a deacon in Podunk this evening. Give my regards to the Prince of Monaco.''

It was scarcely more than a week afterwards when he somberly turned in at the bar room of that same hotel, and almost bumped into Wallingford, who was as somberly coming out. For a moment they gazed at each other in amazement and then both laughed.

"You must have gone over and back by wireless," observed Blackie. "What turned up?"

"Stung!" exclaimed J. Rufus with deep self-scorn. "I got an inside tip on some copper stock the evening you left, and the next morning I looked up a broker and he broke me. He had just started up in the bucket-shop business and I was his first customer. He didn't wait for any more. That's all.''

WALLINGFORD

Daw laughed happily, and he was still laughing when they entered the drawing room of Wallingford's suite.

"It's the one gaudy bet that the biggest suckers of all are the wise people," he observed. "Here you go out West and trim a bunch of come-ons for twenty-five thousand, and what do you do next? Oh, just tarry here long enough to tuck that neat little bundle into the pocket of a bucket-shop broker that throws away the bucket! You'd think he was the wise boy, after that, but he'll drop your twenty-five thousand on a wire-tapping game, and the wire tapper will buy gold bricks with it. The gold-brick man will give it to the bookies and the bookies will lose it on stud poker. I'm a Billy goat myself. I clean up ten thousand last week on mining stock that permits Mr. Easy Mark to mine if he wants to, and I pay it right over last night for the fun of watching a faro expert deal from a sanded deck! Me? Cleaned with-*out* soap!"

"You don't mean to say you're broke, too?" demanded his host.

"If I had any less they'd arrest me for loitering."

Mr. Wallingford glowered upon his twenty-dollar-a-day apartments with a sigh. The

115

latest in heavy lace curtains fluttered at him from the windows, thick rugs yielded to his feet, all the frippery of Louis-Quinze, while it mocked his bigness, ministered to his comfort —but waited to be paid for!

"You don't look as good to me as you did a while ago," he declared. "I'd figured on you for a sure touch, for now it's back to the Rube patch for us. O Fanny!"

"Yes, Jim," answered a pleasant voice, and Mrs. Wallingford, in a stunning gown which, supplementing her hair and eyes, made of her a symphony in brown, came from the adjoining room. She shook hands cordially with Mr. Daw and sat down with an inquiring look at her husband.

"It's time for us to take up a collection," said the latter gentleman. "We're going ay-wye."

"Ya-as, ay-wye from he-*ah!*" supplemented Blackie to no one in particular.

"Won't your ring and scarf pin do?" his wife inquired anxiously of Mr. Wallingford. A "collection," in their parlance, meant the sacrifice of a last resource. and she was a woman of experience.

"You know they won't," he returned in mild reproach. "If I don't keep a front I know where my ticket reads to; the first tank!"

Without any further objection she brought him a little black leather case, which he opened. An agreeable glitter sparkled from its velvet depths, and he passed it to his friend with a smile of satisfaction.

"They'll please Uncle, eh, Blackie?" he observed. "The first thing to do, after I cash these, is to look at the map and pick out a fresh town where smart people have money in banks. It always helps a lot to remember that somewhere in this big United States people have been saving up coin for years, just waiting for us to come and get it."

The two men laughed, but Mrs. Wallingford did not.

"Honest, I'm tired of it," she confessed. "If this speculation of Jim's had only turned out luckily I wanted to buy a little house and live quietly and—and decently for a year or so."

Mr. Daw glanced at her in amusement.

"She wants to be respectable!" he gasped in mock surprise.

"All women do," she said, still earnestly.

"You wouldn't last three months," he informed her. "You'd join the village sewing circle and the culture club, and paddle around in a giddy whirl of pale functions till you saw you had to keep your mouth shut all the time for fear the other women would find out you knew something. Then you'd quit."

"You talk as if you had been crossed in love," she consoled him.

"That's because I'm in pain," confessed Blackie. "It hasn't been an hour since I saw a thousand dollars in real money, and the telegraph company jerked it away from me just as I reached out to bring it home."

"*Is* there that much money in the world?" inquired Wallingford.

"Not loose," replied Blackie. "I thought I had this lump pried off, but now it's got a double padlock on it and to-night it starts far, far back to that dear old metropolis of the Big Thick Water, where the windy river looks like a fresh-plowed field. But they've coin out there, and every time I think of Mr. James Clover and his thousand I'm tempted to go down to his two-dollar hotel and coax him up a dark alley."

"Who does Mr. Clover do?" inquired Wallingford perfunctorily.

Blackie's sense of humor came uppermost to soothe his anguished feelings.

"He's the Supreme Exalted Ruler of the Noble Order of Friendly Hands," he grinned, 'and his twenty-six members at three or eleven cents a month don't turn in the money fast enough; so he took a chance on the cold-iron cage and brought a chunk of the insurance reserve fund to New York to double it. I picked myself out to do the doubling for him."

Mr. Wallingford chuckled.

"I know," he said. "To double it you fold the bills when you put them in your pocket, and when Clover wanted it back you'd have him pinched for a common thief. But how did it get away? I'm disappointed in you, Blackie. I thought when you once saw soft money it was yours."

"Man died in his town. If he'd only put it off for one day the whole burg could have turned into a morgue, for I don't need it. But no! The man died, and the Supreme Exalted Secretary wired the Supreme Exalted Ruler. The telegram was brought to his room just when I had the hook to his gills, and he—went —down—stream! It was perfectly scandalous the names we called that man for having died, but it takes a long time to cuss a thousand dollars' worth."

Mr. Wallingford was thoughtful.

"A fraternal insurance company," he mused. "I've never taken a fall out of that game, and it sounds good. This gifted amateur's going

out to-night? Hustle right down to his hotel
and bring him up to dinner. Tell him I've
been thinking of going into the insurance field
and might be induced to buy a share in his
business. I've a notion to travel along with
that thousand dollars to-night, no matter where
it goes. O Fanny!'' he called again to his
wife in the other room. ''Suppose you begin
to pack up while I step out and soak the
diamonds.''

That was how Mr. James Clover came to obtain some startling new ideas about insurance;
also about impressiveness. When Mr. Wallingford in a dinner coat walked into any public
dining room, waiters were instantly electrified
and ordinary mortals felt humble. His broad
expanse of white shirt front awed the most
self-satisfied into instant submission, and he
carried himself as one who was monarch of all
he surveyed. This was due to complacency,
for though bills might press and cash be scarce,
there never stood any line of worry upon his
smooth brow. Worry was for others—those
who would have to pay. Mr. Clover, himself of
some bulk but of no genuine lordliness whatever, no sooner set eyes upon Mr. J. Rufus
Wallingford than he felt comforted. Here was
wealth unlimited, and if this opulent being

could possibly be induced to finance the Noble Order of Friendly Hands, he saw better skies ahead, bright skies that shone down on a fair, fruitful world where all was prosperity and plenty. Mr. Clover was a block-like man with a square face and a heavy fist, with a loud voice and a cultivated oratorical habit of speech which he meant to be awe-inspiring. Behind him there was a string of failures that were a constant source of wonderment to him, since he had not been too scrupulous!

"He'd be a crook if he knew how; but he stumbles over his feet," Blackie confided to Wallingford. To Clover he said: "Look out for the big man. He's a pretty smooth article, and you'll miss the gold out of your teeth if you don't watch him."

It was a recommendation, and a shrewd one. Mr. Clover was prepared by it to be impressed; he ended by becoming a dazed worshiper, and his conquest began when his host ordered the dinner. It was not merely what he ordered, but how, that stamped him as one who habitually dined well; and to Clover, who had always lived upon a beer basis, the ascent to the champagne level was dizzying. It was not until they had broached their second quart of wine that business was brought up for discussion.

"I understand you've just had a bit of hard luck, Mr. Clover," said Wallingford, laughing as if hard luck were a joke.

Mr. Clover winced within, but put on a cheerful air.

"Merely what was to have been expected," he replied. "You refer, I suppose, to the death of one of our members, but as our Order now has a large enrollment we are only averaging with the mortality tables."

"What is your membership?" asked the other with sudden directness.

"At our present rate of progress," began Mr. Clover, eloquently, squaring his shoulders and looking Mr. Wallingford straight in the eye, "thousands will have been enrolled upon our books before the end of the coming year. Already we are perfecting a new and elaborate filing system to take care of the business, which is increasing by leaps and bounds."

Mr. Wallingford calmly closed one blue orb.

"But in chilly figures, discounting next year, how many?" he asked. "Live ones, I mean, that cough up their little dues every month."

The Supreme Exalted Ruler squirmed and smiled a trifle weakly.

"You might just as well tell me, you know," insisted Mr. Wallingford, "because I shall

122

want to inspect your books if I buy in. Have you a thousand?"

"Not quite," confessed Mr. Clover, in a voice which, in spite of him, would sound a trifle leaden.

"Have you five hundred?" persisted Mr. Wallingford.

Mr. Clover considered, while the silent Mr. Daw discreetly kept his face straight.

"Five hundred and seventeen," he blurted, his face reddening.

"That isn't so bad," said Mr. Wallingford encouragingly. "But how do you clinch your rake-off?"

At this Mr. Clover could smile with smug content; he could swell with pride.

"Out our way, a little knothole in the regulations was found by yours truly," he modestly boasted. "Mine is somewhat different from any insurance order on earth. The members think they vote, but they don't. If they ever elect another Supreme Exalted Ruler, all he can do is to wear a brass crown and a red robe; I'll still handle the funds. You see, we've just held our first annual election, and I had the entire membership vote 'Yes' on a forever-and-ever contract which puts our whole income— for safety, of course—into the hands of a duly bonded company. For ten cents a month from each member this company is to pay all expenses, to handle, invest and disburse its insurance and other funds for the benefit of the Order. It's like making a savings bank our trustee; only it's different, because I'm the company."

His host nodded in approval.

"You have other rake-offs," he suggested.

"Right again!" agreed Clover with gleeful enthusiasm. "Certificate fees, fines for delinquency, regalia company and all that. But the main fountain is the little dime. Ten cents seems like a cheap game, maybe, but when we have two hundred and fifty thousand members, that trifling ante amounts to twenty five thousand dollars a month. Bad, I guess!"

"When you get it," agreed the other. "You're incorporated, then. For how much?"

"Ten thousand."

"I see," said Mr. Wallingford with a smile of tolerance. "You need me, all right. You ought to *give* me a half interest in your business."

Mr. Clover's self-assertiveness came back to him with a jerk.

"Anything else?" he asked pleasantly.

Mr. Wallingford beamed upon him.

WALLINGFORD

"I might want a salary, but it would be purely nominal; a hundred a week or so."

Mr. Clover was highly amused. The only reason on earth that he would admit another man to a partnership with him was that he must have ready cash. His shoe soles were wearing out.

"I'm afraid our business wouldn't suit you, anyhow, Mr. Wallingford," he said with bantering sarcasm. "Our office is very plain, for one thing, and we have no rug on the floor."

"We'll put rugs down right away, and if the offices are not as swell as they make 'em we'll move," Wallingford promptly announced. "I might give you two thousand for a half interest."

Mr. Clover drank a glass of champagne and considered. Two thousand dollars, at the present stage of his finances, was real money. The Noble Order of Friendly Hands had been started on a "shoestring" of five hundred dollars, and the profits of the Friendly Hands Trust Company had been nil up to the present time. This offer was more than a temptation; it was a fall.

"Couldn't think of it," he nevertheless coldly replied. "But I'll sell you half my stock at par. The secretary has ten shares, and dummy directors four. I hold eighty-six.''

"Forty-three hundred dollars!" figured Wallingford. "And you'd charge me that for a brick with the plating worn thin! You forget the value of my expert services.''

"What do you know about fraternal insurance?" demanded Clover, who had reddened under fire.

"Not a thing," confessed Mr. Wallingford. "All I know is how to get money. If I go in with you, the first thing we do is to reorganize on a two-hundred-and-fifty-thousand-dollar basis.''

Mr. Clover pounded his fist upon the table until the glasses rang, and laughed so loudly that the head waiter shivered and frowned. Seeing, however, that the noise came from Mr. Wallingford's corner, he smiled. He was venal, was the head waiter, and he remembered the pleasant, velvety rustle of a bill in his palm.

"That joke's good enough for a minstrel show," Clover declared. "Why, man, even if that stock could be sold, Gabriel's horn would catch us still struggling to pay our first dividend.''

Mr. Wallingford lit a cigarette and smiled in pity.

"Oh, well, if you figure on staying in the business till you drop dead I won't wake you up," he stated. "But I thought you wanted money."

Mr. Clover shook his head.

"We have laws in my State, Mr. Wallingford."

"I should hope so," returned that gentleman. "If it wasn't for good, safe, solid laws I never would make a cent. Why, the law's on my side all the time, and the police are the best friends I've got. They show me the way home at night."

Mr. Clover looked incredulous.

"I'm afraid you don't understand the fraternal insurance business," he insisted. "It takes a lot of hard, patient work to build up an order."

"*You* don't understand the business," retorted the other. "What, for instance, are you going to do with that thousand dollars you're taking back home?"

"Give it to the widow of Mr. Henry L. Bishop, of course," said Mr. Clover, expanding his chest and pursing his mouth virtuously. "The widows and orphans who look to the Noble Order of Friendly Hands for protection shall not look in vain."

"That will look well in a prospectus," admitted Mr. Wallingford with a knowing twinkle of his eyes; "but I'm not going to take out any insurance so you could notice it. Suppose I show you how to have Mrs. Bishop hand you back that thousand with sobs of gratitude? Do I get two hundred and fifty of it?"

"If you can do that legitimately," said Mr. Clover, leaning forward and surprised into sudden warm eagerness, "I'll accept your price for a half interest."

"I'll go with you to-night—if I can get the drawing-room on your train," decided Wallingford, and arose.

The Supreme Exalted Ruler gazed up at him with profound admiration. He looked so much like actual cash. He might be a "smooth article," but was not one Clover also "smooth"? He could guard the gold in his own teeth, all right.

"You're a wonder, Jim," said Mr. Daw to his friend when they were alone for a few minutes; "but where are you going to get that two thousand?"

"Out of the business—if I pay it at all," replied Mr. Wallingford. "Trust your Uncle Rufus."

CHAPTER IX

MRS. BISHOP, a small, nervous-look-
ing woman of forty-five, with her
thin hair drawn back so tightly
from her narrow forehead that it
gave one the headache to look at her, was in
her dismal "front room" with her wrinkled
red hands folded in her lap when Mr. Wallingford and Mr. Clover called. It was only the
day after the funeral, and she broke into tears
the moment they introduced themselves.

"Madam," declaimed Mr. Clover in his
deepest and most sympathetic voice, "it is
the blessed privilege of the Noble Order of
Friendly Hands to dry the tears of the widows
and orphans, and to shed the light of hope
upon their disconsolate pathway. It is our
pleasure to bring you, as a testimonial of your
husband's affection and loving care, this check
for one thousand dollars."

Mrs. Bishop took the check and burst into
uncontrollable sobs, whereat Mr. Wallingford

looked distinctly annoyed. If he could help it, he never, by any possibility, looked upon other than the most cheerful aspects of life.

Mr. Clover cleared his throat.

"But the broad paternal interest of the Noble Order of Friendly Hands does not stop here," he went on, turning for a glance of earned approval from J. Rufus Wallingford. "The family of every member of our Order becomes at once a ward of ours, and they may look to us for assistance, advice, and benefit in every way possible. We are a group of friends, banded together for mutual aid in time of trouble and sorrow."

Mr. Wallingford judged this magnificent flight to be a quotation from the ritual of the Noble Order of Friendly Hands, and he was correct; but, as Mrs. Bishop had ventured to look up at them, he nodded his head gravely.

"It is about that thousand dollars you hold in your hand, Mrs. Bishop," Clover continued, resuming his oratorical version of the lesson he had carefully learned from Wallingford; "and we feel it our duty to remind you that, unless it is wisely used, the plans of your thoughtful husband for your safe future will not have been carried out. How had you thought of investing this neat little sum?"

Mrs. Bishop gazed at the check through her tears and tried to comprehend that it was real money, as it would have been but for the astuteness of Mr. Wallingford. Mr. Clover had proposed to bring her ten new, crisp one-hundred-dollar bills, but his monitor had pointed out that if she ever got that money between her fingers and felt it crinkle she would never let go of it. A check was so different.

"Well," she faltered, "my daughter Minnie wanted me to get us some clothes and pay some down on a piano and lay in the winter coal and provisions and put the rest in a bank for a rainy day. Minnie's my youngest. She's just quit the High School because she wants to go to a commercial college. But my oldest daughter, Hattie, wouldn't hear to it. She says if Minnie'll only take a job in the store where she works they can run the family, and for me to take this thousand dollars and finish paying off the mortgage on the house with it. The mortgage costs six per cent. a year."

"Your daughter Hattie is a very sensible young lady," said Mr. Wallingford with great gravity. "It would be folly to expend this thousand dollars upon personal luxuries; but equally wrong to lose its earning power."

It was the voice of Wall Street, of the Gov

ernment Mint, of the very soul and spirit of all financial wisdom, that spoke here, and Mrs. Bishop felt it with a thrill.

"Madam," orated Mr. Clover, "the Noble Order of Friendly Hands has provided a way for the safe and profitable investment of the funds left to the widows and orphans under its protection. It has set aside a certain amount of high-dividend-bearing stock in the Order itself, or rather in its operating department, of which, by the way, I am the president, and of which the eminent capitalist and philanthropist, Mr. J. Rufus Wallingford, is a leading spirit." His sweeping gesture toward that benevolent multi-millionaire, and Mr. Wallingford's bow in return, were sights worth beholding. "The benevolent gentlemen who organized this generous association have just made possible this further beneficence to its dependents. The stock should pay you not less than twelve per cent. a year, and your original capital can be withdrawn at any time. With this income you can pay the interest on your mortgage, and have a tidy little sum left at the end of each quarter. Think of it, madam! Money every three months, and your thousand dollars always there!"

Mrs. Bishop glanced at him in slow comprehension. The figures that he gave her did not, as yet, mean so much, but the sight of Mr. Wallingford did. He was so big, so solid looking, so much like substantial prosperity itself. A huge diamond glowed from his finger. It must be worth several hundred dollars. Another one gleamed from his scarf. His clothing was of the latest cut and the finest mate rial. Even his socks, in the narrow rim which showed above his low-cut shoes, were silk; she could see that clear across the room.

The door opened, and a girl of seventeen or eighteen came in. That she was unusually pretty was attested by the suddenly widening eyes of Mr. Wallingford.

"And is this your daughter Minnie?" asked the benevolent gentleman, all his protecting and fostering instincts aroused.

Mrs. Bishop, in a flutter, presented her younger daughter to the fortune-bringing gentlemen, and Minnie fluttered a bit on her own account. She knew she was pretty; she read in the eyes of the wealthy-looking, perfectly groomed Mr. Wallingford that she was pretty; she saw in the smile of Mr. Clover that she was pretty, and her vanity was pleased inordinately.

A sudden brilliant idea came to Mr. Wallingford.

"I have the solution to your problem, Mrs. Bishop," he said. "We shall need more help in our offices, and your daughter shall have the place. She can soon earn more money than she ever could in a store, and can secure as good a training as she could in a business college. How would you like that, Miss Bishop?"

"I think it would be fine," replied the young lady, with a large-eyed glance toward Mr. Wallingford.

The glance was more of habit than intent. Minnie's mirror and what she had heard from her boy friends had given her an impulse toward coquetry. It was pleasant to feel her power, to see what instantaneous impression she could make upon grown men. Such a friendly party it was! Everybody was pleased, and in the end Mr. Wallingford and Mr. Clover walked away from the house with Mrs. Bishop's check and her receipt and her policy in their pockets.

Mr. Clover was lost in profound admiration.

"It worked, all right!" he said exultantly to Mr. Neil, as soon as they returned to the dingy little office. "Here's the thousand dollars," and he threw down the check. "Good Lord! I couldn't believe but that thousand was gone; and then if another man died he would put us on the toboggan."

Mr. Neil was a thin young man whose forehead wore the perpetual frown of slow thought. Also his cuffs were ragged. He was the Supreme Exalted Secretary.

"Now may I have fifty?" he inquired in an aside to Clover. "My board bill, you know."

"Certainly not!" declared the Supreme Exalted Ruler with loud rectitude. "This thousand dollars belongs in the insurance reserve fund."

"Tut, tut," interposed Wallingford. "Your alarm clock is out of order. You just now paid a death claim with that money, and the reserve fund is out that much. A private individual, however, just now bought a thousand dollars' worth of stock in the reorganized Friendly Hands Trust Company, and you have the pay in advance. Let Mr. Neil have his fifty dollars, and give me a check for my two hundred and fifty; then we'll go out to hunt a decent suite of offices and buy the furniture for it."

"There wouldn't be much of the thousand left after that," objected Mr. Clover, frowning.

"Why not? You don't suppose we are going to pay cash for anything, do you?" returned Wallingford in surprise. "My credit's good, if yours isn't."

His credit! He had not been in town four hours! As Mr. Clover looked him over again, however, he saw where he was wrong. Mr. Wallingford's mere appearance was as good as a bond. He would not ask for credit; he would take it. Mr. Clover, in a quick analysis of this thought, decided that this rich man's resources were so vast that they shone through his very bearing. Mr. Wallingford, at that same moment, after having paid his enormous hotel bill in New York and the expenses of his luxurious trip, had only ten dollars in the world.

"Now then," suggested Mr. Clover as he passed the hypnotically won check to his new partner, "we might as well conclude our personal business. I'll make you over half my stock in the company, and take your two thousand."

"All right," agreed Wallingford very cheerfully, and they both sat down to write.

Mr. Clover transferred to Mr. Wallingford forty-three shares of stock in the Friendly Hands Trust Company, Incorporated, and received a rectangular slip of paper in return. His face reddened as he examined it.

"Why, this isn't a check!" he said sharply. "It's a note for ninety days!"

WALLINGFORD

"Sure!" said J. Rufus Wallingford. "In our talk there wasn't a word said about cash."

"But cash is what I want, and nothing but cash!" exploded the other, smacking his hairy fist upon his desk.

"How foolish!" chided J. Rufus smilingly. "I see I'll have to teach you a lot about business. Draw up your chairs and get my plan in detail. If, after that, Clover, you do not want my note, you may give it back and go broke in your own way. Here's what we will do. We will organize a new operating company for two hundred and fifty thousand dollars, in twenty-five-dollar shares. We will buy over the old ten-thousand-dollar company for one hundred and fifty thousand in stock of the new company. Dividing this pro rata, you and I, Clover, will each have nearly twenty-six hundred shares. Mr. Neil, in place of his present ten shares, will have six hundred, and we shall have left four thousand shares of treasury stock. These we will sell among your members. We will reduce your present insurance rate one fourth, and use the hundred thousand dollars we take in on stock sales to get new members to whom to sell more stock. In the meantime, we'll see money every day. You and I, Clover, will each draw a hundred

137

a week, and I think Mr. Neil will be pretty well satisfied if he drags down fifty.''

The pleased expression upon Mr. Neil's face struggled with the deepening creases on his brow. Fifteen dollars a week was the most he had ever earned in his life, but he was so full of fraternal insurance figures that his skin prickled.

"But how about the insurance end of it?" he interposed. "How will we ever keep up at that ridiculously low rate? That might do for a while, but as our membership becomes older the death rate will increase on us and we can't pay it. Why, the mortality tables—" and he reached for the inevitable facts and figures.

"Who's talking about insurance?" demanded Wallingford. "I'm talking about how to get money. Put up the little red dope-book. Clover, you get busy right away and write a lot of circus literature about the grand work your members will be doing for the widows and orphans by buying this stock; also how much dividend it will pay them. When the treasury stock is sold, and we have a big enough organization to absorb it, we will begin to unload our own shares and get out. If you clean up your sixty-four thousand dollars in this year, I guess you will be willing to let the stockholders elect new officers and conduct their own Friendly Hands Trust Company any way they please, won't you?"

Mr. Clover quietly folded Mr. Wallingford's note and put it in his pocket.

"Let's go out and rent some new offices," he said.

He came back, at Mr. Neil's call, to write out that fifty-dollar check, and incidentally made out one for himself in a like amount.

"What do you think of him, anyhow?" asked Neil with a troubled countenance.

"Think of him?" repeated Clover with enthusiasm. "He's the greatest ever! If I had known him five years ago I'd be worth a million to-day!"

"But is this scheme on the level?" asked Neil.

"That's the beauty of it," said Clover, exulting like a schoolboy. "The law can't touch us any place."

"Maybe not," admitted Neil; "but somehow I don't quite like it."

"I guess you'll like your fifty a week when it begins to come in, and your fifteen thousand when we clean up," retorted Clover.

"You bet!" said Neil, but he began to do some bewildered figuring on his own account. His head was in a whirl.

CHAPTER X

AN AMAZING COMBINATION OF PHILANTHROPY AND PROFIT IS INAUGURATED

MINNIE BISHOP came to work for the Noble Order of Friendly Hands on the day that they moved into offices more in keeping with the magnificence of Mr. Wallingford, and she was by no means out of place amid the mahogany desks and fine rugs and huge leather chairs.

"Her smile alone is worth fifty dollars a week to the business," Clover admitted, but they only paid her five at the start.

She had more to recommend her, however, than white teeth and red lips. Wallingford himself was surprised to find that, in spite of her apparently frivolous bent, she had considerable ability and was quick to learn. From the first he assumed a direct guardianship over her, and his approaches toward a slightly more than paternal friendship she considered great fun. At home she mimicked him, and when her older sister tried to talk to her seriously about it she only laughed the more. Clover she amused continually, but Neil fell desperately in love with her from the start, and him she flouted most unmercifully. Really, she liked him, although she would not admit it even to herself, charging him with the fatal error of being "too serious."

In the meantime the affairs of the concern progressed delightfully. For the regulation fee, the Secretary of State, after some perfunctory inquiries, permitted the "Trust Company" to increase its capitalization to two hundred and fifty thousand dollars. Even before the certificates were delivered from the printer's, however, that month's issue of "The Friendly Hand" bore the news to the five hundred members of the Order and to four thousand five hundred prospective members, of the truly unprecedented combination of philanthropy and profit. Somewhere the indefatigable Wallingford had secured a copy of a most unusual annual statement of a large and highly successful insurance company, of the flat-rate variety and of a similar sounding name. In the smallest type to be found he had printed over this:

READ THIS REPORT OF THE PROVIDENT FRIENDS TO ITS STOCKHOLDERS

Then followed direct quotations, showing that the Provident Friends had a membership of a quarter of a million; that it had paid out in death claims an enormous amount; that it had a surplus fund expressed in a staggering array of figures; that its enrollment had increased fifty thousand within the past year. Striking sentences, such as:

WE HAVE JUST DECLARED A THIRTY PER CENT. DIVIDEND

were displayed in big, black type, the whole being spread out in such form that readers ignorant of such matters would take this to be a sworn statement of the present condition of the Order of Friendly Hands; and they were invited to subscribe for its golden stock at the rate of twenty-five dollars a share! The prudent members who were providing for their families after death could now also participate in the profits of this commendable investment during life, and at a rate which, while not guaranteed, could be expected, in the light of past experience, to pay back the capital in a trifle over three years, leaving it still intact and drawing interest.

But this, dear friends and coworkers in a noble cause, was not just a hard, money-grinding proposition. The revenue derived from the sale of stock was to be expended in the fur-

ther expansion of the Order, until it should
blanket the world and carry the blessings of
protection to the widows and orphans throughout the universe! Never before in the history
of finance had it been made possible for men
of modest means to further a charitable work,
a noble work, a work appealing to all the highest aspirations of humanity and creditable to
every finest instinct of the human heart, and
at the same time to reap an enormous profit!
And the price was only twenty-five dollars a
share—while they lasted!

Wallingford had secured the data and supplied the human frailty ideas for this flaming
announcement, but Clover had put it together,
and, as he examined the proof sheet, the latter
gentleman leaned back in his chair with profound self-esteem.

"That'll get 'em!" he exulted. "If that
don't bring in the money to make this the
greatest organization in the business, I don't
want a cent!"

"You spread it on too much," objected Neil.
"Why can't we do just as well or better by
presenting the thing squarely? It seems to me
that any man who would be caught by the
self-evident buncombe of that thing would be
too big a sucker to have any money."

Wallingford looked at him thoughtfully.

"You're right, in a way, Neil," he admitted. "The men who have real money wouldn't touch it, but the people we're appealing to have stacked theirs up a cent at a time, and they are afraid of all investments — even of the banks. When you offer them thirty per cent., however, they are willing to take a chance; and, after all, I don't see why, with the money that comes in from this stock sale, we should not be able to expand our organization to even larger proportions than the Provident Friends. If we do that, what is to prevent a good dividend to our stockholders?"

Clover glanced at his partner in surprise. From that overawing bulk there positively radiated high moral purpose, and Neil shriveled under it. When they were alone, Clover, making idle marks with his pencil, looked up at Wallingford from time to time from under shaggy brows, and finally he laughed aloud.

"You're the limit," he observed. "That's a fine line of talk you gave Neil."

"Can't we buy him out?" asked Wallingford abruptly.

"What with? A note?" inquired Clover. "Hardly."

"Cash, then."

WALLINGFORD

"Will you put it up?"

"I'll see about it, for if I have him gauged right he will be hunting for trouble all along the line."

Wallingford went to the window and looked out; then he got his hat. As he stepped into the hall Neil came from an adjoining room.

"Do you want to sell your stock, Neil?" asked Clover.

"To whom?" asked Neil slowly. Wallingford had shaken his slow deductions, had suggested new possibilities to ponder, and he was still bewildered.

"To Wallingford."

"Say, Clover, has he *got* any money?" demanded Neil.

"If he hasn't he can get it," replied the other. "Come here a minute."

He drew Neil to the window and they looked down into the street. Standing in front of the office building was a huge, maroon-colored automobile with a leather-capped chauffeur in front. As they watched, Mr. Wallingford came out to the curb and the chauffeur saluted with his finger. Mr. Wallingford took from the rear seat a broad-checked ulster, put it on, and exchanged his derby for a cap to match. Then he climbed into the auto and went whirring away.

"That looks like money, don't it?" demanded Clover.

"I give up," said Neil.

"How much do you want for your stock?" inquired Clover, again with a smile.

"Par!" exclaimed Neil, once more satisfied. "Nothing less!"

"Right you are," agreed Clover. "This man Wallingford is the greatest ever, I tell you! He's a wonder, a positive genius, and it was a lucky day for me that I met him. He will make us all rich."

His admiration for Wallingford knew no bounds. He had detected in the man a genius for chicanery, and so long as he was "in with it" Wallingford might be as "smooth" as he liked. Were they not partners? Indeed, yes. Share and share alike!

That night Clover and Neil dined with Mr. and Mrs. Wallingford at their hotel, and if Neil had any lingering doubts as to Mr. Wallingford's command of money, those doubts were dispelled by the size of the check, by the obsequiousness shown them, and by the manner in which Mrs. Wallingford wore her expensive clothing. After dinner Wallingford took them for a ride in his automobile, and at a quiet road house, a dozen miles out of town, over sparkling drinks and heavy cigars, they quite incidentally discussed a trifling matter of business.

"You fellows go ahead with the insurance part of the game," Wallingford directed them. "I don't understand any part of that business, but I'll look after the stock sales. That I know I can handle."

They were enthusiastic in their seconding of this idea, and after this point had been reached, the host, his business done, took his guests back to town in the automobile upon which he had not as yet paid a cent, dropping them at their homes in a most blissful state of content.

Proceeding along the lines of the understanding thus established, within a few days money began to flow into the coffers of the concern. Mr. Wallingford's method of procedure was perfectly simple. When an experimentally inclined member of any one of the out-of-town "Circles" sent in his modest twenty-five dollars for a share of stock, or even inquired about it, Wallingford promptly got on a train and went to see that man. Upon his arrival he immediately found out how much money the man had and issued him stock to the amount; then he got introductions to the other members and brought home stock subscriptions to approximately the exact total of their available cash. There was no resisting him. In the meantime, with ample funds to urge it forward, the membership of the organization increased at a rapid enough rate to please even the master hand. New members meant new opportunities for stock sales, and that only, to him, and to Clover, the world, at last, was as it should be. Money was his for the asking, and by means which pleased his sense of being "in" on a bit of superior cleverness. Quite early in the days of plenty he saw a side investment which, being questionable, tempted him, and he came to Wallingford—to borrow money!

"I'll sell some of your stock," offered Wallingford. "I want to sell a little of my own, anyhow."

In all, he sold for Clover five thousand dollars' worth, and the stock was promptly reported by the purchasers for transfer on the books of the company. Some of Wallingford's also came in for transfer, although a much less amount; sufficient, however, it seemed, for he took the most expensive apartments in town, filled them with the best furnishings that were made, and lived like a king. Mrs. Wallingford secured her diamonds again and bought many more. Clover also "took on airs." Neil worried. He had made a study of the actual cost of insurance, and the low rate that they were now receiving filled him with apprehension.

"We're going on the rocks as fast as we can go," he declared to Clover. "According to the tables we're due for a couple of deaths right now, and the longer they delay the more they will bunch up on us. Mark what I say: the avalanche will get you before you have time to get out, if that's what you plan on doing. I wish the laws governed our rate here as they do in some of the other States."

"What's the matter with the rate?" Clover wanted to know. "When it's inadequate we'll raise it."

"That isn't what we're promising to do," insisted Neil. "We're advertising a permanent flat rate."

"Show me where," demanded Clover.

Neil tried to do so, but everywhere, in their policies, in their literature, or even in their correspondence, that he pointed out a statement apparently to that effect, Clover showed him a "joker" clause contradicting it.

"You see, Neil, you're too hasty in jumping at conclusions," he expostulated. "You know that the law will not permit us to claim a flat rate without a sufficient cash provision, under State control, to guarantee it, and compels us to be purely an assessment company. When the time comes that we must do so, we will do precisely what other companies have done before us: raise the rate. If it becomes prohibitive the company will drop out of business, as so many others have; but we will be out of it long before then."

"Yes," retorted Neil, "and thousands of people who are too old to get fresh insurance at any price, and who will have paid for years, will be left holding the bag."

"The trouble with you, Neil, is that you have a streak of yellow," interrupted Clover impatiently. "Don't you like your fifty a week?"

"Yes."

"Don't you like your fifteen thousand dollars' worth of stock?"

"It looks good to me," confessed Neil.

"Then keep still or sell out and get out."

"I'm not going to do that," said Neil deliberately. He had his slow mind made up at last. "I'm going to stick, and reorganize the company when it goes broke!"

When Clover reported this to Wallingford that gentleman laughed.

"How is he on ritual work?" he asked.

"Fine! He has a streak of fool earnestness in him that makes him take to that flubdubbery like a duck to water."

"Then send him out as a special degree master to inaugurate the new lodges that are formed. He's a nuisance in the office."

In this the big man had a double purpose. Neil was paying entirely too much attention to Minnie Bishop of late, and Wallingford resented the interference. His pursuit of the girl was characteristic. He gave her flowers and boxes of candy in an offhand way, not as presents, but as rewards. As the business grew he appropriated her services more and more to his own individual work, seating her at a desk in his private room, and a neat balance-sheet would bring forth an approving word and an offhand:

"Fine work. I owe you theater tickets for that."

The next time he came in he would bring the tickets and drop them upon her desk, with a brusque heartiness that was intended to disarm suspicion, and with a suggestion to take her mother and sister along. Moreover, he raised her salary from time to time. The consideration that he showed her would have won the gratitude of any girl unused to such attentions and unfamiliar with the ways of the world, but under them she nevertheless grew troubled and thoughtful. Noticing this, Wallingford conceived the idea that he had made an impression, whereupon he ventured to become a shade more personal.

About this time another disagreeable circumstance came to her attention and plunged her into perplexity. Clover walked into Mr. Wallingford's room just as the latter was preparing to go out.

"Tag, you're it, Wallingford," said Clover jovially, holding out a piece of paper. "I've just found out that your note was due yesterday."

"Quit joking with me on Wednesdays," admonished Wallingford, and taking the note he tore it into little bits and threw them into the waste basket.

"Here! That's two thousand dollars, and it's mine," Clover protested.

Wallingford laughed.

"You didn't really think I'd pay it, did you? Why, I told you at the time that it was only a matter of form; and, besides that, you know my motto: 'I never give up money,'" and, still chuckling, he went out.

"Isn't he the greatest ever?" said Clover admiringly, to Minnie.

But Minnie could not see the joke. If Wallingford "never gave up money," and Clover subscribed to that clever idea with such enthusiasm that he was willing to be laughed out of two thousand dollars, what would become of her mother's little nest-egg? A thousand dollars was a tragic amount to the Bishops. That very evening, as Wallingford went out, he ventured to pinch and then to pat her cheek, and shame crimsoned her face that she had brought upon herself the coarse familiarities which now she suddenly understood. Neil, who had come in from a trip that afternoon, walked into the office just after Wallingford had gone, and found her crying. The sight of her in tears broke down the reserve that she had forced upon him, so that he told her many things; told them eloquently, too, and suddenly she found herself glad that he had come—glad to rely upon him and confide in him. Naturally, when she let him draw from her the cause of her distress, he was furious. He wanted to hunt Wallingford at once and chastise him, but she stopped him with vehement earnestness.

"No," she insisted, "I positively forbid it! When Mr. Wallingford comes here to-morrow

GET-RICH-QUICK

I want him to find me the same as ever, and I
do not want one word said that will make him
think I am any different. But I want you to
walk home with me, if you can spare the time
want to talk with you."

CHAPTER XI

NEIL TAKES A SUDDEN INTEREST IN THE BUSINESS
AND WALLINGFORD LETS GO

NEIL, the next day after his talk with Minnie Bishop, had a great idea, which was nothing more nor less than a Supreme Circle Conclave, in which a picked degree team would exemplify the ritual, and to which delegates from all the local circles should be invited. They had never held a Supreme Conclave, and they needed it to arouse enthusiasm. Clover fell in with the idea at once. It would provide him with an opportunity for one of the spread-eagle speeches he was so fond of making. As this phase of the business—comprising the insurance and the lodge work—was left completely in charge of Clover and Neil, Wallingford made no objections, and, having ample funds for carrying out such a plan, it was accordingly arranged. Neil went on the road at once about this matter, but letters between himself and Minnie Bishop passed almost daily. An indefinable change had come over the girl. She had grown more earnest, for one thing, but she assumed a forced flippancy with Wallingford because she found that it was her only defense against him. She turned off his advances as jests, and her instinct of coquetry, though now she recognized it and was ashamed of it, made her able to puzzle and hold uncertainly aloof even this experienced "man of the world." It was immediately after she had jerked her hand away from under his one afternoon that, in place of the reproof he had half expected from her, she turned to him with a most dazzling smile.

"By the way, we've both forgotten something, Mr. Wallingford," she said. "Quarter day for the Bishops is long past due."

"What is it that is past due?" he asked in surprise.

"When my mother bought her stock, you know, you promised that she should have twelve per cent. interest on it, payable every three months."

"That's right," he admitted, looking at her curiously, and before she started home that evening he handed her an envelope with thirty dollars in it.

She immediately made a note of the amount and dropped it in the drawer of her desk.

"Never mind entering that in your books," he said hastily, noting her action; "just keep the memorandum until we arrange for a regular dividend, then it can all be posted at once. It's—it's a matter that has been overlooked."

She thanked him for the money and took it home with her. She had been planning for a week or more upon how to get this thirty dollars. On the very next day, while he was absorbedly poring over a small account book that he kept locked carefully in his desk, he found her standing beside him.

"I'm afraid that I shall have to ask you to buy back mother's stock in the company," she said. That morning's mail had been unusually heavy in stock sale possibilities. "We have a sudden pressing need for that thousand dollars, and we'll just have to have it, that's all."

Wallingford's first impulse was to dissuade her from this idea, but another thought now came to him as he looked musingly into his roll-top desk; and as the girl, standing above him, gazed down upon his thick neck and puffy cheeks, he reminded her of nothing so much as a monstrous toad.

"Have you the stock certificate with you?" he inquired presently.

No, she had not.

"Well, bring it down to-night," he said, "and I'll give you a check for it. I'm going away on a little trip to-morrow, and I want you to get me up a statement out of the books, anyhow."

For an instant the girl hesitated with a sharp intake of breath. Then she said, "Very well," and went home.

That night, when she returned, she paused in the hall a moment to subdue her trepidation, then, whether foolish or not, but with such courage as men might envy, she boldly opened the door and stepped in. She found Wallingford at his desk, and she had walked up to him and laid at his elbow the stock certificate, properly released, before he turned his unusually flushed face toward her. In his red eyes she saw that he had been dining rather too well, even for him. She had been prepared for this, however, and her voice was quite steady as she asked:

"Have you the check made out, Mr. Wallingford?"

"There's no hurry about it," he replied a trifle thickly. "There's some work I want you to do first."

"I'd rather you would make out the check now," she insisted, "so that I won't forget it."

158

Laboriously he filled out the blank and signed it, and then blinkingly watched her smooth, white fingers as she folded it and snapped it into her purse. Suddenly he swung his great arm about her waist and drew her toward him. What followed was the surprise of his life, for a very sharp steel hatpin was jabbed into him in half a dozen indiscriminate places, and Minnie Bishop stood panting in the middle of the floor.

"I have endured it here for weeks now, longer than I believed it possible," she shrieked at him, crying hysterically, "because we could not afford to lose this money: stood it for days when the sight of you turned me sick! It seems a year ago, you ugly beast, that I made sure you were a thief, but I wouldn't leave till I knew it was the right time to ask you for this check!"

Dazed, he stood nursing his hurts. One of her strokes had been into his cheek, and as he took his reddened handkerchief away from it a flood of rage came over him and he took a step forward; but he had miscalculated her spirit.

"I wish I had killed you!" she cried, and darted out of the door.

For three days after that episode the man was confined to his room under the care of his wife, whom he told that he had been attacked by a footpad, "a half-crazy foreigner with a stiletto." For a week more he was out of town. A peremptory telegram from Clover brought him in from his stock-drumming transactions, and by the time he reached the city he was ready for any emergency, though finally attributing the call to the fact, which he had almost forgotten, that to-morrow was the first day of the three set apart for the Supreme Circle Conclave of the Noble Order of Friendly Hands.

He arrived at about eight o'clock in the evening, and as his automobile rolled past the big building where their offices were located, he glanced up and saw that lights were blazing brightly from the windows. Anxious to find out at once the true status of affairs he went up. He was surprised to find the big reception room full of hard-featured men who looked uncomfortable in their "best clothes," and among them he recognized two or three, from surrounding small towns, to whom he had sold stock. At first, as he opened the door, black looks were cast in his direction, and a couple of the men half arose from their seats; but they sat down again as Mr. J. Rufus Wallingford's face beamed with a cordial smile.

"Good evening, gentlemen," he observed cheerfully, with a special nod for those he remembered, and then he stalked calmly through the room.

The nights being cool now, Mr. Wallingford wore a fur-lined ulster of rich material and of a fit which made his huge bulk seem the perfection of elegance. Upon his feet were shining patent leather shoes; upon his head was a shining high hat. He carried one new glove in his gloved left hand; from his right hand gleamed the big diamond. His ulster hung open in front, displaying his sparkling scarf pin, his rich scarf of the latest pattern, his fancy waistcoat. He held his head high, and no man could stand before him nor against him. When the door had closed behind him they almost sighed in unison. There went money, sacred money, even the more so that some of it was their own!

In the inner office, Wallingford was surprised to find Minnie Bishop present and working earnestly upon the books. Looking up she met his darkening glance defiantly, but even if he had chosen to speak to her there was no time, for Clover had opened the door of his own private office and greeted him with a curt nod.

"Come in here," said Clover roughly. "I want to talk to you."

It was the inevitable moment, the one for which Wallingford had long been prepared.

"Certainly," he said with aggravating cheerfulness, and, walking in, let Clover close the door behind him. He sat comfortably in the big leather chair at the side of the desk and lit a cigar, while Clover plumped himself in his own swivel.

"Who are the Rubes outside?" asked Wallingford, puffing critically at his half-dollar perfecto.

"Neil's picked degree team," answered Clover shortly. "He had them meet up here to-night for some instructions, I believe, but he's not here yet. It's his affair entirely. I want to see you about something else."

"Blaze away," said Wallingford with great heartiness, carefully placing his silk hat upon a clean sheet of paper. He was still smiling cheerfully, but in his eyes had come the trace of a glitter.

"I'll blaze away all right, whether I have your invitation or not!" snapped Clover. "You've been giving me the double cross. For every share of stock you sold for the company you've sold five of your own and pocketed the money."

"Why shouldn't I?" inquired Mr. Wallingford calmly, his willingness to admit it so pleasantly amounting to insolence. "It was my stock, and the money I got for such of it as I sold was my money."

"*Such* of it as you sold!" repeated Clover indignantly. "I know how much you unloaded. You have placed somewhat over twenty thousand for the company—"

"And five thousand for you," Wallingford reminded him. "I suppose you went South with the proceeds. If you didn't you're crazy!"

Clover flushed a trifle.

"But you got rid of nearly sixty thousand dollars of your own stock," he charged bitterly. It still rankled in him that Wallingford had "handed the lemon" to him. *Him!* Monstrous that a man should be so dishonorable! "You played me for a mark. When you handed out my certificates you instructed every man to send them in for transfer, but when you peddled your own you said nothing about that, and only the few yaps who happened to know about such things sent them in. You're nearly all sold out, and I'm holding the bag."

"Right you are," admitted Wallingford, openly amused. "I have a few shares left in my desk, though, and I'll make you a present of them. I'm going out of the company, you know."

"You're not!" exclaimed Clover, smiting his fist upon his desk. "We were in this thing together, half and half, and I want my share!"

Wallingford laughed.

"I told you once," he informed his irate partner, "that I never give up any money. My action is strictly legal. Now, don't choke!" he added as he saw Clover about to make another objection. "You've not a gasp coming. When I took hold here you were practically on your last legs. You have had a salary of one hundred dollars a week since that time. In addition to that I have handed you five thousand dollars, and you have nearly sixty thousand dollars' worth of stock left. You can do just what I have been doing: sell your stock and get out. As for me I *am* out, and that's all there is to it! I have all I want and I'm going to quit!"

The door had opened and Neil stood on the threshold.

"You bet you're going to quit!" said Neil. His face was pale but his eyes were blazing and his fists were clenched. "You're both going to quit, but not the way you think you are! Come out here. Some of my friends are in the waiting room, and they want to see you right away!"

Clover had turned a sickly, ashen white, but Wallingford rose to his feet.

"You tell them to go plumb to Hell!" he snarled.

His eyes were widened until they showed the whites. He was fully as much cowed by the suggestion as Clover, but he would "put up a front" to the last.

"Come in, boys!" commanded Neil loudly.

They came with alacrity. They crowded into the small room, packing it so snugly that Neil and Wallingford and Clover, forced into the little space before Clover's desk, stood touching.

"What does this mean?" demanded Wallingford, glaring at the invaders.

He stood alm st head and shoulders above them, and where he met a man's eyes those eyes dropped. Some of them who had not removed their hats hastily did so. His lordliness was still potent.

"You can't bluff me!" shrieked Neil, who, standing beside him, shook his fist in Wallingford's face. The contrast between the sizes of the two men would have been ludicrous, had it not been for Neil's intensity, which seemed to expand him, to make him and his passionate purpose colossal. "I know you, and these men don't!" he went on, his neck chords swelling with anger. "Why, think of it, gentlemen, in the four months that he has been here, this man has taken sixty thousand dollars from the hard-working members of this Order, has stuffed it in his pocket and is making ready to leave! The little girl out there, who is getting us up a statement for to-morrow, figured him out for the dog he is while I was still groping for the facts. He tried to take her for a fool, but she — she —" His voice broke and he smacked his fist in his palm to loosen his tongue. "You're a smart man, Mr. Wallingford, but you made a few mistakes. One of them was in sending me on the road so you could—so you—" again his voice broke and he sank his nails into his palms for control. "You thought this meeting was a mere jolly for our members, didn't you? It's not. These men are here solely as representatives of the business interests of their friends. We're going to put this Order back upon a sound basis, and the first thing we're going to do is to cut out graft. Why, you unclean whelp, you have spent over fourteen thousand dollars in the four months you have been here, and you have—or had, up to a week ago—forty-five thousand dollars in the Second National—all of poor men's money! How do I know? You lost your bank book which had just been balanced. As for you, Clover, you're a clog upon the business, too!" Clover had brought this upon himself by darting at Wallingford a glance of hate, which Neil caught. "Now this is what *you're* going to do, James Clover. For having fathered the Order you're to be allowed to keep the five thousand dollars you got for the sale of stock. Your remaining stock you're going to transfer over to our treasury, and then you're going to step down and out. As for you, Mr. J. Rufus Wallingford, you're going to write a check for forty-five thousand dollars, payable to the company."

"What you are asking of me is unjust—and absurd," whined Wallingford.

"Write that check!" Neil almost screamed. "We know you're slick enough to keep your tricks within legal bounds, and that's why these men are here."

The brow of Wallingford contracted and he tried to look angry, but his breath was coming short and there was a curious pallor around the edge of his lips and around his eyes.

"This is coercion!" he charged with dry mouth.

"Put it that way if you want to," agreed Neil hotly.

"We'll break your infernal neck, that's what we'll do!" put in a spokesman back toward the door, and there was a general pressing forward. Neil had lashed them into fury, and one rawboned fellow, a blacksmith, wedged through them with purple face and upraised fist. So heavily that he knocked the breath out of Clover with his chair back, Wallingford plumped down at the desk and whipped out his check book.

"I ask one thing of you," he said, as he picked up the pen with a curious trembling grimace that was almost like a smile, but was not. "You must leave me at least a thousand dollars to get away from here."

There was a moment of silence.

"That's reasonable," granted Neil, after careful consideration. "Give us the check for forty-four thousand."

Wallingford wrote it and then he put it in his pocket.

"I have the check ready, gentlemen," he an-

168

nounced, "but I'll give it to you at the entrance of my home—to a committee consisting of Neil and any two others you may select. If I hand it to you before I pass out at that door, some of you are liable to—to lose your heads."

He was positively craven in appearance when he said this, and with an expression of contempt Neil agreed to it. Wallingford's car was still waiting on the street below, and into it piled the four. Before the rich building where J. Rufus had his apartments, Neil and one of the other men got out first; but if they had anticipated any attempt at escape on Wallingford's part they were mistaken. Without a word he handed the check to Neil and waited while they inspected it to see that it was correctly drawn and signed.

"Now, Mr. Slippery Eel," said Neil exultantly as he put the check in his pocket, "it won't do any good to try to stop this check, for if I can't draw it you can't. I shall be there in the morning when the bank opens. I secured an injunction this afternoon that will tie up your account," and his voice swelled with triumph.

Wallingford laughed. With his hand upon the knob he held the vestibule door open, and he felt safe from violence, which was all he feared.

"Well," said he philosophically, "I see I'm beaten, and there's no use crying over spilled milk."

Neil looked after him dubiously, as he swaggered into the hall.

"I didn't expect it would be so easy," he said to the men. "I knew the fellow was a physical coward, but I didn't know he was such a big one. My lawyer told me he could even beat us on that injunction."

Mr. Wallingford did not go directly to his apartments. He went into the booth downstairs, instead, and telephoned his wife. Then he went out. He was gone for about half an hour, and, when he came back, Mrs. Wallingford, wastefully leaving a number of expensive accumulations that were too big to be carried as hand luggage, and abandoning the rich furniture to be claimed by the deluded dealers, had four suit cases packed.

CHAPTER XII

FATE ARRANGES FOR J. RUFUS AN OPPORTUNITY TO MANUFACTURE SALES RECORDERS

IT was not until their train had passed beyond the last suburb that Wallingford, ensconced in the sleeper drawing room, was able to resume his accustomed cheerfulness.

"Sure you have that bundle of American passports all right, Fanny?" he inquired.

"They're perfectly safe, but I'm glad to be rid of them," she answered listlessly, and opening her hand bag she emptied it of its contents, then, with a small penknife, loosened the false bottom in it. From underneath this she drew a flat package of thousand-dollar bills and handed them to him.

"Forty of them!" gloated Wallingford, counting them over. Then he pounded upon his knees and laughed. "I can see Starvation Neil when he has to tell his jay delegates that I drew out every cent the day after I lost my bank book. I'd been missing too many things that never turned up again. I fixed them to-night, too. Although I didn't need to do it to be on the law's safe side, I hustled out before we started and swore to a notary that I signed that check under coercion; and they'll get that affidavit before the check and the injunction!''

Mrs. Wallingford did not join him in the shoulder-heaving laugh which followed.

"I don't like it, Jim," she urged. "You're growing worse all the time, and some day you'll overstep the bounds. And have you noticed another thing? Our money never does us any good.''

"You'll wake up when we get settled down some place to enjoy ourselves. I don't believe you know how well you like fine dresses and diamonds, and to live on the fat of the land. You know what this little bundle of comfort means? That we're the salt of the earth while it lasts; that for a solid year we may have not only all the luxuries in the world, but everybody we meet will try to make life pleasant for us.''

To that end Wallingford secured a suite of rooms at two hundred dollars per week the moment they landed in New York, and began to live at a corresponding rate. He gave himself no regret for yesterday and no care for to-morrow, but let each extravagant moment take care of itself. It was such intervals as this, between her husband's more than doubtful "business" operations, that reconciled Mrs. Wallingford to their mode of life, or, rather, that numbed the moral sensibilities which lie dormant in every woman. While they were merely spending money she was content to play the *grande dame,* to dress herself in exquisite toilettes and bedeck herself with brilliant gems, to go among other birds of fine feathers that congregated at the more exclusive public places, though she made no friends among them, to be surrounded by every luxury that money could purchase, to have her every whim gratified by the mere pressing of a button. As for Wallingford, to be a prince of spenders, to find new and gaudy methods of display, to have people turn as he passed by and ask who he might be; these things made existence worth while.

Only one thing—his restless spirit—kept him from pursuing this uneventful path until all of his forty thousand dollars was gone. After two months of slothful ease, something more exciting became imperative, and just then the racing season began and supplied that need. Every afternoon they drove out to the track, and there Wallingford bet thousands as another man might bet fives. There could be but one end to this, but he did not care. What did it matter whether he spent his money a trifle more or less quickly? There was plenty of it within his broad hunting grounds, and when what he had was gone he had only to go capture more; so it was no shock one morning to count over his resources and find that he had but a fragment left of what he had laughingly termed his "insurance fund." Upon that same morning an urgent telegram was delivered to him from "Blackie" Daw. He read it with a whistle of surprise and passed it over to his wife without comment.

"You're not going?" she asked with much concern, passing the message back to him.

"Of course I am," he promptly told her. "Blackie's the only man I could depend upon to get me out of a similar scrape."

"But, Jim," she protested; "you just now said that you have barely over six thousand left."

"That's all right," he assured her. "I'd have to get out and hustle in less than a month anyhow, at the rate we're going. I'll just take Blackie's five thousand, and a couple of hundred over for expenses. You keep the balance of the money and we'll get out of these apartments at once. I'll get you nice accommodations at about twenty a week, and before I come back I'll have something stirred up."

Secretly, he was rather pleased with the turn affairs had taken. Inaction was beginning to pall upon him, and this message that called urgently upon him to take an immediate trip out of town was entirely to his liking. Within an hour he had transferred his wife into comfortable quarters and was on his way to the train. He had very little margin of time, but, slight as it was, the grinning Fate which presided over his destinies had opportunity to arrange a meeting for him. Even as he pointed out his luggage to a running porter, a fussy little German in very new-looking clothes which fitted almost like tailor-made, had rushed back to the gates of the train shed where the conductor stood with his eyes fixed intently on his watch, his left hand poised ready to raise.

"I left my umbrella," spluttered the passenger.

"No time," declared the autocrat, not gruffly or unkindly, but in a tone of virtuous devotion to duty.

The little German's eyes glared through his spectacles, his face puffed red, his gray mustache bristled.

"But it's my wife's umbrella!" he urged, as if that might make a difference.

The brass-buttoned slave to duty did not even smile. He raised his hand, and in a moment more the potent wave of his wrist would have sent Number Eighteen plunging on her westward way. In that moment, however, the Pullman conductor, waiting with him, clutched the blue arm of authority.

"Hold her a second," he advised, and with his thumb pointed far up the platform. "Here comes from a dollar up for everybody. He's rode with me before."

The captain of Eighteen gave a swift glance and was satisfied.

"Sure. I know him," he said of the newcomer; then he turned to the still desperately hopeful passenger and relented. "Run!" he directed briefly.

Wallingford, who had secured for Carl Klug this boon, merely by an opportune arrival, was not hurrying. He was too large a man to hurry, so a depot porter was doing it for him. The porter plunged on in advance, springing heavily from one bent leg to the other, weighted down with a hat box in one hand, a huge Gladstone bag in the other and a suit case under each arm. The perspiration was streaming down his face, but he was quite content. Behind him stalked J. Rufus, carrying only a cane and gloves; but more, for him, would have seemed absurd, for when he moved the background seemed to advance with him, he was so broad of shoulder and of chest and of girth. Dignity radiated from his frame and carriage, good humor from his big face, wealth from every line and crease of his garments; and it was no matter for wonder that even the rigid schedule of Number Eighteen was glad to extend to this master of circumstances its small fraction of elasticity.

One of the Pullman porters from up the train caught a glimpse of his approach and came running back to snatch up two of the pieces of luggage. It did not matter to him whether the impressive gentleman was riding in his coach or not; he was anxious to help on mere general principles, and was even more so when the depot porter, dropping the luggage inside the gate, broke into glorious sunrise over the crinkling green certificate of merit that was handed him. The Pullman conductor only asked to what city the man was bound, then he too snatched up a suit case and a bag and raced with the porter to take them on board, calling out as he ran the car into which

the luggage must go. To Wallingford their
activity gave profound satisfaction, and he
paused to hand the conductor a counterpart to
the huge black cigar he was then smoking.
It had no band of any sort upon it, but
he conductor judged the cigar by the man.
It was not less than three for a dollar, he
was sure.

"Pretty close figuring, old man," observed
Wallingford cordially.

The conductor's smile, while gracious enough,
was only fleeting, for this thing of being responsible for Eighteen was an anxious business, the gravity of which the traveling public
should be taught to appreciate more.

"We're nearly a minute off now," he said,
"and I've let myself in to wait for a Dutch-
man I let run out when I saw you coming.
There he is. Third car up for you, sir,"
and he ran up to the steps of the second car
himself.

The missing passenger came tearing through
the gates just as Wallingford went up the car
steps. The conductor held his hand aloft, and
the engineer, looking back, impatiently clanged
his bell. The porter picked up his stepping-box
and jumped on after his tip, but he looked out
to watch the little German racing with all his

might up the platform, and did not withdraw his head until the belated one, all legs and arms, scrambled upon the train. Instantly the wheels began to revolve, both vestibule doors were closed with a slam, and a moment later Carl Klug, puffing and panting, dropped upon a seat in the smoking compartment, opposite to the calm J. Rufus Wallingford, without breath—and without his umbrella.

"Schrecklich!" he exploded when he could talk. "They are all thieves here. I leave my umbrella in the waiting-room five minutes, I go back and it is gone. Gone! And it was my wife's umbrella!"

Under ordinary circumstances Mr. Klug, whose thirty years of residence in America had not altogether destroyed certain old-country notions of caste, would not have ventured to address this lordly-looking stranger, but at present he was angry and simply must open the vials of his wrath to some one. He met with no repulse. Mr. Wallingford was not one to repulse strangers of even modest competence. He only laughed. A score of jovial wrinkles sprang about his half-closed eyes, and his pink face grew pinker.

"Right you are," he agreed. "When I'm in this town I keep everything I've got right

in front of me, and if I want to look the other
way I edge around on the other side of my
grips.''

Mr. Klug digested this idea for a moment,
and then he, too, laughed, though not with the
abandon of Mr. Wallingford. He could not so
soon forget his wife's umbrella.

"It is so," he admitted. "I have been here
three days, and every man I had any business
with ought to be in *jail!*"

A sudden thought as he came to this last
word made Mr. Klug lay almost shrieking em-
phasis upon it, and smack both fists upon his
knees. He craned his head forward, his eyes
glared through his spectacles, his cheeks puffed
out and his mustache bristled. Wallingford
surveyed him with careful appraisement. The
clothing was ready made, but it was a very
good quality of its kind. The man's face was
an intelligent one and told of careful, concen-
trated effort. His hands were lean and rough,
the fingers were supple and the outer joints
bent back, particularly those of the thumb,
which described almost a half circle. The in-
sides of the fingers were seamed and crossed
with countless little black lines. From all this
the man was a mechanic, and a skilled one.
Those fingers dealt deftly with small parts, and

years of grimy oil had blackened those innumerable cuts and scratches.

"Did they sting you?" Wallingford inquired with a dawning interest that was more than courteous sympathy.

"I guess *not!*" snapped Mr. Klug triumphantly, and the other made quick note of the fact that the man was familiar with current slang. "I was too smart for them." Then, after a reflective pause, he added: "Maybe. They might steal my patent some way."

Patent! Mr. Wallingford's small, thick ears suddenly twitched forward.

"Been trying to sell one?" he asked, pausing with his cigar half way to his mouth and waiting for the answer.

"Three hundred dollars they offer me!" exploded Mr. Klug, again smiting both fists on his knees. "Six years I worked on it in my little shop of nights to get up a machine that was different from all the rest and that would work right, and when I get it done and get my patent and take it to them, they already had a copy of my patent and showed it to me. They bought it from the Government for five cents, and called me the same as a thief and offered me three hundred dollars!"

Wallingford pondered seriously.

"You must have a good machine," he finally announced.

Mr. Klug thought that he was "being made fun of."

"It *is* a good machine. It's as good a machine as any they have got. There is no joke about it!"

"I'm not joking," Wallingford insisted. "Who are the people?"

Mr. Klug considered for a suspicious moment, but the appearance of this gentleman, the very embodiment of sterling worth, was most reassuring. Beneath that broad chest and behind that diamond scarf pin there could rest no duplicity. Moreover, Mr. Klug was still angry, and anger and discretion do not dwell together.

"The United Sales Recording Machine Company of New Jersey," he stated, rolling out the name with a roundness which betrayed how much in respect and even awe he held it.

Wallingford was now genuinely interested.

"Then you *have* a good patent," he repeated. "If they offered you three hundred dollars it is worth thousands, otherwise they would not buy it at any price. They have hundreds of patents now, and you have something that they have not covered."

182

"Four hundred and twelve patents they own," corrected Mr. Klug. "I have been over every one in the last six years, every little wire and bar and spring in them, and mine is a whole new machine, like nothing they have got. They have got one man that does nothing else but look after these patents. You know what he said? 'Yes, you have worked six years for a chance to hold us up. But we're used to it. It happens to us every day. If you think you can manufacture your machine and make any money, go at it.' He told me that!"

Wallingford nodded comprehendingly.

"Of course," he agreed. "They have either fought out or bought out everybody who ever poked their nose into the business. They had to. I know all about them. If you have a clean invention you were foolish to go to them with it in the first place. They'd only offer you the cost of the first lawsuit they're bound to bring against you. That's no way to sell a patent. Inventors all die poor for that very reason. The thing for you to do is to start manufacturing, and make them come to you. Throw a scare into them."

Mr. Klug was frightened by the very suggestion.

"Jiminy, no!" he protested, shaking his head

vigorously. "I got no big money like that.
I'd lose every cent and all my little property."

"It don't take so much money, if you use it
right," insisted Wallingford. "Use as little
capital as you can for manufacturing, and save
the most of it for litigation. I'll bet I could
sell your patent for you." He pondered a
while with slowly kindling eyes, and smiled out
of the window at the rushing landscape. "I
tell you what you do. Get up a company and
I'll buy some stock in it myself."

"Humbug with that stock business!" Mr.
Klug exclaimed with explosive violence, his
mustache bristling now until it stuck straight
out. "I would not get up any such a business
with stock in it. I had all the stock I want,
and I never buy nor sell any any more. I got
some I'll give away."

Wallingford smiled introspectively.

"Oh, well, form a partnership, then. You
have four or five friends who could put up five
thousand apiece, haven't you?"

Mr. Klug was quite certain of that.

"I am president of the Germania Building
Loan Association," he announced with pardon-
able pride.

"Then, of course, you can control money,"
agreed the other in a tone which conveyed a

thoroughly proper appreciation of Mr. Klug's standing. "I'll invest as much as anybody else, and you put in your patent for a half interest. We'll start manufacturing right away, and if your machine's right, as it must be if they offer to buy the patent at all, I'll make the United people kneel down and coax us to take their money. There are ways to do it."

"The machine is all right," declared Mr. Klug. "Wait; I'll show it to you."

He hurried out to his seat, where reposed a huge box like a typewriter case, but larger. He lugged this back toward the smoker, into which other passengers were now lounging, but on the way Wallingford met him.

"Let's go in here, instead," said the latter, and opened the door into the drawing room.

It was the first time Mr. Klug had ever been in one of these compartments, and the sense of exclusiveness it aroused fairly reeked of money. The dreams of wealth that had been so rudely shattered sprang once more into life as the inventor opened the case and explained his device to this luxury-affording stranger, who, as a display of their tickets had brought out, was bound for his own city. It was a pneumatic machine, each key actuating a piston which flashed the numbered tickets noiselessly into view. It was perfect in every particular, and Wallingford examined it with an intelligent scrutiny which raised him still further in Mr. Klug's estimation; but as he compared patent drawings and machine, intent apparently only upon the mechanism, his busy mind was ranging far and wide over many other matters, bringing tangled threads of planning together here and there, and knotting them firmly.

"Good," said he at last. "As I said, I'll buy into your company. Get your friends together right away and manufacture this machine. I'll guarantee to get a proper price for your patent."

CHAPTER XIII

MR. WALLINGFORD OFFERS UNLIMITED FINANCIAL
BACKING TO A NEW ENTERPRISE

THE hotel at which Mr. Wallingford had elected to stop was only four blocks from the depot, but he rode there in a cab, and, having grandly emerged after a soul-warming handshake with Mr. Klug, paid liberally to have his friend the inventor taken to his destination. His next step, after being shown to one of the best suites in the house, was to telephone for a certain lawyer whose address he carried in his notebook, and the next to make himself richly comfortable after the manner of his kind. When the lawyer arrived, he found Wallingford, in lounging jacket and slippers and in fresh linen, enjoying an appetizer of Roquefort and champagne by way of resting from the fatigue of his journey. He was a brisk young man, was the lawyer, with his keen eyes set so close together that one praised Nature's care in having inserted such a hard, sharp wedge of nose to keep them apart. He cast a somewhat lingering glance at the champagne as he sat down, but he steadfastly refused Mr. Wallingford's proffer of a share in it.

"Not in business hours," he said, with over-disdain of such weak indulgence. "In the evening some time, possibly," and he bowed his head with a thin-lipped smile to complete the sentence.

"All right," acquiesced J. Rufus; "maybe you will smoke then," and he pointed to cigars.

One of them Mr. Maylie took, and Wallingford was silent until he had lit it.

"How is this town?" he then asked. "Is the treasury full, or are the smart people in power?"

The young man laughed, and, with a complete change of manner, drew his chair up to the table with a jerk.

"Say; you're all right!" he admiringly exclaimed, and—shoved forward the extra glass. "They're in debt here up to their ears."

"Then they'd rather have the bail than the man," Wallingford guessed, as he performed the part of host with a practiced hand.

"Which would you rather have?" asked Maylie, pausing with the glass drawn half way toward him.

"The man."

"Then everybody's satisfied," announced the lawyer. "If the authorities once get hold of that five thousand dollars cash bail and the man leaves town, they'll post police at every train to warn him away if he ever comes back."

"That's what I thought when I looked at the streets. You can even get the bond reduced."

"I don't know," replied the other, shaking his head doubtfully. "I've tried it."

"But you didn't go to them with the cash in your hand," Wallingford smilingly reminded him, and from an envelope in his inside vest pocket he produced a bundle of large bills. "This is a purchase, understand, and it's worth while to do a little dickering. Hurry, and bring the goods back with you."

"Watch me," said Mr. Maylie, taking the money with alacrity, but before he went out he hastily swallowed another glass of wine.

He was gone about an hour, during which his distinguished client was absorbed in drawing sketch after sketch upon nice, clean sheets of hotel stationery; and every sketch bore a strong resemblance to some part of Mr. Klug's pneumatic sales recording device Mr. Wallingford was very busy indeed

over the problem of selling Mr. Klug's
patent.

"Come in," he called heartily in answer to
a knock at the door.

It opened and the voice of Mr. Maylie announced: "Here's the goods, all right." And
he ushered in a tall, woe-begone gentleman, who,
except for the untidiness of black mustache and
hair, and the startlingly wrinkled and rusty condition of the black frock suit, bore strong resemblance to a certain expert collector and disseminator of foolish money—one "Blackie" Daw!

Mr. Wallingford, who, in his creative enthusiasm, had shed his lounging coat and waistcoat, and had even rolled up his shirt sleeves,
lay back in his chair and laughed until he shook
like a bowl of jelly. Mr. Daw, erstwhile the
dapper Mr. Daw, had gloomily advanced to
shake hands, but now suddenly burst forth in a
volley of language so fervid that Mr. Maylie
hastily closed the door. His large friend, with
the tears streaming down his face, thereupon
laughed all the more, but he managed to call
attention to a frost-covered silver pail which
awaited this moment, and while Mr. Daw
pounced upon that solace, Mr. Maylie, smiling
unobtrusively as one who must enjoy a joke
from the outside, proceeded to business.

"I got him for four thousand," he informed Mr. Wallingford and laid down a five-hundred-dollar bill. The remainder, in hundreds, he counted off one at a time, more slowly with each one, and when there were but two left in his hand Mr. Wallingford picked up the others and stuffed them in his pocket.

"That will about square us, I guess," he observed.

"Certainly; and thank you. Now, if there's anything else—"

"Not a thing—just now."

"Very well, sir," said Mr. Maylie with a glance at the enticing hollow-stemmed glasses; but it was quite evident that this was a private bottle, and he edged himself out of the door, disappearing with much the effect of a sharp knife blade being closed back into its handle.

Mr. Daw had tossed three bumpers of the champagne down his throat without stopping to taste them, and without setting down the bottle. Now he poured one for Mr. Wallingford.

"Laugh, confound you; laugh!" he snarled. "Maybe I look like the original comic supplement, but I don't feel like a joke. Think of it, J. Rufus! Four days in an infernal cement tomb, with exactly seventeen iron bars in front of me! I counted them twenty hours a day, and I know. Seven-teen!"

He glanced down over his creased and wrinkled and rusty clothing with a shudder, and suddenly began to tear them off, not stopping until he had divested himself of coat, vest and trousers, which he flung upon a chair. Then he rushed to the telephone, ridiculously gaunt in his unsheathed state, and ordered a rulet and a barber.

"Give me one of those hundreds, Jim, quick! I want it in my hand. Maybe I'll believe it's real money after a while."

Mr. Wallingford chuckled again as he passed over one of the crisp bills. "Cheer up, Blackie," he admonished his friend. "See how calm I am. Have a smoke."

Mr. Daw seized eagerly upon one of the cigars that were proffered him; but he was still too much perturbed to sit down, and stalked violently about the room like a huge pair of white tongs.

"I notice you turn every seven feet," observed Wallingford with a grin. "That must have been the size of your cell. Well, you never know your luck. Why, out here, Blackie, your occupation is called swindling, and it's a wonder they didn't hang you. You see, in these harvest festival towns there's not a yap over twenty-five who hasn't been fanged on a fake gold mine or something of the sort, and when twelve of these born boobs get a happy chance at a vaselined gold brick artist like you, nothing will suit them but a verdict of murder in the first degree."

Mr. Daw merely swore. The events of the past four days had dampened him so that he was utterly incapable of defense. There was a knock at the door. In view of his *déshabillé* the lank one retreated to the other room, but when the caller proved to be only the valet, he came prancing out with his clothes upon his arm. "I want these back in half an hour," he demanded, "and have this bill changed into money I can understand. I feel better already," he added when the valet had gone. "I've ordered somebody to do something, and he stood for it."

Wallingford brought from his closet a bathrobe in which Mr. Daw could wrap himself two or three times, and continued his lecture.

"It's too bad you don't understand your profession," he went on, still amused. "Sometimes I think I'll buy you another acre of Arizona sand and start a new mining company

with you, just to show you how the stock can
be sold safely and legally."

For the first time Mr. Daw was able to
grin.

"Who's that clattering down the street?" he
exclaimed with fine dramatic effect. "Why, it's
me! Notice how my coat tails snap as I top
yon distant hill. See how pale my face as I
turn to see if I am still pursued. Oh, no, J.
Rufus. We've been friends too long. I'd hate
to think of us losing sleep every night, trying
to figure how to give each other the double
cross."

"I got you at a bargain just now, and I
ought to be able to sell you cheap," retorted
the other. "By the way, it's a mighty lucky
thing for you that Fanny had some money
soaked away from that insurance deal of mine.
I had to all but use a club to get it, too. She
don't think very much of you. She thinks you
might lead me astray some time."

"*Can* limburger smell worse?" growled Mr.
Daw, but there he stopped. Four days in jail
had taken a lot of his gift of repartee away.
When barber and bootblack and valet had restored him to his well-groomed ministerial as-
pect, however, his saturnine sense of humor
came back and he was able to enjoy the elab-

orate midday luncheon which his host had served in the room.

"Amuse yourself, Blackie," invited Wallingford after luncheon. "Get orey-eyed if you want to, and don't mind me, for I'm laying the wires to locate here."

"Don't!" advised his friend. "This is a poison town. Every dollar has a tag on it, and if you touch one they examine the thumb marks and pinch you."

"Not me! My legitimate methods will excite both awe and admiration." And he set to work again.

Not caring to show himself in daylight, Mr. Daw read papers and took naps and drank and smoked until his midnight train; but, no matter what he did, Mr. Wallingford sat steadily at the little desk, sketching, sketching, sketching. Along about closing time he went down to make friends with the bartender, and before he went to bed he had secured an unused sales recording machine which was kept on hand for use during conventions, and this he had taken up to his rooms for leisurely study and comparison. In the morning he drove out to Carl Klug's clean little model making shop in the outskirts of the town, and here he found an interested group gathered about the pneumatic device that he had seen the day before. On a bench lay the patent—a real United States Government patent with a seal and a ribbon on it!

"Different from all the four hundred and twelve patents, every place!" Mr. Klug had just a shade pompously reiterated before Wallingford came.

"So-o-o-o!" commented big Otto Schmitt, the market gardener, as he pushed down the dollar key and then the forty-five-cent key with a huge, earth-brown finger that spread out on the end like a flat club. "And how much does it cost to make it?"

"Not twenty-five dollars apiece," claimed Carl; "and the United Sales Recording Machine Company sells them for two and three hundred dollars. We can sell these for one hundred, and when we get a good business they must buy us out or we take all their trade away from them. That's the way to sell a patent. Because they don't do this way is why inventors never get rich."

"Sure!" agreed Henry Vogel, the lean, raw-boned carpenter. "When they buy us out, that's where we make our money."

"Sure!" echoed Carl, and the three of them laughed. It was such a pleasant idea that they would be able to wrest some of its hoarded thousands from a big monopoly.

"It is a good business," went on Carl. "When I showed this machine to this Mr. Wallingford I told you about, he said right away he would come in. He is one of these Eastern money fellows, and they are all smart men."

Over in the corner sat Jens Jensen, with a hundred shrewd wrinkles in his face and a fringe of wiry beard around his chin from ear to ear. Up to now he had not said a word. He was a next door neighbor to Carl, and he had seen the great patent over and over.

"It is foolishness," declared Jens. "He is a skinner, maybe; and, anyhow, if there's money to be made we should keep it at home."

Big Otto Schmitt pushed down the two-dollar key. The dollar ticket and the forty-five-cent ticket disappeared, the two-dollar ticket came up with a click, the drawer popped open and a little bell rang. It was wonderful.

"I say it too," agreed Otto. His face was broad and hard as granite, his cheekbones were enormous and the skin over them was purple.

The four men were near the front windows of the shop, and it was at this moment that Wallingford's cab whirled up to the door. It was a new looking cab, its woodwork polished like a piano, the glass in it beveled plate. The driver sprang down and opened the door. Out of that small opening stepped the huge promoter, resplendent in a new suit of brown checks, and wearing a brown Derby, brown shoes and brown silk hose, all of the exact shade to match, while from his coat pocket peeped the fingers of brown gloves.

"That's him," said Carl.

"I knew it," announced Jens Jensen. "He is a skinner."

Nothing could exceed the affability of Mr. Wallingford. He shook hands with Mr. Klug, with Mr. Schmitt, with Mr. Vogel, with Mr. Jensen; he smiled upon them in turns; he made each one of them feel that never in all his life had he been afforded a keener delight than in this meeting.

"You have a fine little shop, Mr. Klug," he said, looking about him with an air of pleased surprise. "There is room right here to manufacture enough machines to scare the United Sales Recording Machine Company into fits. Gentlemen, if no one else cares for a share in Mr. Klug's splendid invention, I am quite willing to back him myself with all the capital he needs."

This was an exceptionally generous offer on

Mr. Wallingford's part, particularly as the six hundred dollars he had in his pocket was all the capital he controlled in the world. In justice to him, however, it must be said that he expected to have more money—shortly. The prospects seemed good. They looked him over. Twenty-five thousand, fifty thousand, a hundred thousand dollars; it was easy to see that the gentleman could supply any or all of these sums at a moment's notice.

"No!" said Jens Jensen, voicing the suddenly eager sentiment of all. "We're all going in it, and another man."

"Two other men," corrected Carl. "Doctor Feldmeyer and Emil Kessler."

Otto Schmitt shook his head dubiously.

"Emil owes on his building loan," he observed.

"Emil's coming in," firmly repeated Carl Klug. "He is a friend of mine. I will lend him the money and he pays me when we sell out."

Mr. Wallingford glanced out of the window at the shining cab and smiled. With business people like these he felt that he could get on.

"When, then, do we form the partnership?" he asked.

"To-morrow!" Jens promptly informed him. "We all put in what money we want to, and we take out according to what we put in."

Jens, who had condemned Mr. Wallingford at sight as a "skinner," now kept as close to him as possible, and beamed up at him all the time; one cordial handshake from the man of millions had won him over.

"Carl," he suggested, "you must take Mr. Wallingford over to the cellar."

"Oh, we all go there," said big Otto Schmitt, and they all laughed, Carl more than any of them.

"Come on," he said.

Right at the side of the shop stood Mr. Klug's brick house, in the midst of a big garden that was painfully orderly. Every tree was whitewashed to exactly the same height, and everything else that could be whitewashed glared like new-fallen snow. The walks were scrubbed until they were as red as bricks could be made, and all in between was velvet-green grass. There were flowers everywhere, and climbing vines were matted upon the porch trellises and against the entire front of the house. In the rear garden could be seen all sorts of kitchen vegetables in neat rows and beds. Down into the front basement the five

men crowded and sat on rough wooden
benches. Jens Jensen hastened to spread a
clean newspaper on the bench where Mr. Wallingford was to sit. Carl disappeared into another part of the cellar and presently came out
again with a big jug and five glasses, all of different shapes and sizes. Out of the jug he
poured his best home-made wine, and they settled down for a jovial half hour, in which they
admitted the guest of honor to full fellowship.

"You must come over to church to-night,"
Jens Jensen insisted as they came away. "We
have a raffle and Doctor Feldmeyer will be
there. He is a swell. He will be glad to know
you. There will be plenty to eat and drink.
Look; you can see the church from here," and
he pointed out its tall spire.

Mr. Wallingford shook hands with Mr. Jensen impulsively.

"I'll be *there!*" he declared with enthusiasm.
When he had gone, Carl Klug asked:

"Well, what do you think of him?"

"He is a swell," said Jens, and no voice
dissented.

CHAPTER XIV

SHOWING HOW FIVE HUNDRED DOLLARS MAY DO
THE WORK OF FIVE THOUSAND

AT a total cost of twenty-five dollars, Mr. Wallingford made himself a Prince of the Blood at the church raffle that night, throwing down bills and refusing all change, winning prizes and turning them back to be raffled over again, treating all the youngsters to endless grabs in the "fish pond"; and Jens Jensen proudly introduced him to everybody, beginning with the minister and Emil Kessler—the latter a thin, white-faced man with a high brow, who looked like a university professor and was a shoemaker — and ending with Doctor Feldmeyer, who came late. Wallingford's eyes brightened when he saw this gentleman. He was more or less of a dandy, was the doctor, and had great polish and suavity of manner. He had not been with Mr. Wallingford five minutes until he was talking of Europe. Mr. Wallingford had also been to Europe. The doctor was very keen on books, on music, on art, on all the re-

finements of life, also he was very much of a
ladies' man, he delicately insinuated, and not
one expression of his face was lost upon the
Eastern capitalist. It transpired that the doctor was living at Mr. Wallingford's hotel, and
they went home together that night, leaving
behind them the ineffaceable impression that
the rich Mr. Wallingford was an invaluable
acquisition to Mr. Klug and his friends, to the
community, to the city, to any portion of the
globe which he might grace with his presence.
But when the invaluable acquisition was left
alone in his rooms he penned a long letter to
his wife.

"My dear Fanny," he wrote, "come right
away. I have in sight the biggest stake I have
made yet, in a clean, legitimate deal; and I
need your smiling countenance in my business."

He meant more by that than he would have
dared to tell her, but he laughed and mused
on Doctor Feldmeyer as he sealed the letter;
then he sent it out to be mailed and turned his
earnest attention to the inside of his sales recorder. This time he found the one little point
for which he had been looking: the thing that
he knew must be there, and the next morning,
bright and early, he drove out to Mr. Klug's
shop.

"Mr. Klug, you are in bad," he said with portentous gravity. "Look here." And he pointed out the long, spring-actuated bar which kept all the tickets from dropping back when they sprang up, and released them as others were shot into place. "This is an infringement of the United Sales Recording Machine Company's machine," he declared.

"Nothing like it!" indignantly denied the inventor, bristling and reddening and puffing his cheeks.

"The identical device is in every machine they manufacture," insisted Wallingford; "and I would bet you all you expect to make that before you're on the market two days they will have an injunction out against you on that very point. Now let me show you how we can get around it."

Mr. Klug reluctantly and protestingly followed his mechanical idea, a logical application of the pneumatic principle, as he made it plain by sketches and demonstration on the machine.

"Another thing," went on Mr. Wallingford. "It occurs to me that all these little pistons multiply the chances of throwing your machine out of order. Why don't you make one compressible air chamber to actuate all the ticket pistons and to be actuated by all the keys, the keys also opening valves in the ticket pistons? It would save at least five dollars on each machine, make it simpler and much more practical. Of course, I'll have to patent this improvement, but I'll turn it over to you at practically no cost to the company.''

Mr. Klug merely blinked. Six long years he had worked on this invention, following the one idea doggedly and persistently, and he had thought that he had it perfect. He had all the United Company's patents marked in his copies of the patent record, and now he went through the more basic ones one after the other.

''It is not there,'' he said in triumph, after an hour's search, during which Wallingford patiently waited. One book he had held aside, and now he put his finger quietly upon a drawing in it.

''No,'' he admitted, ''not in the form that you have used it; but here is the trick that covers the principle, and this patent still has four years to run.''

Carl examined it silently. In form the device was radically different from his own, but when he came to analyze it he saw that Wallingford was probably right; the principle had been covered, at least nearly enough to leave a loophole for litigation, and it worried him beyond measure.

"Don't look at it that way," comforted Wallingford. "Only be glad that we found it out in time. I'll apply for this patent right away and assign it to you. All I'll want for it will be a slight credit on the books of the company; say fifteen hundred."

Again Carl Klug blinked.

"I'll let you know this afternoon."

He needed time to figure out this tangled proposition; also he wanted, in simple honor, to talk it over with his friends.

"All right," said Wallingford cheerfully. "By the way, we don't want to form such a big partnership in a lawyer's office, where people are running in and out all the time. I'll provide a room at my hotel. That will be better, don't you think?"

"Sure," slowly agreed Mr. Klug. He was glad to decide upon something about which a decision was easy.

"Can you get word to the others?" asked the promoter. "If not I'll go around and notify them."

"Oh, they're going to meet here. They all live up this way except Doctor Feldmeyer. You see him. I'll bring the lawyer along."

"All right," said Wallingford, quite convinced that a lawyer other than Maylie would be secured, and after he had driven from sight he took out his pocketbook and counted again his available cash.

He had a trifle over six hundred dollars, and in the afternoon he would be expected to pay over the difference between five thousand dollars and the fifteen hundred he was certain would be allowed for his patent. Thirty-five hundred dollars! At the present moment there was no place on earth that he could raise that amount, but nevertheless he smiled complacently as he put up his pocketbook. So long as other people had money, the intricacies of finance were only a pleasant recreation to him, and it was with entire ease of mind that he set the stage for his little drama at the hotel. He had Doctor Feldmeyer to await Carl Klug and his friends in the lobby and conduct them up to a private dining room, where the man of specious ideas, at the head of a long table and strictly in his element, received them with broad hospitality. In his bigness and richness of apparel and his general air of belonging to splendid things, he was particularly at home in this high, beam-ceilinged apartment, with its dark woodwork, its rich tapestry, its stained-glass windows, its thick carpet, its glittering buffet. Around the snowy clothed table were chairs for eight, and at each plate stood a generous goblet. As the first of the visitors filed in, Wallingford touched a button, and almost by the time they were seated a waiter appeared with huge glass pitchers of beer. The coming of this beverage necessarily put them all in a good humor, and there was much refilling and laughing and talking of a purely informal character until Doctor Feldmeyer arose to his feet and tapped with his knuckles upon the table, when deep gravity sat instantly upon the assemblage.

"Since our host is already seated at the head of the table," said the doctor with easy pleasantry, "I move that he be made temporary chairman."

The doctor had lunched with Mr. Wallingford at noon, and now knew him to be a thoroughbred in every respect; a *bon vivant* who knew good food and good wine and good fellowship; a gentleman of vast financial resources, who did not care how he spent his money just so he got what he wanted when he wanted it; and he was quite willing to vouch for Mr. Wallingford, in every way, upon a gentleman's basis! The election of Mr. Wal-

lingford as temporary chairman and of Doctor
Feldmeyer as temporary secretary were most
cordial and pleasant things to behold. The
lawyer, a dry little gentleman who never ventured an opinion unless asked for it, and always put the answer in his bill, thereupon read
the articles of agreement which were to bind
these friends in a common partnership,
whereby it was understood that Mr. Klug, in
virtue of his patents, was to have one half interest in the company, no matter to what size
it might be increased, and that the other gentlemen were to put in such money as was
needed to carry on the business, each one to
share in the profits in exact proportion to the
amount of his investment. It appeared to be
the unsmiling consensus of the meeting that
this agreement was precisely what they wanted,
and after it had been read again, very slowly
and distinctly, the simply honorable gentlemen
interested solemnly signed it. While this little
formality was being looked after, with much
individual spelling out of the document, word
by word, under broad forefingers, the waiter
filled the glasses again and Wallingford turned
to Mr. Klug.

"By the way," he asked, in a voice low
enough to be taken as confidential but loud

enough to be heard by those nearest, "have you told the gentlemen about the new patent?"

Jens Jensen, seated next to Mr. Klug, took it upon himself to answer.

"That is all right," he said, nodding his head emphatically. "We know all about that," and a glance at the nodding heads about the table disposed of that question. It was quite understood that Mr. Wallingford was to have a fifteen-hundred-dollar credit for the invaluable addition and correction he had made to their principal asset, the wonderful sales recorder patent.

"Very well, then," said Mr. Wallingford, with a secret relief which he carefully kept out of his voice, "as temporary chairman I would instruct the secretary now to take the list of subscriptions."

A sigh went around the table. This was serious business, the letting go of toil-won money, but nevertheless they would go sturdily through with it. It appeared upon a canvass that Mr. Schmitt and Mr. Jensen and Doctor Feldmeyer and Mr. Wallingford were each prepared immediately to invest five thousand dollars, while Mr. Vogel and Mr. Kessler were each ready to invest two thousand.

"Twenty-four thousand dollars," announced

the doctor roundly, whereupon Mr. Wallingford arose.

"Gentlemen," said he, "there is no use to have idle capital. This is more money than we shall need for some time to come, and that is not good business. I therefore propose that the total assessment from any one member at this time be restricted to two thousand dollars. That will allow Mr. Schmitt and Mr. Jensen, Doctor Feldmeyer and myself each to keep three thousand dollars of our money in our savings banks, building associations and other places where it is earning good interest, until the company needs it, which may perhaps be a matter of six months. I would like to have a vote upon this proposition."

There could be but one answer to this. Interest! The savings of all these men throughout their lives had been increased at three, four and scarcely to exceed five per cent. rates, and they had grown to reverence interest almost more than capital. He was a smart man, this Wallingford, to think of the interest!

Money was already appearing from deep pockets when the crabby little lawyer, as if it gave him pain to volunteer information, wrenched from himself the fact that before any money could be paid in some one must be appointed to receive it. Thereupon, though not a corporate association, they held an election, and, naturally, Mr. Klug was made president. Mr. Wallingford firmly declined the vice presidency and also the secretaryship. He might even have had the post of treasurer, but he was too modest, also too busy, to hold office. No, he kindly stated, he would be a mere investor, ready to aid them with what little advice and experience he could give them, and ready to back them to any extent if the time should ever arise when their own finances would prove insufficient to carry the Pneumatic Sales Recorder Company on to the undoubted success which awaited it! Thereupon the treasurership was voted to Jens Jensen, and Emil Kessler proposed that they pay in their respective assessments and adjourn. He had two thousand dollars of Carl Klug's money in his pocket, and it made him a trifle uncomfortable.

"I forbid anybody to leave this room," laughingly announced Mr. Wallingford, and gave a nod to the waiter, who disappeared. "We'll pay in our money, but we have some other very important business."

Doctor Feldmeyer also became jolly, to show

that he was in the secret. He drew a fountain
pen and a check book from his pocket.

"Mr. Wallingford wants us to eat, drink
and make merry on the United Sales Recording Machine Company of New Jersey," he
told them as he wrote.

The joke was thoroughly appreciated. It
was a commendable and a holy thing to con-
spire to get the money of a monopoly away
from it, as every newspaper proved to them.
In pleasant pursuance of this idea, the United
Company, by methods that should proceed in
comfort and ease and entire absence of worry,
such as was foreshadowed by this luxurious
dining room and by the personal grandeur of
Mr. Wallingford, was to be brought suppli-
antly to its knees; so, with the utmost cheerfulness, each of these men paid over his subscription. Doctor Feldmeyer was the only man
among them who paid by check. The rest was
in cash, but the host, busy with his hospitable
duties, held back his payment until the waiters
brought in a luncheon which was a revelation
in the way of "cold snacks." It was during
this appetite-whetting, gayety-promoting con-
fusion that Wallingford quietly paid over his
five hundred dollars — this, with the fifteen
hundred dollars' credit on the coming patent.

making his contribution total to two thousand, the same amount as that put in by every other member of the company except Carl Klug. This done, the clever gentleman surreptitiously wiped his brow and sighed a little sigh all to himself. It had taken him three days to figure how to fasten upon Mr. Klug's patent and prospects with as little money as five hundred dollars!

It was a happy crowd that dispersed an hour later — a crowd upon which Fortune already beamed; but the last of them had scarcely left the room when their princely entertainer telephoned for his own lawyer.

"I want you," said Wallingford to Mr. Maylie, when he arrived, "to find out all you can for me about the United Sales Recording Machine Company of New Jersey. I want to know the outcome of every suit they have brought against infringers of their patents, and the present addresses of the people with whom they fought; also all about the companies they have been forced to buy out. Got that?"

"I'll get it," replied Mr. Maylie confidently, and helped himself to a glass of champagne. He looked longingly at the bottle as he finished his first glass, but as Mr. Wallingford did not invite him to have a second he went out.

CHAPTER XV

WALLINGFORD GENEROUSLY LOANS THE PNEUMATIC
COMPANY SOME OF ITS OWN MONEY

THE arrival of Mrs. Wallingford set
upon a much higher plane her husband's already well-established reputation as a capitalist of illimitable resources, and had any one of his partners
paused to reflect that Mr. Wallingford had secured an active interest in the concern for five
hundred dollars, Doctor Feldmeyer's report
of the capitalist's charming lady was enough
to make that trifling incident forgotten. To
Carl Klug and Jens Jensen at Carl's shop, the
doctor, without knowing it, did the missionary
work that Wallingford had planned for him to
do.

"She is a stunner," he declared, with the
faintest suggestion of a smirk, "and carries
herself like a queen. She wears a fur coat
that cost not less than six or seven hundred
dollars, and not a woman in this town has
such diamonds. We all went to the theater
last night, and there were more opera glasses

turned on our box than on the stage. I
tell you, our friend Wallingford has the best
there is, in women, as well as in wine,
and as for wealth, he could buy and sell us
all."

"I believe it," said Jens Jensen. "But
why should such a rich man go into a little
business?"

"Because," said Doctor Feldmeyer, with
profound wisdom, "a rich man never over-
looks a thousand per cent. like this. That's
why they are rich. Why, this man's daily expenses would keep every one of us. He had
fine apartments at the hotel himself, but when
his wife came he got the best in the house—
four fine, big rooms. Last night after the
theater he took me to his own dining room, and
we had a supper that cost not less than thirty
or forty dollars!"

Such gossip would go far to establishing any
man's reputation for wealth, especially among
such simple natured people as these, and it
was quite certain that Otto Schmitt and Henry
Vogel and Emil Kessler would hear every scrap
of it. Had Doctor Feldmeyer heard the conversation that took place after he left the Wallingford suite the night before, his report might
have been slightly different.

"Well, Jim," Mrs. Wallingford had asked with a trace of anxiety, "what are you doing this time?"

"The United Sales Recording Machine Company of New Jersey," he replied with a laugh. "You remember how they turned me down a long time ago when I tried to sell them a patent?" She nodded. "You made me go right to them and try what you called 'straight business,' and I got what was coming to a mollycoddle. I'm going to sell them a patent this time, but in the right way, and for a good, big round chunk."

"Whose patent?" she inquired.

"What's the difference?" he queried, and laughed again. "It serves him right for being an inventor."

She did not laugh with him, however. She sat in frowning disquiet, and he watched her curiously.

"What's the matter with you?" he presently complained. "It used to be enough for you that I could not be jailed for having a few dollars."

"We're nearly middle-aged, Jim," she replied, turning to him soberly. "What will we be like when we are old?"

"Cheer up, Fanny, and I will tell you the

worst!" he declaimed. "You'll be gray and
I'll be bald!"

She was compelled to laugh herself, and gave
up the idea of serious conversation with him,
for that time at least.

Doctor Feldmeyer, encouraged by Wallingford, became an unofficial attaché of the family
in the following weeks. Vain, susceptible, and
considering himself very much of a ladies'
man, he exerted himself to be agreeable, and
J. Rufus helped him to opportunities. If he
had any ulterior purpose in this he did not
confide it to his wife, or even let her suspect
it. It would not have been safe. In the meantime the affairs of the Pneumatic Sales Recorder Company moved speedily onward. One
entire end of his shop Carl Klug devoted to its
affairs, putting in special machinery and hiring as many men as he could use, and here
Wallingford reported every day, his suggestions being nearly always sound and inspiring
Mr. Klug's respect. He held his standing
with the rest of them in a different way.
When they called at the shop they found
Wallingford's cab always standing outside,
and it was soon noised about that this cab
was hired by the day! "Blackie" Daw,
levying his dubious contributions on a gul-

lible public, was paying for this and wiping
out his debt.

But little more than two months had elapsed
when Carl had his first lot of recorders ready
for the market, and the treasury was depleted.
Now it became necessary to have money for
marketing, and that meant the remaining
three thousand dollars of J. Rufus Wallingford's subscription or an evasion of it. Prepared for this, he took the floor as soon as the
matter was mentioned at the meeting which
was called to levy this assessment.

"What is the use?" he demanded to know.
"Why use our own money? I understand that
Mr. Schmitt must get his three thousand from
the building loan association, to which he must
pay six per cent. I understand that Mr. Jensen has his now out at five per cent. Let me
show you how to finance this concern. I will
put in ten thousand at once, and take the company's note. This note I can then discount,
and put the money right back into my business, and in that way my ten thousand dollars
is doing twenty thousand dollars' worth of
work — a bank carrying the burden of both
operations."

It was a financial argument entirely new to
these men, unused to tricks of money manipu-

lation, and it took them some little time to grasp it. When they did, however, they were as pleased as a boy with his first watch, and Wallingford was a dazzling hero, as, with a nonchalant air, after glancing at the clock to make sure that it was after banking hours, he wrote them a check on "his bank in Boston" for ten thousand, and took their note, signed by the Pneumatic Sales Recorder Company and indorsed jointly by all its members.

That night Wallingford drove up in hot haste to Jens Jensen's house.

"Let me see that check I gave you this afternoon," he demanded, with an air of suspecting a good joke on himself. Jens, wondering, produced it from a little tin box. "That's what I thought," said Wallingford as he glanced at it. Then, smiling, he handed it back. "I have made it out on the Fifth National of Boston. They'd probably honor it, but it's the wrong bank. I have a balance there, but am not sure that it is sufficient to cover this check. Just hold that, and I'll wire them in the morning. If my balance isn't large enough I'll give you a check on the First, with which I do most of my business."

"Sure," said Jens, and put back into the tin

box the worthless paper which called for ten
thousand dollars.

The next morning Wallingford called at one
of the local banks and had no difficulty whatever in discounting the quite acceptable note.
He gained a full day by forwarding the proceeds, special delivery, to the Fifth National
Bank of Boston, where his balance at that moment was considerably less than a hundred dollars; then he told Jensen to deposit the check:
that his balance in the Fifth National was all
right.

It was financial jugglery of a shrewd order,
and the juggler prided himself upon it. He
was not yet through, however. Having loaned
the company ten thousand dollars of its own
money at six per cent. interest, he was now
confronted by the necessity of securing money
for his own enormous personal expenses. For
replenishment, however, he had long planned,
and now he went to his new source of income
—Doctor Feldmeyer. The time was ripe, for,
though Mrs. Wallingford had given him no
more encouragement than the ordinary courteous graciousness which is so often misinter-
preted by male coquettes, the doctor was
aflame with foolish imaginings, and, within
the past week or so, had felt guilty upon every

meeting with Mr. Wallingford, betraying it as Wallingford had planned that he should, growing nervous at a sharp glance, a sudden movement, an obscure remark. He was as uncomfortable as guilty conscience ever made a coward, and when the big man, on the plea of sudden business and personal needs, went to him almost peremptorily for a loan of rather staggering proportions, the doctor was an easy victim. Thus provided and at ease, Wallingford "consented" to become the salesman for the first output of Pneumatic Sales Recorders, going directly to a list of cities supplied to him by Maylie; and in those cities he went to see certain gentlemen whose names came to him from the same source! Incidentally, he sold a number of sales recorders with a celerity that was most gratifying to the delighted members of the company. Why, even if the United Sales Recording Machine Company of New Jersey did not care to buy them out, a fortune was in sight through the legitimate manufacture and sale of this device! Before the salesman returned from his trip, however, a blow, entirely unexpected by Klug and his friends, fell on them from a clear sky. An injunction and a notice of suit was served, not only upon the company, but upon every purchaser of

their contrivance. The injunction restrained
the buyers from using and the company from
manufacturing or selling any further machines,
and the suit was for infringement of patent.
The device by which the drawer flew open
after the keys had been pressed, the United
Sales Recording Machine Company of New
Jersey claimed to be modeled upon their own.
The news was wired to Wallingford. He had
been waiting for it, and he came home at once,
where he found that Maylie had been appointed the local legal representative of the
big New Jersey concern; but as this had been
a matter of Wallingford's own contriving, he
was not nearly so much surprised over it as he
might have been. He also found direst con-
sternation in the company's ranks, and himself
shook his head sadly when questioned, though
he spoke bravely.

"What we have to do," he declared, "is to
keep a stiff upper lip and fight it."

They did so. Within a couple of months they
had the suit decided in their favor, and Carl
Klug was vindicated in the eyes of his friends.
Again they were jubilant, again they prepared for an era of commercial triumph; but
on the very next day another injunction and
suit were brought, and from the very start of

this proceeding delays were encountered. The weakest case had been brought first, the stubborn one being held back for a longer and more discouraging fight. When that was over there would be a third suit and a fourth. With their millions of capital and their knowledge of such matters, gleaned from vital struggles with others who had demanded either their money or their business life, they could continue such a fight indefinitely, or until the Pneumatic Sales Recorder Company should be choked out of existence.

There never was a more discouraged lot of men than those who met in Carl Klug's shop upon the day after notice of this second suit was brought. Wallingford was the most inconsolable of all. Of course, if the others felt like putting in any more money to fight this company with its millions they could do so; in fact, they ought to do so, but his own business affairs were in such shape that, at the present moment, he could not spare a dollar. He said this in such a hesitant way, with a five-hundred-dollar diamond gleaming from his finger and another from his scarf, that they felt sure he had plenty of capital, but would not risk it further in such a losing fight; and it helped them to realize that all the capital they could command would be but as a wisp of straw to be brushed aside by this formidable giant, which not only could crush them, but had the disposition to do so.

Wallingford left them in this hopeless spirit, and went "back East to look after his other business." That business took him directly to the offices of the United Sales Recording Machine Company of New Jersey, and into an immediate conference with the man who had charge of all its patent affairs.

"I have come to sell you the Pneumatic Sales Recorder Company," said Wallingford, by way of introduction.

"The Pneumatic Sales Recorder Company?" repeated Mr. Priestly vaguely, trying to convey the impression that the name was unfamiliar to him, and he looked into his desk file. "Oh, yes; we have a suit pending against them."

"Exactly," agreed his caller. "Suit number two is now pending. We won suit number one. We will win suits number two, three, four, five and six, if need be, but it is such a waste of money on both sides. You might just as well buy us out now as later."

Mr. Priestly shook his head without a smile. He was almost gloomy about it, even. He was a small man with gray mutton-chop whiskers, and nothing could exceed his deep gravity. From another file he produced a copy of the patent taken out by Mr. Klug, and of the one just issued to Mr. Wallingford, assignor to Mr. Klug's company.

"The Pneumatic Sales Recorder Company," he stated, tossing down the papers as if they were too trifling to examine after he had found them, "has nothing whatever that we wish to purchase."

"Oh, yes, it has," Wallingford insisted. "It has two patents, and the absolute certainty of a business that in three years will take trade enough and profits enough away from you to buy the company several times over."

Again Mr. Priestly shook his head sadly.

"We shall have to wait three years to determine that," he hinted, with no sinister intonation whatever to go with the veiled threat. "We must defend our very existence here every day of our lives. If we did not we would have been put out of the business years ago."

"Exactly," again agreed the other. "In your files you have comprehensive reports on Mr. Carl Klug, Mr. Jens Jensen, Mr. Otto Schmitt and the others of the company. You know their small resources to a penny, and you can figure almost to the day how long they can last. But that, Mr. Priestly, is where you have made your error, for these men will soon be out of the game. I have here another list about which you will not need to collect any information, for you have it even in memory, no doubt."

He laid before Mr. Priestly a neatly-type-written slip, containing barely over half a dozen names. In spite of his excellent facial command, Mr. Priestly could not repress a start of surprise, and he shot across at Mr. Wallingford one quick little glance, which had in it much more of respect than he had hitherto shown.

"*J. B.* Hammond," read Mr. Priestly, clutching at a straw. "The last name is familiar, but the initials are not."

"No," agreed Wallingford. "By the terms under which he sold out to you, Mr. W. A. Hammond is not to go into the sales recorder business at all. Allow me to read you a letter," and from a pocketbook he took a folded paper.

"My dear Mr. Wallingford," he read. "Under no circumstances could I participate in the manufacture of sales recorders; but my son,

Mr. J. B. Hammond, is quite convinced that the
Klug patent is both practical and tenable, and
he advises me that he is willing to invest up to
two hundred thousand dollars, provided a company of at least one million *bona fide* capitalization can be formed."

"It is a curious coincidence," added Wallingford, passing over this letter with a smile,
"that two hundred thousand dollars is exactly
the price you paid William Hammond for his
business, after five years of very bitter litigation. The son, no doubt, would take a keen
personal interest in regaining the losses of the
father through a company that has so excellent
a chance to compete with yours. You see, a
company with a million dollars, composed of
men who know all about the sales recorder business, would set aside these suits of yours in a
jiffy, because they are untenable, and you know
it, although I do not expect you to admit it
just now. Mr. Keyes, whose name is next on
the list, had nothing left to sell after losing
almost a quarter of a million in fighting you,
and so is unbound. It just happens, however,
that he has been left quite a comfortable leg-
acy, and would like nothing so much as to sink
part of it in our company. Here is the letter
from Mr. Keyes," and he spread the second

document in the case before Mr. Priestly, who now laid down the first letter and, readjusting his glasses, took up the second one in profound silence.

Mr. Wallingford lit a cigar in calm content and waited until Mr. Priestly had finished reading the letter of Mr. Keyes, when he produced another one.

"Mr. Rankley," he observed, "has never been in the sales recorder business, but he apparently has his own private and personal reasons for wishing to engage in it," and at the mention of Mr. Rankley's name Mr. Priestly broke the toothpick he was holding and threw it away.

Mr. Rankley, as he quite well knew, was Mr. Alexander's bitterest enemy, and Mr. Alexander was practically the United Sales Recording Machine Company of New Jersey. Wallingford went on down the list in calm joy. It was composed entirely of men of means, who would put into this enterprise not only experience and shrewd business ability, but a particularly energetic hatred of the big corporation and its components.

"I see," said Mr. Priestly, laying down the final letter upon the previous ones, and with great delicacy and precision placing a glass paperweight squarely in the middle of them. "Permit me to retain these letters for a short time. I wish to take them before our board of directors."

"When?" asked Wallingford.

"Well, our regular monthly meeting——" began Mr. Priestly.

"No, you don't," interrupted the other. "I think a few minutes of conversation with Mr. Alexander himself would do away entirely with the necessity of consulting the board of directors. You think it possible, I know, that by going directly to Mr. Klug and his friends you would be able to purchase the patents cheaper than you can from me, but I am quite sure I can convince Klug and his company that these gentlemen will raise the price on you."

"Why didn't you form this new company in the first place, then?" demanded Mr. Priestly sharply, implying a doubt. "Why do you come to us at all?"

"Because I personally," patiently explained Wallingford, "can make more money by quietly selling the patent to you than I personally can make by selling it openly to them, as you will see if you reflect a moment. At present I own a twelfth share in the company. If I induce this other company to take hold of it I must divide the purchase price into twelve equal shares, of which I receive but one. Is Mr. Alexander in the city?"

"I believe so," hesitated Mr. Priestly.

"Is he in his office?"

"Possibly," admitted the other.

"Oh, he's in, then," concluded Wallingford sagely. "Well, I think you can give me my answer in an hour. I'll be down at the Hotel Vandyne. You might telephone me. I want to go back West this evening."

It did not take Mr. Priestly and Mr. Alexander sixty minutes to conclude that they could save a lot of money by doing business with Mr. Wallingford, and they asked him to drive up to their office and see them again. When they got through "dickering," Mr. Wallingford had agreed, in writing, to deliver over to them, within sixty days, the Pneumatic Sales Recorder Company patents, for the sum of one hundred and seventy-five thousand dollars, the receipt of a ten-thousand-dollar advance payment being acknowledged therewith.

Before he started West, Wallingford wired Maylie: "Note due in morning. Advise bank on quiet to sue."

CHAPTER XVI

A STORM that he had scarcely expected awaited Wallingford when he returned. His wife met him furiously. She had all her belongings packed separately from his own, and would have been gone before his arrival but that she could not express her anger in a mere letter.

"It is the last straw, Jim!" she charged him. "You're growing worse all the time. I saw that you were throwing me with this puppy Feldmeyer deliberately, but was foolish enough to think that you were doing it only so that I might be amused while you were busy. As well as I know you, I did not suspect that you could possibly bring yourself to use me as a lever to borrow money from him!"

A twinkle that he could not help came into Wallingford's eyes as he thought of how easily Feldmeyer had been bent to his own ends, and it was most unfortunate for him, for she caught the look and interpreted it instantly.

232

"You're even proud of it!" she cried. "There's nothing in this world sacred to you. Why, only last night he made open love to me and insisted that I 'disappear' with him on a trip he is taking. He only laughed when I told him how I hated him. He had been drinking, and he and Maylie had been together. They are on to you, Jim. Maylie has found out something about you and has told Feldmeyer, and now the man would believe anything of you. He showed me your notes, and as good as told me that I was in partnership with you in getting money out of him. And you exposed me to this!"

"Where is he?" asked Wallingford unsteadily.

"I shan't tell you. He has left the city. He left this morning, and I have been considering whether, after all, I had not better stay sold."

They were in the parlor. Now she opened the door into the next room.

"Where are you going?" he asked, stepping toward her.

For reply she only laughed, the most unpleasant laugh he had ever heard from her, and, stepping through, closed the door. Before he could reach it she had bolted it. He went immediately into the hall, but all the other doors to their suite were also locked.

Maylie stepped out of the elevator as he was pondering what to do.

"Heard you had come in," said the lawyer, in a jaunty tone of easy familiarity. "How are tricks?"

The fellow stood in front of the open parlor door, and the light streamed upon his face. Wallingford, in the dimness, could study his countenance without exposing his own to such full scrutiny. There sat upon Maylie a new self-possession that had something insolent about it. Fanny had been right. Maylie had been getting reports upon him.

"Step in," he cordially invited, and Maylie walked into the parlor. It was noticeable that he kept his hat on until after he had sat down. "Tricks are very fair indeed," continued Wallingford in answer to the offhand question. "We're going to get through with it in good shape."

Maylie laughed.

"You're all right," he said. "From all accounts you're a wonder. No matter what you tackle, the milk stopper business, carpet tacks, insurance, sales recorders, you're always a winner," and after this hint that he knew

something of Wallingford's past he lit a cigarette with arrogant nonchalance, then got up
to close the hall door which had been left
slightly ajar.

Wallingford's half-closed eyes followed him
across the room with a gleam in which there
boded no good for Mr. Maylie. Turning, however, Maylie found his host laughing heartily.

"I seldom pick up the hot end of it," asserted Wallingford. "How about the bank?"

"They're offering suit right now, and the
Pneumatic will not pay the note. The company hasn't the money, and the tightening up
of the local financial situation that has come
about in the past month will make it almost
impossible to realize on such trifling securities
as the members have. Moreover, if they had
money they're scared stiff, and not one of
them would put up a dollar, except Klug,
perhaps. They'll let the company go to a
forced sale. I guess that's what you wanted,
isn't it?"

"I'm not going to say about that," replied
Wallingford. "The less we talk, even with the
doors locked, the better."

"That's so," agreed Maylie; "only there's
one point of it we *must* talk about. How did
you come out in the East?"

235

"I have just told you not to try to know too much."

"I don't want to know too much. I only want to know where I come in."

"Your experience with me ought to tell you that you will have no occasion to quarrel with your fee."

"I thought so," retorted Maylie, leaning forward with a laugh that was more like a sneer; "but I want more than a fee, and I'm going to have more than a fee!"

For just one instant Wallingford almost lost his suavity, but whatever game he played he held all its tangled ends continuously in view.

"So we're all thieves together, eh?" he said, smiling, and the gleam of gratification upon Maylie's face assured him that he was upon the right track. "Of course, I know that you have a string on me in this matter and can hold me up," he admitted, as if reluctantly, "so suppose we say ten thousand for you, if the deal goes through the way I want it."

"Now you're shouting!" exclaimed Maylie, and rising impulsively he shook hands with great enthusiasm. "You may count on me."

"I do," said Wallingford, also rising; and, still keeping his grip of the lawyer's hand, he turned his back squarely to the window, so that Maylie would be compelled to face it. "I consider you as mine from this minute."

As he said the words there came that little flicker in Maylie's close set eyes for which he had been looking. It told of negation—that Maylie still held his own plans in reserve. So adroit himself in plot and counterplot, it was no trick for Wallingford to fathom this amateur, and he let the lawyer go away hugging the delusion that he had this experienced schemer under his thumb; then Wallingford once more turned his attention to the locked door.

The silence within those other rooms had become oppressive, and a panic began to come over him. He knocked, but there was no response. He went out into the hall once more, and trying each of the knobs shook them. The far door, to his surprise, opened under his hand. Not one valued possession of Mrs. Wallingford's was in evidence. Empty dresser drawers were open, and two suit cases were gone. A trunk in the corner stood wide, and its bulky articles of lesser worth were strewn upon the floor. He immediately telephoned from that room. Yes, Mrs. Wallingford had gone. No, they did not know to which depot.

She had merely called a cab and had hurried away. He ordered up time tables and studied them feverishly. Almost at this very moment trains were leaving from two different depots, and these were more than three miles apart. There was no chance of finding quickly to which one she had gone. A horrible fear oppressed him. That she had joined Feldmeyer was almost inconceivable, but that she might have taken even this revenge for the slight that had made her furious was a thought in harmony with the principles by which, through his own moral warp, he judged humanity, and he was frantic. At Feldmeyer's office he found the door also locked and the rooms for rent!

The next train for the East found Wallingford upon it. He spent days in attempting to get on the track of them, and he finally found out about Feldmeyer. He had gone to Europe. On the sailing list almost any name might conceal his wife, and to Europe went Wallingford, misled by his own worse self. It was characteristic of him that, having found Feldmeyer and being convinced that Mrs. Wallingford had never joined that gentleman, he should remind the doctor that he had been "chased" with his own money; and then he hurried home, more worried than ever, but his precious ten thousand dollars still intact and with some to spare. He needed that ten thousand for a specific purpose. Finally it occurred to him to enlist the services of "Blackie" Daw, and hunted that enterprising salesman of insecure securities. Blackie laughed at him and handed him a letter. Partly to punish her husband and partly to satisfy certain vague, mistaken longings she had cherished for a "quiet life," Mrs. Wallingford had immured herself in a little village, living most comfortably upon her diamonds; but now she was tired of it—and anxious for "Jim!"

"It's no use," she confessed when he had hurried to her. "Your way is wrong, but you've spoiled me with luxury."

"I'll spoil you with more of it," he assured her, petting her with an overgrown playfulness that seemed strange in one of his bigness of frame, and made of his varied character a most complex thing; "but if I don't hurry back on the job I'll get the hooks."

It was, in fact, high time for him to return to business, for he could get no wire from Maylie about the forced sale; and this was the strategic point for which he had been planning since the day he met Carl Klug. Three telegrams drew no response, and there was no

one else to whom he dared wire in the present
condition of affairs. Leaving his wife where
she was for the present, he took the first train
for the West and, arriving on the day before
the sale, drove directly from the train to Carl
Klug's, where he found a mournful assembly.

"That's him!" exclaimed Jens Jensen, as
he came into the shop. "I always said he was
a skinner."

Klug looked at him with dull eyes. Otto
Schmitt arose to his threatening, rawboned
height. Henry Vogel put his hand on Otto's
arm.

"Wait a minute," he cautioned. "You don't
know anything for sure about things."

"What's the matter?" Wallingford asked,
stopped in the midst of his intended cordial
greeting by the hostile air of the gathering.

"You done it a-purpose," charged Jens,
shaking his skinny fist. "You got from us that
note, and now it shuts us up in business. You
say you back the company for all you're worth.
Maybe you ain't worth anything. If you ain't
you're a liar. If you are worth something you
don't back us up. Then you're a liar again, so
that makes you a skinner!"

"Gentlemen," said Wallingford sternly, "I
am surprised. The question of whether I have

or have not money is not worth arguing just
now. The point is this: if any one of you had
money would you be willing to invest it against
the millions of the United Sales Recording Machine Company of New Jersey? Would you,
Mr. Jensen?"

"I don't know," said Jens sullenly. "I
think you're a skinner."

Wallingford shrugged his shoulders.

"Would you, Mr. Schmitt?"

"No," said Otto, and unclenched his huge
fists.

"Would you, Vogel?"

Vogel was positive about it, too. It would
be throwing good money after bad.

"I ask Mr. Klug. Would you, Carl?"

"Yes," sturdily asserted Carl, his mustache
bristling, his face puffing red. "Every cent.
It is a good patent. It is a good machine.
There's money in it."

"Maybe," admitted Mr. Wallingford; "but
let me tell you something I found out during
my trip East. For five years the Hammond
Automatic Cashier Company fought the United
Sales Recording Machine Company of New
Jersey tooth and toe nail, and finally sold out
to them for two hundred thousand dollars, a
net loss of over a quarter of a million, besides

all their time. During the same period, the Keyes Accounting Device Company, with a capital of three hundred thousand dollars, was fought out of existence and quit without a cent. The Burch Company, the Electric Sales Checking System Company and the Wakeford and Littleman Store Supply Company, all rich, all met the same fate. That note you gave me was a mere incident. You had the ten thousand dollars, have used it in the business, and it is gone. If you had a hundred thousand dollars more on top of it, that would drop into the same hole, for I am told that the United Company lays aside twenty-five dollars from every sale for patent litigation. But since Jensen seems to think I am not a man of my word I will do this: There are seven of us in the company. I will put in ten thousand dollars if the rest of you will raise 'thirty. We will pay this note and hire lawyers as long as we last, and as a proof that I mean what I say here is ten thousand dollars that I will put into the hands of your treasurer the minute the rest of you are ready to make up your share.''

From his pocket he drew ten bills of one thousand dollars each. It was the first time they had any of them seen money of such large denomination, and it had a visible effect.

"I can raise five thousand dollars on my house and shop," offered Carl Klug hopefully, but one glance at the glum faces of his friends was enough to discourage that idea.

Wallingford was rehabilitated, but not their faith in Carl Klug's unlucky device. The sale of the company must bring something, possibly enough to settle the note. If they could get out of it without losing any more they would consider themselves lucky.

"When is this sale?" asked Wallingford.

"To-morrow morning at ten o'clock. Here."

"Very well," said Wallingford. "If before that time any of you want to take up the offer I have just made, you are welcome to do so," and he put the money back in his pocket.

He had found out what he wanted to know, and drove away well satisfied with the results of his visit. His proposition to put further cash into the concern "if they would raise thirty thousand dollars" had wrought the effect he had calculated upon. It had scared them out completely.

At his hotel he found three telephone memoranda waiting for him. They were all from the same source: room number 425 of the only other good hotel in the city. He did not answer this call until he got to his own rooms, and then he spoke with much briefness.

"No, do not come over," he peremptorily insisted. "I have no time to-day nor to-night, nor until after the sale. It is at ten o'clock, at 2245 Poplar Street. Stay right where you are. I'll send you over the stuff within an hour," and he rang off.

As soon as he could get connection he called up Maylie, but if the latter contemplated any trickery he did not show it by any hesitation of speech when he recognized Wallingford's voice. As a matter of fact, he already knew Wallingford to be in town. He was cordiality itself. Why, certainly, he would be right over! His cordiality, however, could not be exceeded by that of Mr. Wallingford when they met.

"You simply must stay for dinner with me, old man," said Wallingford. "I have a lot of things to talk over with you."

"I really have an engagement," Maylie hesitated. He had not, but he would much rather have been alone, this night of all nights.

"Nonsense," insisted Wallingford. "This is more important. It means money, and big money, to both of us, and we'll just have dinner up here. We want to be alone to-night.

There might always be somebody at the next table, you know.''

Within ten minutes Maylie was glad he had stayed, and the dinner he heard Wallingford order had reconciled him. He had been doing yeoman work for himself, and he felt entitled to a certain amount of indulgence. Within another ten minutes a bottle of champagne was opened, and Wallingford, taking one glass of it, excused himself to remove the stains of travel. When he came back, refreshed and clean, the quart of wine was nearly emptied, and Maylie, leaning back in a big leather chair, was puffing smoke rings at the ceiling in huge content.

CHAPTER XVII

WHEREIN A GOOD STOMACH FOR STRONG DRINK IS WORTH THOUSANDS OF DOLLARS

WINE was the *pièce de résistance* of that dinner. There were other things, certainly, course after course, one of those leisurely, carefully blended affairs for which Wallingford was famous among his friends, a dinner that extended to nearly three hours, perfect in its ordering and appointments; but champagne was, after all, its main ingredient. It was on the table before the first course was served, and half emptied bottles and glasses of it were there when they came to the coffee and the cordials and the fat black cigars. In all, they had consumed an enormous quantity, but Wallingford was as steady as when he began, while Maylie was flushed and so buoyant that everything was a hilarious joke. Wallingford, on their first encounter, had detected this appetite in the young man, and had saved it for just such a possibility as this. It was half past nine before they arose from the table, and by that time Maylie was ripe for any suggestion. Wallingford's proposal that they pile into a carriage and take a ride met with instant and enthusiastic acquiescence. There were clubs to which Wallingford had already secured the *entrée* by his personality and his free handling of money, and now he put them to full and extravagant use.

Dawn was breaking when the roisterers finally rolled back to Wallingford's apartments. Wallingford was holding himself right by a grim effort, but Maylie had passed to a pitiable condition of imbecility. His hair was stringing down over his forehead, and his face was of a ghastly pallor. In the parlor, however, he drew himself together for a moment and thought that he was capable of great shrewdness.

"Look yere, ole man," he stammered, trying to focus his gaze upon his watch; "this 's mornin' now, an' i'ss all off. Tha's sale's at ten o'clock an' we godda be there."

"We'll be there all right," said Wallingford. "What we need's a little nap. There are two bedrooms here. We'll leave a call for nine o'clock. Three hours of sleep will do us more good than anything else."

"Aw ri'," agreed Maylie, and winked labo-

riously to himself as an absurdly foolish idea
came to him that he would let Wallingford get
to sleep first, and would then change the call
to his own room. He would answer that call,
take a hasty plunge, dress and walk out, leaving Wallingford to sleep on for a week! Wallingford, in the dining room, sought for the
thing he had ordered left there: one more bottle, packed tightly in its ice, and this he now
opened. Into Maylie's glass he poured two or
three drops of a colorless liquid from a little
vial he carried, filled it with wine and set it
before him. Maylie pushed it away.

"Do' wan' any more wine," he protested.

"Sure you do. A nightcap with your dear
old pal?" Wallingford persisted, and clinked
glasses with him.

Maylie obeyed that clink as he would not
have responded to any verbal urging. He
reached for the glass of champagne and drank
half of it, then collapsed in his chair. Wallingford sat opposite to him and watched him
as intently as a cat watches a mouse hole, sip-
ping at his own wine quietly from time to time.
His capacity was a byword among his friends.
Maylie's hand slipped from his chair and
hung straight down, the other one curling
awkwardly upon his lap. His head drooped

and he began to snore. He was good for an all-day sleep. Only a doctor could arouse him from it.

Wallingford still waited. By and by he lifted up the hanging hand and dropped it roughly. Maylie made not the slightest motion. Wallingford stood above him and looked down in smiling contempt; and the ghastly blending of the artificial light with the morning, where it struggled bluely in around the edges of the blinds, touched the smile into a snarl. Suddenly he stooped to the limp figure in the chair and picked it up bodily in his arms, and, staggering slightly under the burden, carried the insensate lump to the far sleeping apartment and laid it upon the bed. He loosened the man's collar and took off his shoes, then, as calmly and unconcernedly as he might read a newspaper, he went through Mr. Maylie's clothing.

Nothing worth mentioning in the outside coat pockets; nothing in the inside coat pockets; in the inside vest pocket a few yellow papers! He did not even stop at the window of this dim room to make sure of what he held. He was sure without looking. Into the parlor and to an easy chair he took them and opened them with grim satisfaction. They were tele-

grams, all from the United Sales Recording
Machine Company of New Jersey, and they
told an absorbingly interesting story. There
were four, and in the order of their receipt
they read thus:

Were already informed our Mr. Bowman
will report to you in time for sale

Since you think Bowman's presence might
hurt negotiations he will not come   look to you
to bid us in at lowest possible figure

Up to one hundred and fifty thousand   if
bidding goes above that wire for further instructions

Yes keep all under fifty thousand for your fee

Business! All pure business! The United
Sales Recording Machine Company of New
Jersey was being held up, and it was good business for them to see that they were mulcted of
as little as possible. Wallingford rather admired them for it. Since the property was at
open sale they had as much right to buy it
as he had. He read these telegrams over and
over in profound content. He had foreseen
them. Moreover, he had read not only May-

fie's intention, but his plan and every detail
of it, and for him he felt no admiration whatever. Maylie was too clumsy.

There was a small serving table in the
dining room, and Wallingford carried that in
to the sleeper's bedside. Upon this he spread
the four telegrams in neat order, and weighted
them down with *empty glasses* for Mr. Maylie's absorbed study if he should happen to
awaken. Next he drew his favorite chair into
that room, and placed it at the opposite end of
the serving table. He put upon this the champagne bottle and his own glass, and lighting a
big and extremely black cigar he sat down to
watch his erstwhile comrade, for he was taking no chances. Whenever he felt himself
nodding or letting that cigar lax in his fingers
he took a tiny sip of the champagne. Sometimes he went in and held his head under the
cold water faucet.

At the end of the first hour sleep threatened
to overcome him, in spite of all that he could
do, and going into the bathroom he undressed
and took a cold shower. That refreshed him
exceedingly, and the feel of cool, fresh linen
upon him brightened him still more, for in his
personal habits he was clean as a cat. It
crossed his mind once or twice to send down

and get newspapers, but he knew that the least strain upon his eyes would send him to sleep quicker than anything else. The second hour passed; the third, then the fourth one dragged wearily by. At the beginning of the fifth he began to stumble as he walked from room to room to keep awake, but never for more than five minutes at a time did he let that sleeping man out of his sight.

It seemed an eternity until the telephone bell rang in the parlor with startling insistence. With a glance of triumph toward the bed, he hurried in to obey the welcome call.

"Yes, this is Wallingford," he answered huskily. "How about it? . . . Good. How much? . . . What? All right, come straight up."

He stood scratching his head and trying to think for a few minutes, endeavoring to recall a certain number that he had in mind. Then he turned to the telephone book and fumbled through its leaves, backward and forward. His thumbs and fingers were like clubs. They had no feeling whatever. It took him whole minutes to separate two leaves from each other, swaying upon his feet and muttering to himself, but finally he found the name he wanted and put in the call. Slowly and with tremendous effort he delivered his message, then slapped the receiver on the hook and staggered back to his chair. His fight against sleep for the next ten relaxed minutes was like a drowning man's fight for life, but he conquered, and when, a few moments later, there came a knock at his door, he was able to open it briskly.

"Hee-avings hee-elp us!" exclaimed Blackie Daw when he came in. "What a bat you've been on! Have you looked at yourself, J. Rufus?" and kicking the door shut he walked his friend up in front of the mantel mirror.

Wallingford focused his attention upon his own puffed face, on the swelled and reddened eyelids, on the bloodshot eyes, and laughed hoarsely.

"It's worth it," he declared. "I win over one hundred and fifty thousand clean, cold simoleans. But how did you come to have to pay eight thousand for the patents?"

"Klug," replied Blackie. "I thought for a minute he'd top my pile. He'd raised a little money some place, but he spent four thousand of it bidding in some machinery. It never flashed on him that the patents would have to be sold, too, and he nearly took a fit when he found it out. Game, though. He bid 'em up to his last cent. We had been going in five-hundred-dollar raises until it got up to six thousand. That was Mr. Klug's last bid, for I piled two thousand square on top of it and tried to look like I could go two thousand at a jump for the next two hours, and then Klug laid down.''

"Eight thousand and four thousand. That's twelve thousand, and the bank's note is ten,'' figured Wallingford with painful slowness. "The costs will run about two hundred, and that lets the company have eighteen hundred dollars to divide among the partners. Why, say, Blackie, I get one twelfth of that! There's about a hundred and fifty dollars coming to me. Suppose we go over and get it.''

He laughed, but even as he did so he swayed and caught at a chair, and his eyelids dropped.

"I've got to keep up now until we get into a Pullman,'' he mumbled with halting effort. "Sleep? I'll sleep all the way to New Jersey. Did you arrange to pay for the patents?''

"Did I?'' triumphed Mr. Daw. "Trust your uncle for that. Say, J. Rufus, what'll you give me to transfer them over to you?''

Wallingford turned to his friend a countenance that was almost ferocious in its sudden alertness.

"I'll give you twenty minutes to do it in," he said with a growl. "There's a lawyer on the way here now, and I can have a policeman here in two minutes. You know you jumped bail in this town, don't you?"

Mr. Daw was shocked.

"There's no need for you to be so ugly about it, J. Rufus," he protested. "I wouldn't take a cent away from you."

"Wouldn't you!" sneered J. Rufus. "Do you know why? I'd never give you a chance. Let me show you the last man that tried to do me up," and he led the way into the apartment where Mr. Maylie still lay in profound slumber.

Mr. Daw grinned.

"He makes you look perfectly sober," he confessed; "but what are those papers on the table?"

Mr. Wallingford laughed quite naturally this time.

"Poor boob!" he said. "He just lost forty thousand, and those telegrams are his fee."

CHAPTER XVIII

SLEEP, blessed sleep! Desperately Wallingford fought it off until the lawyer had arrived and the necessary documents had been signed, and then, more dead than alive, he allowed himself to be bundled into a cab.

"Now, J. Rufus," said Blackie Daw as he jumped in beside him, "we have your affairs all wound up and a red ribbon tied around them, so let's 'tend to Happy Horace. I'm a bridegroom! Congratulate muh."

"Huh?" grunted J. Rufus, and immediately there followed another succession of unintelligible sounds. Wallingford was snoring.

It was precisely twenty-four hours before Mr. Daw could convey this important information to his friend and make him understand it, and it was not until they had arrived in Jersey City that J. Rufus, still dull from his nerve-racking experience, was normal enough to ask:

WALLINGFORD

"Who's the lucky lady?"

"The Star of Morning and the Queen of Night," responded Blackie with vast enthusiasm. "The one best bet of blazing Broadway. The sweetest peach in the orchard of joy. The fairest blossom in Cupid's garden. The—"

"It's a fine description," interrupted Wallingford. "I'd be able to pick her out any place from it; but what was her name before she shortened it?"

"You want to know too quick," complained Blackie. "You ought to have waited till I explained something more about her; but you always were an impatient cuss, and I'll tell you. Her name was and is, upon the bill-boards and in the barber-shop windows, Violet Bonnie, whose exquisite voice and perfect figure—"

"Is *she* divorced again?" once more interrupted Wallingford.

"Last week," answered Blackie with no abatement of his enthusiasm, "and Happy Horace happened to be on the spot. I was introduced to her over at Shirley's the night she was celebrating the granting of her decree, and I had so much money with me it made my clothes look lumpy. She took an awful shine to that bank roll; not so much the diameter of it but the way I rolled it. It never rested, and by two in the morning she had transferred her affections from the swiftly flowing mezuma to me. At four o'clock G. M. we waded out from among the ocean of empties and, attended by a party so happy they didn't care whether it was day before yesterday or day after to-morrow, we took passage in seaworthy taximeters and floated to the Little Church Around the Corner, where the bright and shining arc light of musical comedy became Mrs. Violet Bonnie Daw. It was a case of love at first sight.''

"For how long have you secured a lease?'' inquired Wallingford.

"I don't know,'' replied Blackie reflectively. "She was married the first time for three years, the second for two and the third for one. According to those figures Number Four would have a right to look forward to about six months of married bliss.''

"I never was drunk for six months at a time in my life,'' reflected Wallingford, "but I can see how it could happen. When it's all over, come around to me and I'll lead you to a sanitarium. In the meantime, when am I to have a chance to congratulate the lady?''

"Right away. She is now awaiting yours truly with quite yearning yearns. You know,

WALLINGFORD

J. Rufus, your urgent telegram interrupted the howlingest honeymoon that ever turned the main stem into the Great Purple Way. Here's the address. Come over as soon as you have held up the United people, and interrupt us. If you don't find us at home, just go charter a car and roll up and down the avenue until you see the speediest automobile cab outdoors. Chase that, because it's us."

When he called at two o'clock on the following afternoon, however, after having seen Mr. Priestly to their mutual satisfaction, he found them at home just preparing for breakfast, and blinking at the gray world through the mists of a champagne headache. He found Violet Bonnie Daw, seen thus intimately, to be an extremely blond person with a slight tendency toward *embonpoint*, but her eyes were very blue, and her complexion, even without a make-up, very clear, able even to dominate her charming morning gown of a golden shade that exactly matched her hair. True, if one looked closely there were already traces of coming crow's-feet about the eyes, but one must not look closely; and her very real cordiality made amends for any such slight drawbacks.

"So you're my husband's old pal!" she exclaimed as she shook hands with him warmly.

Then she surveyed him from head to foot with an expert appraisement. "You look like a good sport all right," she concluded. "Blackie tells me you just cleaned up a tidy wad of pin money out West, and that you could give Pittsburgh's Best cards and spades on how to spend it. And Blackie's no slouch himself," she rattled on. "My, you ought to have been with us last night."

Blackie grinned dolefully.

"We left a string of long-necked bottles from the Café Boulevard to Churchill's," he stated somberly, but still with quite justifiable pride, "and when we rolled home this morning even the bankers were coming to work."

"It was something fierce," smiled his wife reminiscently, "but I guess we had a good time. Anyhow, it was so hilarious that we can't tell this morning what to take for a pick-me-up."

"That's where I won my first gold medals," boasted Wallingford, chuckling. "What sort of a bar outfit have you?"

"Everything from plain poison to prussic acid," Blackie informed him. "The preceding husband of Mrs. Daw was a swell provider."

"You bet he was," agreed Mrs. Daw as she led the way to the dining room and threw open the cupboard of the sideboard. "Harry was a good sport all right, but his stomach gave out."

The sideboard, given over in most apartments to cut glass and other ordinary dining-room adornments, was in this case stocked with fancy bottles of all shapes and colors and sizes, and in the lower part of it was ice.

"Pardon the bartender, mum," observed J. Rufus, his eyes lighting up with the dawning of creative skill as he removed his coat.

Mrs. Daw watched him musingly through the open door of the dining room as he worked deftly among those bottles and utensils.

"He's a good sport all right," she confided to her present husband, and she was still more of that opinion when Wallingford served three tall, thin glasses with sugared edges, crowned with cracked ice and filled with a golden green-ish liquid from which projected two straws. One sip and a sigh of satisfaction from both Mr. and Mrs. Daw, and then they drained the glasses.

"Our hero!" declaimed Mrs. Daw, looking up at him in gratitude. "You have saved our lives. Which will you have, Mr. Wallingford, breakfast or lunch?"

By evening she was calling him Jimmie, and any trifle of disapproving impression that Wal-

lingford had at first harbored was gone. As
Blackie claimed, she was born to adorn the
night and became more beautiful as dusk fell.
Perhaps clothes and consummate art in toilet
had something to do with this, but before the
three had parted in the morning, Wallingford
had decided to introduce his wife after all, a
matter about which he had been in considerable doubt. Now, however, he was convinced
that the lady was thoroughly respectable. No
breath of scandal had ever attached itself to
her name. She was always off with the old
love before she was on with the new, and
could hold up her head in any society!

Mrs. Wallingford came to town the next day,
and at no time did she share the enthusiasm
of these two men for the incomparable Mrs.
Daw. There was a striking contrast between
the women, and even their beauty was not only
of a strikingly different kind but of a strikingly different nature. Mrs. Daw was a flaming poinsettia, Mrs. Wallingford a rose, and
the twain were as antagonistic as were their
hues of cheek. Mrs. Daw, however, was more
at ease, for she was in her natural environment, the niche to which her nature had fash-
ioned her and of which she had made delib-
erate choice; but Mrs. Wallingford, in spite

of her surroundings, had much in her—though
she did not recognize it—of the quantities that
would go to make up a Lady Godiva. Her
proper sphere, one of calm, pure domesticity,
she had never known, though she had vaguely
yearned for it; but she was adaptable, and,
particularly throughout her married life, she
had been thrown with all sorts and conditions
of chance nomads such as her husband was
likely to pick up; so she accepted Mrs. Daw
as a matter of course and got on with her
without friction. Nevertheless, her face fell a
trifle when her husband joyously announced
one afternoon that he had just thought up a
great stunt—a honeymoon party for the Daws.
He had acted the moment the suggestion had
come to him. He had already chartered a
private car and had given orders to have it
stocked with the very best of everything. He
had telephoned the Daws. Mrs. Daw had
only the day before signed a contract with a
leading dramatic producer, but what was a
contract?

The next day, in all the luxury that car
builders and fitters had yet been able to de-
vise, they started upon a hilarious tour across
the continent; but so far as their mode of life
and amusement was concerned they might just

as well have stayed on Broadway, for their nights were spent in drinking, their mornings in sleep and their afternoons in sobering up, though in all this Mrs. Wallingford held herself as much reserved and aloof as she could without spoiling the content of the others. They were merely moving a section of the rapid hotel life of New York across the country with them, and the only things which made their hours seem different were the constantly changing scenic environment and the sensation of speed. So long as they were moving swiftly they were satisfied, but a slow rate brought forth howls of discontent. It was on a small connecting line in the middle west that this annoyance reached its climax, and after an hour of exceptionally slow travel Wallingford sent for the conductor and put in a vigorous protest. Yes, there was a faster train on that road. Then why hadn't they been attached to that fast train? The conductor did not know. It was orders.

"You go get different orders!" demanded Wallingford, and for another hour he made life a burden to that official.

Goaded to desperation, wiring at every stop, the conductor finally, with a sigh of relief, saw the polished private car "Theodore" shunted off on the siding at Battlesburg and left behind.

To the quartette of riotous travelers Battlesburg was only an uninteresting detail of their trip, which had intruded itself unbidden upon their sight; but to Battlesburg the arrival of a private car with real people in it was an epoch. Why, it might be the President! Long-legged Billy Ricks, standing idly upon the platform because the dragging hours passed by there as well as anywhere else, did not even wait to take a good look at it, but loped up the one long street, so fired with enthusiasm that he scarcely wobbled as his bony knees switched past each other in their faded blue overalls. He did not bother with people near the depot —they would find out soon enough; but at the little frame office of "Judge" Lampton, Justice of the Peace, Notary Public and Real Estate Dealer, he bobbed his head in for a moment.

"Private car on the sidin'!" he bawled. "Name's 'Theodore'!" and he was gone.

Judge Lampton, smoking a long, ragged stogie, jerked his feet down from among the dust-covered litter of ages upon his combination bookcase-desk. Doc Gunther, veterinary surgeon and proprietor of the livery stable across the way, lifted his head forward from against the dark-brown spot it had made during the past years upon the map of Battlesburg, where it hung upon the wall, and vigorously took a fresh chew of tobacco. Then the two friends, without exchanging one word, stalked solemnly out of the office and toward the depot. In the meantime Billy Ricks had paused to hurl his startling information in at the door of Joe Warren's cigar store, of Ben Kirby's cash grocery, of Tom Handy's Red Front saloon, of the Dogget Brothers' furniture and undertaking establishment, of the Barret & Lucas dry goods and notion store, and of every other place of business on that side of the street, including the Palace Hotel, until he came to Gus Newton's drug store and confectionery, where the real dyed-in-the-wool sports of the town shot dice and played penny-ante in a little back room. Here he met a round half dozen of these high-spirited youths piling out upon the street with their eyes depot-ward.

"Private car on the sidin'!" Billy shouted to them. "Name's 'Theodore'!"

"Uh-huh," agreed Gus Newton, "I ordered it. It's late," and, shouting back further ready mendacity, his crowd hurried on.

Just in front of the Battles County Bank, Billy met Clint Richards, owner and city editor of the Battlesburg *Blade*. Clint was also reporter, exchange and society editor and advertising solicitor of the *Blade,* and, as became a literary man, he wore his hair rather long. He was in a hurry, and had his broad-brimmed black felt hat pulled down determinedly upon his head.

"Private car—" began Billy Ricks.

"Yes," interrupted Clint, "I know about it. Thank you," and his coat tails fluttered behind him.

Billy stopped in dejection. The street which, when he started, had been so lazy and deserted, was now alive. People were pouring from all the places of business beyond him and hurrying toward him. Back of him they were all hurrying away from him. He had been outstripped by the telephone, and ungrateful Battlesburg would fail to connect him with the sensation in any way. Well, he might as well go down to the depot himself, and he turned in that direction; but now his feet shuffled.

At the siding, the denizens of Battlesburg—men, women, children and dogs—were packed four deep around the glistening, rolling palace

"Theodore." Agitated groups of two and three and four, scattered from the depot platform to the siding, were discussing the occurrence excitedly, and Dave Walker, the station agent, turned suddenly crisp and brusque with importance, was refusing explanations and then relenting in neighborly confidence with each group in turn. Clint Richards, pale but calm and confident, bustled through the quivering throng, and they all but set up a cheer as they recognized the official and only authorized asker of important questions. The vestibule being open, he pulled himself up the steps and tried the door. It was locked.

"Push the button, Clint," advised Gus Newton, who knew a thing or two, you bet! and Clint, with a smile and a nod in his direction, for Gus was an advertiser, rang the bell.

A brisk and clean-looking young negro in a white apron and jacket came to the door and Clint handed in his card. The porter disappeared. A moment later the news gatherer was admitted. A sigh of relief went up from the waiting crowd, and they swayed in unison from side to side as they stood on tiptoe and craned their necks to see farther in through those broad windows.

Through the wicker-furnitured observation

library the porter led the way into a rich compartment the full width of the car, where at luncheon sat the honeymoon quartette, rich in gay apparel and brave in sparkling adornment. They had evidently just sat down, for an untouched cocktail stood at each place. The extremely large and impressive Mr. Wallingford, the breadth of whose white waistcoat alone proclaimed him as a man of affairs, arose to greet the representative of the Battlesburg *Blade* with great cordiality.

"The members of the progressive press are always welcome," he announced, clasping Mr. Richards' hand in a vast, plump palm, and exuding democratic good will from every square inch of his surface. "We're just going to have a bit of luncheon. Join us."

"I wouldn't think of intruding," hesitated Mr. Richards, his eyes leaping with an appreciation of the rare opportunity and his brain already busy framing phrases like "priceless viands," "toothsome delicacies," "epicurean luxuries."

"Nonsense!" insisted Wallingford heartily, and introduced his visitor with much pompous ceremony to Mr. Horace G. Daw, mine dealer and investment specialist; to Mrs. Violet Daw, formerly Violet Bonnie, the famous comic-

opera queen, but now the happy bride of a
month; to Mrs. Fanny Wallingford; to himself as a recently retired manufacturer and
capitalist; then he placed Mr. Richards in a
chair with a cocktail in front of him.

Mr. Richards was naturally overwhelmed at
this close contact with two of America's leading millionaires, and he agreed with his host
that the P. D. S. Railroad was positively the
worst-conducted streak of corrugated rust in
the entire United States. He was even more
indignant than the travelers that, after having
been promised a through train, they had been
hitched to the local egg accommodation, and
was even more satisfied than they that Mr.
Wallingford had given the chills and ague to
the entire transportation system of the P. D.
S. until their car had finally been dropped off
here to wait for the 3.45, which was a through
train and the one which should have carried
them in the first place. Why, Wallingford
ought to buy the P. D. S., plow up the right
of way and sow it in pumpkins!

"Sir," declared Mr. Richards, "the P. D.
S. is a disgrace to the science of railroading!
Why, its through trains stop only on signal at
this thriving manufacturing center of four
thousand souls. From your car windows here

you may see the smoke belching forth from the chimneys of the Battlesburg Wagon Works, of the G. W. Battles Plow Factory, of the Battles & Handy Sash, Door and Blind Company, of the Battles & Son Canning Company, of the Battles & Battles Pure Food Creamery and Cheese Concern; and yet the only two through trains of the 'Pretty Darn Slow Railroad,' as we call it here, clink right on through! The Honorable G. W. Battles himself has taken up this matter and can do nothing, and when he can do nothing—"

The utter hopelessness of a situation for which the Honorable G. W. Battles himself could do nothing was so far beyond mere words that Mr. Richards turned from the subject in dejection and inquired about the financial situation back East. He found out all about it, and more. Mr. Daw and Mr. Wallingford, their faculty of invention springing instantly to the opportunity, helped him to fill his notebook to the brim, and turned him loose at last with one final glowing fabrication about the priceless sparkling Burgundy which was served during the seven courses of the little midday morsel. Adorned with a big cigar, from which he did not remove the gold band, Mr. Richards hastened from the car, and to

GET-RICH-QUICK

the pressing throng outside he observed, from the midst of an air of easy familiarity with the great ones of earth:

"That's Colonel Wallingford, the famous Eastern millionaire, and he's a prince! You certainly want to see the *Blade* to-night," and he hurried away to put his splendid sensation into type.

CHAPTER XIX

MR. WALLINGFORD WINS THE TOWN OF BATTLES-
BURG BY THE TOSS OF A COIN

"COLONEL" Wallingford looked at his watch. "Two hours yet!" he exclaimed with a yawn. "Two solid hours in a yap town that's not on the map. What shall we do with the time? Play cards?"

"What's the use?" demanded "Blackie" Daw. "If I'd win your money you'd choke me till I gave it back, and if you won mine I'd have you pinched."

"Let's get off then and look at the burg," suggested J. Rufus.

It was Mr. Daw's turn to yawn. He looked out on one side of the manufacturing portion of Battlesburg, and on the other side at the mercantile and residence portion.

"I think I can see all I want to remember of it from here," he objected; "but anything's better than nothing. Shall we go, Vi?"

"That's us," replied the vivacious bride, who was already beginning to respond to all Mr.

Wallingford's suggestions with more alacrity than either Mrs. Wallingford or Mr. Daw quite approved. "Let's go wake 'em up, Jimmy. Ring for a carriage."

The invaluable porter was already exchanging his white coat and apron for his dark-blue coat and derby, and, in another moment, that dusky autocrat, his face calm with the calmness of them who dwell near to much money, had asked the crowd outside the way to a livery stable.

Billy Ricks projected himself instantly through the assemblage. "I'll show you," he said eagerly.

The autocrat surveyed Billy Ricks briefly and gauged him accurately.

"Suppose you go get the best two-horse carriage, to seat four, that you can find in town," and in Billy's palm he pressed a half dollar.

The excitement grew intense! The millionaires were positively to appear! Doc Gunther's best "rig," his rubber-tired one, came rolling down Main Street, turned, and drew up near the car. The porter, now wearing his official cap, jumped down with his stepping box. Ah-h-h! Here they came! First emerged huge, sleek Mr. Wallingford, looking more like a million cleverly won dollars than the money itself. Mr. Daw stepped down upon the gravel, tall and slender, clad in glove-fitting "Prince Albert," his black mustache curled tightly, his black eyes glittering. Descended the beautiful, brown-haired Mrs. Wallingford, brave in dark-green broadcloth. Descended the golden-haired Mrs. Daw, stunning in violet from hat to silken hose. Perfectly satisfactory, all of them; perfectly adapted to fill the ideal of what a quartette of genuine nabobs should look like! Under the skillful guidance of Mr. Wallingford they pranced up Main Street, of fully as much interest and importance as any circus parade that had ever wended its way along that thoroughfare.

The town of Battlesburg, converting a level, dusty country road into "Main Street" for a space, lay across the railroad like a huge tennis racquet, its hand grip being the manufacturing district, its handle the business quarter, its net the residence section; and here were the first cross streets, little, short byways, the longest of them ten or twelve blocks in extent, and all ending against the fences of level fields. As they rode through the town, however, its pavements stirred to unusual liveliness by the great event, the impression that here was a place of merely sleeping money

grew and grew upon J. Rufus Wallingford and
appealed to his professional instincts.

"Some town, this," he concluded, turning to
Mr. Daw. "They have rusty wealth here, and,
if somebody will only give it a start, it will
circulate till it gets all bright and shiny again.
Then you can see by the flash where it is and
nab it."

"Heads or tails to see who gets it," suggested Mr. Daw, and drew a dollar from his
pocket.

"Heads!" called Mr. Wallingford, pulling on the reins, and just in front of the
Baptist Church the fate of Battlesburg was
decided.

Mr. Daw flipped the coin in the air over
Mrs. Wallingford's lap. Upon the green
broadcloth the bright silver piece came down
with a spat, and the Goddess of Liberty faced
upward to the sky.

"I win the place!" exulted J. Rufus as they
rolled on out past the cemetery and toward
Battles' Grove. "I don't know just yet how
I'll milk it, but the milk is here."

"You wouldn't honestly come back to this
graveyard, would you?" inquired Mrs. Daw.
"Why, you'd die."

"If I did, I'd die with money in both hands,"

responded Wallingford. "I can smell money, and I don't think there's a pantry shelf in this town without some spare coin tucked away in the little old cracked blue teapot. All you have to do is to play the right music, and all that coin will dance right out. I shouldn't be surprised that I'd come back here and toot a tune."

"There's no danger just yet a while," laughed Mrs. Wallingford. "You have too much wealth. In spite of this trip I never saw you get rid of money so slowly."

"He's a good enough spender for me," stated Mrs. Daw, with a sidelong glance at him from her round blue eyes. "He's a good sport, all right."

"I rather like this town, Jim," interposed Mrs. Wallingford quickly, catching that glance. "Let's do come back here and start up a business of some sort."

"I'm glad I lost," declared Mr. Daw vehemently. "It's too far away from a push button."

He also had seen that glance. It was nothing to which he could object, of course, but he did not like it. A damper had somehow been put upon the spirits of the party, and, after they had driven far out of sight of the

277

town, Mrs. Wallingford suggested that they had better turn back.

"I don't know," said her husband, looking at his watch. "We have nearly an hour and a half yet, and we can easily make it from here in half an hour."

"But what a long, long ways we are from a drink, if we wanted one," objected Mrs. Daw. "Just think of all that fizzy red wine in the ice box."

"You're a smart woman," declared J. Rufus with laughing enthusiasm, "and you win! Back we go."

They had scarcely proceeded a mile upon the return trip, however, when a shrill whistle screamed behind them. They turned, and there across the fields they saw a passenger train whizzing along at tremendous speed. The same thought came to them instantly.

"I thought there wasn't another train in that direction until 3.45," exclaimed Mr. Daw, "and now it is only 2.40!"

The team was abruptly stopped, and both men gazed accusingly at their watches. Suddenly Wallingford swore and whipped up the horses.

"We've Western time!" he called over his shoulder.

278

The explanation, though depressing, was correct. They had thought that they were over the line in the morning, and had set their watches ahead. When they discovered their error they had let it stand and had forgotten about it. They made the trip back to Battlesburg at record speed, and just beyond the cemetery they met Billy Ricks, in the middle of the road. He had been running.

"Number Two's jus' been through, an' it took away your private car!" gasped Billy.

Mr. Wallingford, gazing straight ahead, made no intelligible answer, but he was muttering under his breath.

"Your colored gentleman tried to stop 'em," Billy went on with enthusiasm, delighted to be the bearer of good or ill tidings so long as it was startling, "but the conductor cussed an' said he had orders to stop here and take on private car 'Theodore,' an' he was goin' to do it. Number Two didn't even stop at the depot. It jus' backed on to the sidin' an' took your private car an' whizzed out, an' the conductor stood on the back platform damnin' Dave Walker till he was plumb out o' hearin'!"

Mrs. Wallingford smiled. Mr. Daw chuckled. Mrs. Daw laughed hilariously.

"Ain't that the limit?" she demanded. "Let's *all* be happy!"

"I jus' thought I'd come on out and tell you, 'cause you might want to know," went on Billy expectantly.

For the first time Mr. Wallingford looked at him, and the next minute his hand went in his pocket. Billy Ricks drew a long breath. Two half dollars for officious errands in one day was a life record, and he trotted behind that carriage all the way to the depot, where Mr. Wallingford, with the aid of Dave Walker, immediately began to "burn up the wires." It seemed that the management of the P. D. S. positively refused to haul the "Theodore" back to Battlesburg. It was not their fault that the passengers had not been aboard at the time they were warned Number Two would stop for them. They would hold the car at the end of that division, and instruct their agent at Battlesburg to issue transportation to the four on the next west bound train; and that was all they would do!

The only west bound train that night was a local freight; the only west bound train in the morning was the accommodation which had brought them to Battlesburg; then came Number Two, the next afternoon. They drove

straight to the Palace Hotel and met the only
man in Battlesburg who was not impressed by
the high honor that a lucky accident had be-
stowed upon the city and upon his hostelry.
Suspicion, engendered by thirty years of contact with a traveling public which had invari-
ably either insulted his accommodations or
tried to cheat him—and sometimes both—had
soured the disposition of the proprietor of the
Palace and cramped his soul until his very
beard had crinkled. Suspicion gleamed from
his puckered eyes, it was chiseled in the
wrinkles about his nose, it rasped in his voice;
and the first and only thing he noted about
Mr. J. Rufus Wallingford and his splendid
company was that they had no luggage!
Whereupon, even before the multi-millionaire
had finished inscribing the quartette of names
upon his register, he had demanded cash in
advance.

Judge Lampton, who had edged up close to
the register, was shocked by this crass demand, and expected to see the retired capitalist give Pete Parsons the dressing down of
his life. Instead, however, Mr. J. Rufus Wallingford calmly abstracted, from a pocketbook bulging with such trifles, a hundred-dollar bill which he tossed upon the desk, and

went on writing. As impassive as Fate, Pete Parsons turned to his safe, slowly worked the combination, and still more slowly started to make change. In this operation he suddenly paused.

"Billy," said he to the ever-present Ricks, "run over to the bank with this hundred-dollar bill and see if Battles'll change it."

For just one instant the small eyes of Wallingford narrowed threateningly, and then he smiled again.

"Show us to our rooms," he ordered. "Send up the change when it comes."

He laid down the pen, but his hand had scarcely left the surface of the book when it was clutched by that of Judge Lampton.

"In the name of the judiciary and of the enterprising citizens of this place, I welcome you to Battlesburg," he announced.

Mr. Wallingford, "always on the job"—to use the expressive parlance of his friend Mr. Daw—drew himself up and radiated.

"Thank you," he returned. "I have already inspected your beautiful little city with much pleasure, and all that you need to make this a live town is a good hotel."

The Judge shot at Pete Parsons a triumphant grin. Ever since Mr. Lampton had been denied credit beyond the amount of two dollars at the Palace Hotel bar, himself and Mr. Parsons had been "on the outs."

"Let me show you the very piece of property to build it on," he eagerly returned.

Only for a moment Wallingford considered.

"I'll look at it to-morrow morning," he said.

"I shall have the facts and figures ready for you, sir," and Judge Lampton swaggered out of the Palace Hotel on a bee-line for a little publicity.

It was scarcely half an hour later when Clint Richards called at Wallingford's room with four copies of the Battlesburg *Blade*.

"I brought these up myself, Mr. Wallingford," he explained, "to show you that Battlesburg is not without its enterprise. Twice this afternoon the *Blade* was made over after it was on the press; once when the P. D. S. stole your private car—stole, sir, is the word —and again upon Judge Lampton's report of his important conversation with you. If you should decide to invest some of your surplus capital in Battlesburg, I am sure that you will find her progressive citizens working hand in hand with you to make that investment profitable."

GET-RICH-QUICK

The Battlesburg *Blade* consisted of four pages, and the first one of these was devoted entirely to that eminent financier, Mr. J. Rufus Wallingford.

EASTERN MILLIONS HERE

was the heading which, in huge, black type, ran entirely across the top of the page just beneath the date line. Beneath this was a smaller black streamer, informing the public that these millions were represented in the persons of those eminent captains of industry, Mr. J. Rufus Wallingford and Mr. Horace G. Daw. Beneath this, in the center four columns of the six-column page, was another large type headline:

ROBBED OF THEIR PRIVATE CAR "THEO-DORE" BY THE BUNGLING P. D. S.

In the center two columns was this boxed-in, large type announcement:

LATER!

It is rumored upon good authority that these wide-awake millionaires may invest a portion of their surplus capital in wide-awake Battlesburg. *Huge hotel projected!*

WALLINGFORD

The article which filled the balance of the page was an eloquent tribute to the yellow genius of Mr. Richards. With flaming adjectives and a generous use of exclamation points it told of the marvelous richness of the private car "Theodore," owned, of course, by the gentlemen who were traveling in it; of the truly unparalleled sumptuousness of the feast that had been served by these charmingly democratic gentlemen to the humble representative of the *Blade;* of the irresistible beauty and refinement of their ladies; of the triumphs of Mr. J. Rufus Wallingford in the milkstopper business, the carpet tack industry, the insurance field, the sales recorder trade, successive steps by which he had arisen to his present proud eminence as one of the powers of Wall Street; of Mr. Daw's tremendously successful activity in gold mining, in rubber cultivation, in orange culture and in allied lines, where deft and brilliant stock manipulations had contributed to the wealth of the nation and himself; of the clumsy and arrogant blundering of the P. D. S. Railroad, which, until this lucky accident, had always been a detriment to the energetic city of Battlesburg.

It was easy to see by the reading of this article that the P. D. S. R. R. did not advertise

in the Battlesburg *Blade,* and that it now issued
no passes to the press, and Mr. Richards took
occasion to point out, as he had so often before urged, that, if a traction line could only
be induced to parallel the P. D. S. and enter
Battlesburg, it would awaken that puerile railroad from its lifelong lethargy and infuse a
new current of life and activity into the entire
surrounding country, besides earning for itself
a handsome revenue.

It was this last clause which plunged Wallingford into profound meditation.

"A traction line," he said musingly, by and
by. "I'm a shine for overlooking that bet so
long, but when we get through this voyage of
joy, just watch my trolleys buzz. I'm coming
back here and jar loose all the money that's
not too much crusted to jingle."

"But, Jim," protested Mrs. Wallingford
thoughtfully, "you couldn't build a traction
line with only a little over a hundred thousand
dollars!"

"How little you know of business, Fanny,"
he rejoined, with a wink at Mr. Daw. "I can
tear up a street, level a small hill and buy two
tons of iron rails with one thousand, and have
the rest to marry to other money. Blackie, I'm
glad I won this town from you. I'd hate to

think of all the good coin hidden away under the cellar stairways here being paid over for your fine samples of four-color printing. They don't need phoney gold mining stock in this burg. What they need is something live and progressive, like a traction line."

"I know," agreed Mr. Daw with a grin. "You'll organize an air line and sell them the air."

"Don't, Jim," protested Mrs. Wallingford. "You're clever enough to make honest money, and I know it. Other people do. A hundred thousand is a splendid nest-egg."

"To be sure it is," assented Mr. Daw. "Watch Jim set on it! If he don't hatch out a whole lot of healthy little dollars from it I'll grow hayseed whiskers and wear rubber boots down Broadway."

There was another knock at the door. This time it was Judge Lampton, and with him was a nervous, wiry man, in black broadcloth and wearing a vest of the same snowy whiteness as his natty mustache.

"Mr. Wallingford," said Judge Lampton, tingling with pride, "permit me to introduce the Honorable G. W. Battles, president of the Battles County Bank, of the Battlesburg Wagon Works, of the G. W. Battles Plow Factory, of the Battles & Handy Sash, Door and Blind Company, of the Battles & Son Canning Company, of the Battles & Battles Pure Food Creamery and Cheese Concern, and of the Battlesburg Chamber of Commerce."

As one seasoned financier to another these two masters of commerce foregathered gravely upon matters of investment and profit. The Honorable G. W. Battles was a man who believed in his own enthusiasm and had command of many, many words, a gift which had been enhanced by much public speechmaking, and now, in a monologue that fairly scintillated and coruscated, he laid before J. Rufus Wallingford the manifold advantages of investment in the historic town that had been founded by his historic grandfather. Before he was entirely through all that he could, would or might have said, there came another knock at the door. Judge Lampton, who had retired immediately upon introducing the Honorable G. W. Battles, had returned, and with him was Max Geldenstein, proprietor of the Rock Bottom clothing stores, not only in Battlesburg, but also in Paris, London, Dublin, Berlin and Rome, all six cities being in or adjacent to Battles County. He was also a director in the Battles County Bank and in the Battles & Son Canning Company, a city councilman and a member of the Chamber of Commerce. He, too, extended a welcoming hand to the chance millionaire and invited him most cordially to become one of them. Came shortly after, in tow of the indefatigable Judge Lampton, the Honorable Timothy Battles, mayor of Battlesburg and illustrious son of the Honorable G. W. Battles, bearing with him the keys of the city. Came, too, Lampton-led, Mr. Henry Quig, coal and ice magnate, and the largest stockholder, except the Honorable G. W. Battles, in the Battlesburg Gas and Electric Light Plant; also a member of the City Council and of the Chamber of Commerce.

It became necessary to subsidize the dining room after eight o'clock, and until far into the night Mr. Wallingford and Mr. Daw entertained the leading gentlemen of the city, who, under the efficient marshalship of Judge Lampton, came to help the Judge sell a building lot and to present their respects to these gentlemen of boundless capital. What need is there to tell how J. Rufus Wallingford, he of the broad chest and the massive dignity, arose to the opportunity of presiding as informal host over Battlesburg's entire supply of twenty-one bottles of champagne? Suffice it to say that, when the last callers had gone, he mopped his perspiring brow and turned to Blackie Daw with a chuckle in which his entire body participated.

"They will do it, eh, Blackie?" he commented. "Just come and beg to be skinned! What will you give me for one side of Main Street?"

"It would be a shame to split it," declared Mr. Daw. "Keep it all, J. Rufus. I'm only a piker. If I make ten thousand on a clean-up I think I'm John W. Gates, and if I made more I'd start mumbling and making funny signs. I can't trot in your class."

But J. Rufus was in no humor for banter. He looked at the array of empty bottles and glasses upon the long dining-room table and nodded his head in satisfaction.

"It's been a good night's work, Blackie," he concluded, "and, when I come back here, I'm going to jam a chestnut burr under the tail of this one-horse town. To-morrow morning I'm going to be an investor in Battlesburg real estate, and the traction line idea must be kept under cover for a while. Don't breathe a word of it."

The next morning, in pursuance of this idea, Mr. Wallingford went forth with Judge Lampton and looked at property. Between the

Palace Hotel and the depot was an entire vacant block, used at present for mere grazing purposes by Doc Gunther, and Mr. Wallingford agreed that this would be an admirable site for an up-to-date, six-story, pressed-brick hotel. He even went so far as to sketch out his idea of the two-story marble lobby—a fountain in the center—balcony at the height of the first floor ceiling—arched orchestra bridge! On the other side of the street, a little above the bank and on a block occupied at present by a black-smith shop and a prehistoric junk heap, he gave a glowing word picture of the new Grand Opera House that should be erected there. Farther up the street was another cow pasture, over which he thought deeply; but his thoughts he carefully kept to himself, and both Clint Rich-ards and Judge Lampton dreamed great, puz-zling dreams by reason of that very silence. Up in the residence district Mr. Wallingford picked out three splendid lots, one of which he did not hesitate to say would make an admi-rable site for an up-to-date apartment house, and one of the others — he had not decided which—would make an admirable location for a private residence.

He bought none of this property, but he took ninety-day options on all seven pieces, paying therefor from ten to fifty dollars upon each one, and leaving in the town of Battlesburg, aside from his hotel and livery bill and other expenses, not less than two hundred and fifty dollars of real money, each dollar of which glowed with a promise of many more to come. It is needless to say that the Battlesburg *Blade* that evening did full honor to these wholesale transactions. It took all of the first page and part of the last to do that; even the telegraphic account of the absorbing and scandalous Estelle Lightfoot murder romance, clipped from the Chicago morning papers, had to be condensed for that day to half-a-dozen lines.

CHAPTER XX

BILLY RICKS, shambling after dandelion greens, stepped out of the road to let a great, olive-green touring car go tearing by and bounce over the railroad track. A second or so later he breathlessly dashed into the near-by office of the wagon works and grabbed for the telephone.

"That millionaire that went through here in his private car a couple o' weeks ago has come back to town in his automobile," he told Clint Richards.

"I know it," was the answer. "He's just stopped in front of the Palace Hotel," and with a sigh Billy Ricks hung up the telephone receiver, eying that instrument in huge disfavor.

In the mean time, Main Street, which had relapsed into slumber for two weeks, was once more wide awake. Hope and J. Rufus Wallingford had come back to town. There was no avenue of trade that did not feel the quickening influence within an hour. Even his appear-

293

ance, as he stepped from the touring car, clad
richly to the last detail of the part, conveyed
a golden promise. Mrs. Wallingford, mostly
fluttering veil, was another promise, and even
the sedate G. W. Battles so far forgot his dignity as to come across from the bank in his
bare head and shake hands with the great
magnate. Quick as he was, however, Judge
Lampton was there before him. His half of
the option money left behind by Mr. Wallingford had wrought a tremendous change in the
Judge, for now the beard that he had worn
straggling for so long was cut Vandyke and
kept carefully trimmed—and instead of a stogie
he was smoking a cigar.

Warmed by their enthusiastic reception, the
Wallingfords amiably forgot the purely private and personal quarrel between Mrs. Wallingford and Mrs. Daw, which had disrupted
the happy quartette and nipped in the bud an
itinerary that had been planned through to San
Francisco, and they plunged into a new life with
great zest. For years J. Rufus had been content to make a few thousand dollars and spend
them, but his last haul of a hundred and fifty
thousand that he had received from the perfectly legitimate sale of another man's patent,
for which the inventor got nothing, had stirrec

in him the desire not merely to live like a multi-millionaire, but to be one. As the first step in his upward and onward progress he transferred his hundred odd thousand dollars from an Eastern depository to the Battles County Bank. Next he took ninety-day options upon all the unoccupied property in Battlesburg, including several acres of ground beyond the Battles & Battles Pure Food Creamery and Cheese Concern. He was not so improvident as to pay cash for these options, however; instead, he gave ninety-day notes, writing across the face of each one: "Not negotiable until after maturity." The first of these notes Judge Lampton took to the Honorable G. W. Battles inquiringly. The autocrat of Battles County merely smiled.

"I'll lend you face value on it, Tommy, any time you want it," he observed; and that was the last notch in establishing the local credit of J. Rufus Wallingford, for Judge Lampton was in his way as persistent a disseminator as Billy Ricks himself.

But Battlesburg alone was not a large enough field for Wallingford. Having tied up about half the town, he left "for a little pleasure jaunt;" but before he went away he bought the Star Boarding House and gave

Judge Lampton *carte blanche* to fit up that magnificent ten-room structure as a private residence, according to certain general plans and requirements laid down by the purchaser. When Mr. and Mrs. Wallingford came back two weeks later, that palatial dwelling was perfect in all its arrangements and appointments, even to the stocking of its cellars and the hiring of Letty Kirby as cook and Bessie Walker as maid, and of Billy Ricks as gardener and man-of-all-work. The vast sensation that might have been created by the hiring of three servants, and by the other lusciously extravagant expenditures faithfully chronicled in the daily issues of the Battlesburg *Blade*, was, however, swallowed up in a still greater sensation; for during the absence of the noted financier Mr. Wallingford had become a vast throbbing mystery to the town of his adoption. He had been gone only two days, when, in the *Blade*, there appeared the heading:

OUR MILLIONAIRE

Favors Paris with Crumbs of the Good Fortune Falling
from Battlesburg's Table

The article that followed was a clipping from the Paris *Times,* and from this it seemed that Colonel J. Rufus Wallingford, the famous multi-millionaire, late of Boston and New York but now of their neighbor and county seat, Battlesburg, had been purchasing property liberally along the main street of Paris, giving in exchange his promissory notes for ninety days, which notes, upon the telephonic advice of the Honorable G. W. Battles, of Battlesburg, were as good as gold. Similar reports were reprinted later on from the London *News*, the Dublin *Banner*, the Berlin *Clarion*, the Rome *Vindicator*, and from the papers of other towns still farther away. It was Clint Richards who became the Sherlock Holmes of Battlesburg and found the solution to this mystery, being led thereto by the fact that the only towns where Mr. Wallingford was purchasing this property were along the direct east and west highway, which, running through Battlesburg, paralleled the P. D. S. Railroad from Lewisville to Elliston. These two towns were not only the terminals of the P. D. S. Railroad, but were also the respective outposts of the great Midland Valley traction system and the vast Golden West traction system. The conclusion was obvious that either Colonel Wallingford intended to finance a traction road connecting those two great terminal points, or that he had absolute knowledge that such a line was to be

ouilt; *and Colonel Wallingford had chosen Battlesburg for his headquarters!*

It was exhilarating to see how Battlesburg arose to the vast possibilities of this conjecture. Men who but a brief two weeks before had slouched to their work in the morning as to a mere daily grind, now stepped forward briskly with smiles upon their faces and high courage in their hearts. Every man who had a dollar lying idle looked upon that dollar now not as so much rusting metal, but as being a raft which might float him high upon the shore of golden prosperity. Only Pete Parsons, of all that town, croaked a note of discord. He never for one moment forgot that J. Rufus Wallingford, upon the day he first registered at the Palace Hotel, had no baggage with him!

The return of Mr. Wallingford after the *Blade's* revelation was the occasion of a tremendous ovation. Clint Richards had fairly to paw his way through the crowd that surrounded him on the steps of the bank, where he had stopped to draw a mere five hundred or so for his pocket money; but, once inside the closely packed circle, Clint pinned Colonel Wallingford down to an admission of his plans. Yes, the Lewisville, Battlesburg and Elliston

WALLINGFORD

Traction Line was a thing of the near future.
All that remained was to secure rights of way.
Battlesburg would, in all probability, be headquarters, and the L., B. & E. might even build
its car shops here if the citizens of Battlesburg
were willing to do their share. Mr. Richards
reached out impulsively to grasp the hand of
Colonel Wallingford, but it was already in possession of Judge Lampton, who, thrilled with
emotion, guaranteed Colonel Wallingford that
the city of Battlesburg would not only be glad,
but would be proud, to perform her part in
this great work. He might have said more,
but that the Honorable G. W. Battles, who had
emerged upon the steps of the bank just above
and behind Colonel Wallingford, publicly
thanked that gentleman, on behalf of his fellow citizens, for this vast boon. Appreciating
the opportunity thus thrown upon his very
doorstep, Mr. Battles, by merely beginning to
speak, quickly packed the street to the opposite
curb with his admiring fellow townsmen, and
gave them a half hour of such eloquence as
only a Battles could summon upon the spur of
the moment; and Colonel Wallingford, looming
beside him as big and as impressive as the
Panama bond issue, looked his part, every
inch!

GET-RICH-QUICK

No open-air political meeting, no Fourth of July speechmaking, no dedication or grand opening had ever given rise to such tumultuous fervor as this. There were cheers and tigers galore for Colonel Wallingford, for the Honorable G. W. Battles, for Judge Lampton, for the Battlesburg *Blade*, for the L., B. & E. Traction line, for the city of Battlesburg, for everything and everybody, until the ecstatic throng was too hoarse to cheer any more; and then, at Colonel Wallingford's cordial solicitation, the entire town moved down to the mansion which, by the magic of his money, this great benefactor had built within and without the shell of the one-time Star Boarding House. They filled his yard, they trampled his grass, they invaded the newly carpeted house, and the male portion of them passed in earnest review before his sideboard. Cakes and sandwiches were on the way in hot haste from Andy Wolf's bakeshop, boxes of cigars stood open upon the porch, ice cream appeared for the ladies. Suddenly there arose sweet strains of music upon the air, and down the street at a quick march, accompanied by happy Billy Ricks, came the Battlesburg brass band. Never before was Battlesburg so spontaneously aroused. Amid that happy throng, Colonel Wallingford,

300

laughing from the sheer joy of feeding people into allegiance, moved like a prince in the midst of his devoted subjects; and while he smilingly accepted their homage, came copies of the Battlesburg *Blade*, wet from the press, an extra special edition. Great piles of these were kept replenished upon the porch throughout the evening, so that every inhabitant of the city of promise should know all the golden future that lay before him—and learn to subscribe. Battlesburg was at last to become the New Metropolis of the West; her citizens were to be in the very vortex of a vast whirlpool of wealth, and not one of them but should wax rich. From the East and from the West, from villages and farms, trade would rush in an endless stream aboard the trolley cars of the L., B. & E. traction line; Main Street of Battlesburg should become a Mecca where countless pilgrims would leave their stream of bright and shining dollars; as business increased, property values would rise; with the first singing of the trolleys a hundred-dollar lot would be worth a thousand. And all this through the advent of that master magician of the modern commercial world, Colonel J. Rufus Wallingford!

Marked copies of that issue of the *Blade*

were sent to Paris, to London, to Dublin, to Berlin, to Rome and to all the other towns between Lewisville and Elliston, and all the papers on the route of the proposed new traction line caught up the information eagerly. Within three days a boom had leaped along every foot of what had been before but a lazy, dusty hundred miles of country road. It was a magnificent effect. Even Mrs. Wallingford read the accounts of this stupendous movement, which her husband had inaugurated, with wonder and amazement, and laid down the first *eight-page issue* of the *Blade* with sparkling eyes.

"Jim," she exclaimed, "I'm proud of you! It is worth something to have started thousands of people into new activity, new hope, new life; to have, by your own unaided efforts, doubled and tripled and quadrupled within just a few days the value of hundreds of thousands of dollars' worth of property!"

Mr. Wallingford at that moment was pouring himself out a glass of champagne, and now he laughed.

"It is a big stunt, Fannie," he agreed; "especially when you come to think that outside of our traveling expenses it was all done at an expense of two-fifty cash, the amount I

paid Lampton when I bought those first
options."

It was almost unbelievable, but it was true,
that all these huge impulses had been set in
motion by mere commercial hypnotism. The
public, however, saw in them only the power
of unlimited money. Money! At last its magic
presence hovered over Battlesburg, a vast
beneficent spirit that quivered in the very
air and rendered the mere act of breathing
an intoxication. Its glitter enhanced the glory
of the very sunlight, and to its clinking music
the staid inhabitants of the town that had
slumbered for half a century quickened their
pace as if inspired by the strains of a martial
air. The same quickening that applied to
individuals applied also to the town as a
whole. Civic pride and ambition were aroused.
The day after Wallingford returned, the Chamber of Commerce convened in special session,
and a committee, composed of Henry Quig and
Max Geldenstein, escorted Colonel Wallingford
before that august board, where the Honorable
G. W. Battles, as president, asked of the
eminent capitalist a pregnant question. Battlesburg wanted the shops of the L., B. & E.
traction line. What did the L., B. & E. want?

His requirements were modest, Colonel Wallingford assured them. He demanded no cash bonus whatever. If they would merely provide him the ground to build the shops, and a lot conveniently placed in the center of the city for a freight, baggage and passenger station, and would use their influence with the city council to secure him a franchise, he would be content. He had secured options upon the very pieces of property that would be ideal for the purposes of the L., B. & E., but upon these he would ask no profit whatever, notwithstanding their enhanced value and his right to share in the wealth he had created. If the Chamber of Commerce would merely take up his options, repaying him the amounts he had paid to secure them, he would ask no more, and, further than that, he would take the option money, would add to it a like sum — or more — and with the total amount would purchase a fountain for Courthouse Square as an earnest of his sincere regard for Battlesburg and its enterprising and gentlemanly citizens.

The enthusiasm that greeted this announcement was distinctly audible for two blocks each way on Main Street, and in the midst of it the Honorable G. W. Battles arose to once more make the speech of his life. He could assure

NEVER IN ALL HER MARRIED LIFE HAD SHE ENJOYED ANY
POSITION APPROACHING THIS

Colonel Wallingford that there would be no trouble in influencing the City Council to grant him a franchise, for the Chamber of Commerce had means of coercing the City Council; which was a splendid joke, for every member of the City Council was also a member of the Chamber of Commerce, and they were all present. Such a quantity of mutual good will and esteem was never before uncorked in so limited a space as the social room of Odd Fellows' Hall, and Clint Richards was quite lost to find new adjectives for the front page of the next day's issue of the *Blade*. The glorious news, together with some striking illustrations of the healthy advance of Battlesburg real estate, was copied in the papers of Paris, London, Dublin, Berlin and Rome. In those towns, too, the same civic activity was exhibited, the same golden hopes were aroused, the same era of prosperity set in; and the papers of those villages vied with each other in chronicling the evidences of increased wealth that had come upon them. Franchises, therefore, were to be had by the munificent Colonel Wallingford without the asking. Before he could even appeal to them, village councils had given him the exclusive use of their only desirable streets for fifty years without money and with-

out price. Ground for stations was donated
everywhere, and when Wallingford started out
to secure a right of way from the regenerated
farmers, who in these days kept themselves
posted by telephone and rural free delivery,
his triumphant progress would have sickened
with envy the promoters of legitimate traction
lines.

Discarding the big touring car, he secured a
horse and buckboard, and donning yellow
leather boots with straps and buckles at the
calf, appeared upon the road the very apothe-
osis of a constructive engineering contractor;
and when he stepped to the ground, big and
hearty, and head and shoulders above nearly
every man he went to see, when he gave them
that cordial handclasp and laughed down upon
them in that jovial way, every battle was half
won. The thorough democracy of the man—
that was what caught them! Moreover, the
value of every foot of ground along the traction line was to be enhanced; at every farm-
house was to be an official stopping point with
a platform; cars were to be run at least every
hour; it would be possible to go to town in
either direction, perform an errand and get
back quickly, at infinitesimal cost and without
sparing a horse from the field; sidings were

to be made everywhere, and wheat cars, whenever required, would be loaded directly from the fields, the cost of transportation being guaranteed to remain less than one half that charged by the railroad; express cars were to be inaugurated, and upon these, milk, butter, eggs, produce of all kinds, could be shipped at trifling expense.

While Wallingford was enjoying this new *rôle* he had created, his wife had also her taste of an entirely new life. She had no more than settled down in her new house than Mrs. G. W. Battles called upon her. Following her lead came Mrs. Geldenstein and Mrs. Quig and Mrs. Dorsett and the other acknowledged social leaders of the town. True, they criticised her house, her gowns, her manner of speech, her way of doing up her hair, but, this solemn duty performed, they unanimously agreed that she was a distinct acquisition to the polite life of the place. Never in all her married existence had she enjoyed any position approaching this. They had been nomads always, but now she had actual calls to make, actual, sober, formal friendships to cement, all these made possible by her husband's vast importance in the community; and upon Wallingford's triumphant return from his campaign for the right of way

he was surprised to find her grown so young
and care-free.

"I like this place, Jim," she told him in explanation. "Let's fix it to stay here always."

He gazed down at her and laughed.

"What have you been doing?" he inquired.
"Giving pink teas? Getting full credit for
your diamonds and those Paris dresses and
hats?"

She laughed with him in sheer lightness of
spirit.

"It's more than that," she said. "It is because I'm a human being at last. I have a
chance to be a real woman like other women,
and it is nice to have everybody looking up to
you as the biggest man in town, not even ex-
cepting Mr. Battles. Why, you could go to
the Legislature from here! You could be
elected to any office they have! You could
even be governor, I think."

He laughed again and shook his head.

"There isn't enough in it," he assured her.
"I'd rather promote a traction line. This is
the best ever. Why, Fanny, the entire popu-
lation, on both sides of the road for a solid
hundred miles, is laying awake nights and turning handsprings by day, all just to make money
for yours truly."

WALLINGFORD

"They owe it to you," she insisted. "Look how much money you're making for them. The only thing I don't like about it is that you're away so much. You must manage, though, to be home the twenty-first. I'm going to give a lawn reception."

"Fine!" he exclaimed. "Every little bit helps. It's a good business move," and he walked away, laughing.

CHAPTER XXI

IN WHICH THE SHEEP ARE SHEARED AND SKINNED AND THEIR HIDES TANNED

A N engineer appeared upon the scene and ran a line straight down the center of Main Street, amid intense excitement on the part of the populace; then he trailed off into the country, and farmers driving into town reported seeing him at work all along the line. It was strange the amount of business that farmers found in town of late. Never before had so brisk a country trade been enjoyed at this season of the year, and the results were far-reaching. The Honorable G. W. Battles, on the occasion of one of Wallingford's visits to the bank, invited him into the back room.

"Are you going to build that hotel, Colonel?" he asked as soon as they were seated.

"I scarcely think so," replied Wallingford with apparent reluctance. "The traction line itself is going to take all my time to look after it, and I really do not see how I can take part in any other work of magnitude."

310

"That lot, then," began Mr. Battles hesi-
tatingly. "You know that property belongs
to me. Judge Lampton, on the very day you
first stopped here, came for a power of attorney to dispose of it. Of course your option
hasn't expired yet, but if you don't figure on
using the ground I might consider the building of a hotel myself."

"Good investment," declared Wallingford.
"Just pay me the difference in increased valuation and take over the site."

"The difference in valuation?" mused Mr.
Battles. "Of course, I appreciate the fact that
you are entitled to some of the wealth you produce for us. About how much do you think the
property has increased?"

"Oh, about four times," estimated Wallingford. "The lot's probably worth two thousand
by now."

He had looked for a vigorous objection to
this, but when the other turned to a scratch
pad and began figuring, he was sorry that he
had not asked more, for presently Mr. Battles
turned to him with:

"Well, in the way property has been going,
I presume the lot *is* worth about two thousand. You paid a twenty-five-dollar option to
hold it for ninety days, and that, of course,

you lose. You owe me five hundred for the property and I owe you two thousand.''

With no further words he took from his desk his private check book and wrote Mr. Wallingford an order for fifteen hundred dollars. Then, as by a common impulse, they walked straight up to the office of the Battlesburg *Blade*. That evening's issue flamed anew. The big hotel was a certainty. It would be called the Battles House. It would be four or five stories in height, and ground would be broken for it as soon as the plans could be prepared. In the same item were published the details of the real estate transaction. Mr. Battles had paid two thousand dollars for his own property, which, less than two months before, he had agreed to sell at five hundred dollars! Battlesburg was waking up.

Mr. Geldenstein and Henry Quig came to Mr. Wallingford with another proposition. Did he intend to build the new opera house, or would he care to dispose of the property he had secured with that end in view? As a favor to them he would dispose of it. With the money he had received from Mr. Battles he had already taken up his option on this and other property, and he let the opera-house syndicate have it for three thousand, four

times what it had cost him. In the papers of
Paris, London, Dublin, Berlin, Rome, these
things were retold, and the temperature of
those places went up another degree or two.
Keeping his fingers carefully upon the pulse
of the town, Wallingford began to draw upon
his capital and close in his options. Men
whose property he had been holding in leash,
accepted that money with wailing and gnash-
ing of teeth, but, within a week, whatever of
selfish bitterness they might have held was forgotten in the fever of speculation; for by the
end of that time there appeared on the hill
just east of town a gang of men with horses
and scrapers—and they began chipping off
the top of that hill! Wallingford was out
there every morning in his buckboard and yellow leggings and yellow leather cap. The
Battlesburg *Blade* and all the other papers
from Lewisville to Elliston blazed with the
fact that actual construction work had begun
upon the L., B. & E., and the time when trolleys would begin to whiz through the main
streets of a dozen villages was calculated to a
second. Supply men, the agents of street car
shops, of ironworks, of electrical machinery
and the like, began flocking to Battlesburg
until even Pete Parsons woke up and raised

his hotel rates; and the arrival of each one of them was heralded in Colonel Wallingford's invaluable adjunct, the Evening *Blade*. From these men Wallingford secured "cuts," which he distributed gratis, and pictures of the palatial L., B. & E. cars appeared in all the papers along its right of way; photographs of the special wheat cars, of the freight and express cars, even of the through sleeping cars which would traverse the L., B. & E., carrying passengers from the western limit of the Midland Valley traction system to the most eastern point of the Golden West traction system.

Ground for the opera house and the hotel was broken within a month, and, immediately upon this, small gangs of men were set to work grading near half a dozen different towns at once upon the projected route. The supreme moment of Wallingford's planning had arrived, for now leaped into devouring flame the blaze that he had kindled. What had at first been a quickening of business became a craze. At a rapidly accelerating pace property began to change hands, with a leap in value at every change. Men thought by day and dreamt by night of nothing but real estate speculation. A hundred per cent. could be made in a day by a lucky trade. A mere "suburban" lot that was purchased in the morning for two hundred and fifty dollars, by night could be sold for five hundred, and every additional transaction added fuel to the flames. The papers chronicled these deals as examples of the wonderful wealth that had suddenly descended upon their respective towns. Money, long hoarded, leaped forth from its hiding places. Everybody had money, everybody was making money. Even the farmers made real estate purchases in the towns, not to hold, but to turn over. The craze for speculation had at last seized upon them all, and it was now that Wallingford began to reap his harvest. A sale here, a sale there, with an occasional purchase to offset them, and he gradually began to unload, making it a rule never to close a deal that did not net him ten times the amount that he had invested. He was on the road constantly now, first in one village and then in another, ostensibly to look after details of the building of his route, but in reality to snap up money that was certain to be offered him for this or that or the other piece of property that he held.

And all this time the people to whom he sold were raving of the wealth that he had made for them! Battlesburg nor any other town stopped for a moment to consider that he had brought it not one cent of new wealth; that the money they were passing so feverishly from hand to hand was their own; that the values he had created for them were purely artificial. They would only realize this after he had gone, and then would come gradually the knowledge that, in place of creating wealth, he had lost it to them in the exact amount that he carried away. Never in all his planning had it crossed his mind really to build a traction line. Throughout a stretch of a hundred miles he had succeeded in starting a mad, unreasoning scramble for real estate, and he, having bought first to sell last, was the principal gainer. He was unloading now at floodtide from one end of the line to the other, and the ebb would see all these thousands of people standing dazed and agape upon the barren beach of their hopes. Some few shrewd ones would be ahead, but for the most part the "investors" would find themselves with property upon their hands bought at an absurd valuation that could never be realized.

At no time did Wallingford talk to his wife about his plans and intentions. She, like the rest of them, saw the work apparently pushing forward, and gave herself up to the social triumphs that were hers at last. She was supremely happy, and her lawn reception upon the twenty-first was, to quote the Battlesburg *Blade*, "the most exclusive and *recherché al fresco* function of a decade," and Wallingford, hurrying in late from the road, scarcely recognized his wife as, in a shimmering white gown, she moved among her guests with a flush upon her cheeks that heightened the sparkling of her eyes. The grounds had been wired, and electric lights of many colors glowed among the trees. On the porch an orchestra, recruited from the ranks of the Battlesburg band, discoursed ambitious music, and Wallingford smiled grimly as he thought of the awakening that must come within a week or so. He had reached the house unobserved, and paused for a moment outside the fence to view the scene as a stranger might.

"I made it myself," he mused, with a strange perversion of pride. "I'm the Big Josh, all right; but it will be a shame to kick the props out from under all this giddy jubilee."

His wife discovered him and came smiling to meet him, and on his way into the house to change his clothing Tim Battles met him at the porch steps with a cordial handshake.

"Well, how goes it, Colonel?" asked the mayor. "We're listening now for the hum of the trolleys almost any day."

"Maybe you're deaf," retorted Wallingford enigmatically, and laughed. "What will you do if the golden spike is never pounded in?"

"Drop dead," replied the other promptly. "Every cent I could lay my hands on is invested in property for which I'm refusing all sorts of fancy prices, and I'm not going to sell any of it until your first car whizzes through Main Street. Lucky you got back to-night. You'd regret it if you didn't hear my speech at the fountain dedication to-morrow."

"Is it up?" inquired Wallingford perfunctorily.

"Up and ready to spout; and so is father."

He said this because his father was approaching them, and all three of them laughed courteously at the sally. When Wallingford, cleansed and dressed, came downstairs again, he was more jovially cordial than usual, even for him, and made his guests, as he always did, feel how incomplete the evening would have been without his presence; but after they had all gone he withdrew into the library, where, after she had seen to the setting of her house to rights, his wife joined him. He had taken

318

WALLINGFORD

a bottle of wine in with him, but it stood upon
the table unopened, while he sat close by it,
holding an unlighted cigar and gazing thoughtfully out of the window. She hesitated in the
doorway and he looked up slowly.

"Come in, Fanny," he invited her soberly.
"Sit down!" and opening the wine he poured
out a glass for her.

She sipped at it and set it back upon the
table.

"What's the matter, Jim?" she asked solic-
itously. "Don't you feel well? Aren't things
going right?"

"Never felt better in my life," he declared,
"and things never panned out half so good.
I guess I'm tired. I never pulled off anything
near so big a game, but my end of the boom is
over. To-day I sold the last piece of property I own, except this. Of course, I've been
too wise to sell any of the ground that was
given to me for shops and depots and terminal
stations. I'd lay myself open to the law if I
did that; and the law and I are real chummy.
I'm particular about the law. But I am rid of
everything else, and, in the five months we
have been here, I have cleaned up over two
hundred thousand dollars."

"The most money we ever did have!" she

exclaimed. "Is that in addition to what we had when we came here?"

"All velvet," he assured her. "We have considerably over three hundred thousand now, all told; a full third of a million!"

"I knew you could do it if you only set yourself to it," she declared. "And all of that fortune, for it is a fortune, Jim, was made in a clean, honorable way."

He looked up at her, puzzled. Could it be possible that she did not understand?

"*Is* a dollar honest?" he responded dryly, and he talked no more of business that night.

The next morning ushered in a great day for Battlesburg. Early in the dawn two carpenters appeared in Courthouse Square and began putting up a platform; but, early as they were, boys were already on the ground, trying to peer beneath the mysterious swathings of the "veiled" fountain. Dan Hopkins set up his ice cream and candy stand, and hoarse Jim Moller appeared with his red and blue and green toy balloons. About nine o'clock the farm wagons came lumbering into town with the old folks. About ten, smart "rigs" drawn by real "high steppers" came speeding in ahead of whirling clouds of dust, and these rigs carried the young folks. By noon there were horses tied to every hitching-post, and genuine throngs shuffled aimlessly up one side of Main Street and down the other. There was the sound of shrieking whistles and of hoarse tin horns; there was the usual fight in front of Len Bradley's blacksmith shop. At one o'clock strange noises were wafted out upon the street from Odd Fellows' Hall. The Battlesburg brass band was practicing. At one-thirty Courthouse Square was jammed from fence to fence, and the street was black with people, the narrow lane between being constantly broken by perspiring mothers darting frantically after Willie and Susie and Baby Johnnie.

Za-a-a-am! At last here came the band, two and two, down the street, to the inspiriting strains of "Marching Through Georgia," with Will Derks at the head in a shako two feet high and performing the most marvelous gyrations with a shining brass baton. Throw it whirling right over a telephone wire, for instance, and never miss a stroke! Right through the crowd went the band, and in about ten minutes it came back to the lively step of "The Girl I Left Behind Me." Following the music came carriages, trailed off by Ben Kirby's gayly decorated grocery wagon; and in the first carriage of all were the Honorable G. W. Battles, the Honorable Timothy Battles, Judge Lampton, and last, but not least, that master of golden plenty, Colonel J. Rufus Wallingford! Ah, there rode the progress and prosperity, the greatness and power, the initiative and referendum not only of Battlesburg, but of a dozen once poor, now rich, villages between Lewisville and Elliston! Amid mingled music and huzzas the noble assemblage took their places upon the platform, the gentlemen in the front row, the ladies in the rear; and, at one side, was a table and a chair for that thoroughly alive representative of the press, Clint Richards.

The band stopped abruptly. The Honorable G. W. Battles had held up his hand for silence. He had the honor to introduce the speaker of the day, Mayor Timothy Battles, but before doing so he would take up a trifle of their time, only a few brief moments, to congratulate his beloved fellow citizens upon the brave and patriotic struggle they had made to bring Battlesburg to such a thriving condition that it could attract Eastern capital; and in vivid, glowing, burning words he depicted the glorious future that awaited Battlesburg when she should become the new Queen of the Prairies, the new Metropolis of the Middle West, the new Arbiter of Commerce and Wealth! No-

body escaped the Honorable G. W. Battles.
From the farmer's hired hand who tilled the
soil to the millionaire whose enterprise had
made so much possible to them, he gave to every
man his just and due meed of praise, and there
was not one within hearing of his voice who did
not ache at that very moment to vote for the
Honorable G. W. Battles, for something, for
anything! For full forty-five minutes he introduced the speaker of the day, sitting down
at last amid deafening cheers that were so aptly
described in that evening's issue of the Battlesburg *Blade* as "salvos of applause."

The Honorable Timothy Battles, mayor of
Battlesburg, had also but very little to say.
He also would not take up much of their time.
It was merely his privilege to introduce a
gentleman whom they all knew well, one who
had come among them modestly and unobtrusively, asking nothing for himself, but bringing to them precious Opportunity, of the
golden fruits of which they had already been
given more than a taste; a gentleman of masterful ability, of infinite resources, of magnificent
plans, of vast accomplishment; in short, a
gentleman who had made famous, across five
counties and to thousands of grateful people,
his own name as a synonym for all that was pro-

gressive, for all that was vigorous, for all that was ennobling—the name of Colonel J. Rufus Wallingford!

"Wallingford!" That was the magic word for which they had waited. Through all of the Honorable G. W. Battles' speech of introduction the name itself had not been used, although the address had bristled with allusions to the gentleman who bore it. In the same manner the Honorable Timothy Battles, trained in the same effective school of oratory, had held back the actual name until this dramatic moment, when, with hand upraised, he shouted it down upon them and waited, smiling, for that tumultuous shout of enthusiasm which he knew to be inevitable.

"WALLINGFORD!" Courthouse Square fairly rang with the syllables. Patiently the Honorable Timothy Battles awaited the subsidence of the storm he had so painstakingly created, smiling upon his beloved people with ineffable approval. Not yet was the Honorable Timothy Battles through, however. He had a few words to say about the political party which he had the honor to represent in his humble capacity, and how it had laid the ground work of the prosperity upon which their friend and benefactor, Mr. J. Rufus Wallingford, had reared such a magnificent super-structure; and amid the deadly silence of enforced respect he made them a rousing political speech for a solid half hour, after which he really did introduce that splendid benefactor, Colonel J. Rufus Wallingford!

The Colonel, all that a distinguished capital-ist should be in externals, arose hugely in his frock coat of black broadcloth and looked at his watch. He was not an orator, he said; he was a mere business man, and as he had lis-tened to the earnest remarks of his very dear friends, the Honorable G. W. Battles and the Honorable Timothy Battles, he felt very humble indeed. He had done but little that he should deserve all the glowing encomiums that had been pronounced upon him. The energetic citizens who stood before him were themselves responsible for the new era of prosperity, and what trifle he had been able to add to it they were quite welcome to have. He only wished that it were more and of greater value. He would remember them, and how they had all worked hand in hand together, throughout life, and in the meantime he thanked them, and he thanked them again for their cordial treatment ever since that first and most happy moment that he had come among them. Thanking them yet once more, he mopped his brow and sat down.

Again the Honorable G. W. Battles was upon his feet. He had now, beloved citizens, to call their attention to the beautiful and generous gift that had been made them by their esteemed fellow townsman, Colonel J. Rufus Wallingford (great applause) and the honor, moreover, to introduce to them the charming wife of that esteemed fellow townsman, to whose fair hand should be committed the cord that was to reveal to Battlesburg its first official glimpse of this splendid gift. The cord was placed in her hand; the Battlesburg Band, at a signal from the Honorable G. W. Battles, struck into "The Star-Spangled Banner;" the wife of their esteemed fellow townsman, confused, yet secretly elated, gave a tug at the silken cord; the gray shroud that had enveloped the new bronze fountain fell apart; Jim Higgins, waiting at the basement window of the courthouse for his signal, turned on the cock and the water spouted high in air, a silver stream in the glorious sunlight of midday, falling back to the basin in a million glittering diamonds. At that moment, gathering these descriptive facts into words as he went, Clint Richards grabbed his notes from the table, and, springing over the railing of the platform, forced his way through the cheering, howling crowd to strike out on a lope for the office of the Battlesburg *Blade*.

Well, it was all over. The grand shakedown was accomplished; he had milked his milk; he had sheared his sheep and skinned them, and nailed their hides up to dry. To-morrow, or in two or three days at most, he would quietly disappear and leave all these Reubens to wake up and find themselves waiting at the morgue. But it had been a skyrocket finish, anyhow, and he reflected upon this with a curious satisfaction as he made his slow progress to the street, stopping at every step to shake hands with those who crowded up to greet him as the incomparable human cornucopia. It was with a sigh of relief, however, that he finally reached home, where he could shut himself away from all this adulation.

"Honest, Fanny," he confessed with an uneasy laugh, "it's coming too strong for me. I want to get away from it."

"'Away'!" she echoed. "I thought you liked all this. I do. I like the place and the people—and we amount to something here."

"That's right, puff up," he bantered her. "I like that tight-vest feeling, too, but I can't keep it going, for the yeast's run out; so it's us for

Europe. Next spring I'll try this game again.
A couple more such deals, and then I'll jump on
Wall Street and slam the breath out of it. I
have an idea or two about that game ——"

He stopped abruptly, checked by the dawning
horror in his wife's face, then he laughed a bit
nervously.

"Go away from here: from the only place
where we've ever had respect for ourselves and
from others?" she faltered. "Not build the
traction line? Make all this happiness I've had
a theft that is worse than stealing money?
Jim! You can't mean it!"

"You don't understand business," he protested. "This is all perfectly legal, and the
traction line wouldn't make me as much in ten
years as I've already cleared. I'd be a rank
sucker —— Hello, who's this?"

They were standing before the window of the
library, and at that moment a road-spattered
automobile, one of the class built distinctively
for service, stopped in front of the door. Out of
it sprang a rather undersized man with a steel-
gray beard and very keen gray eyes, but not at
all impressive looking. His clothing was very
dusty, but he did not even shake his ulster as
he strode up to the porch and rang the bell.
Of all their household not even Billy Ricks had

as yet returned, and Wallingford himself opened the door.

"Is this the residence of Colonel Wallingford?" asked the man crisply.

"I am Mr. Wallingford."

"I am E. B. Lott, of the Midland Valley Traction System, which was yesterday consolidated with the Golden West group. I dropped in to talk with you about your Lewisville-Elliston line."

Mrs. Wallingford stopped for only a moment to gather the full significance of what this might mean, and then hurried upstairs. She was afraid to remain for fear she might betray her own eagerness.

"Step in," said Wallingford calmly, and led the way to the library.

CHAPTER XXII

THE Battlesburg *Blade* was full of the
big consolidation for a week following the providential visit of Mr. Lott.
The Lewisville, Battlesburg and Elliston traction line was not merely an assured
fact—it had always been that since the coming
of Colonel Wallingford—but it was now even
a bigger and better thing than ever, the key
to a vast network of trolleys which, with this
connecting link, would have its ramifications
across more than the fourth part of a continent.
The only drawback to all this good was that
they were to lose as a permanent resident their
esteemed fellow citizen, Colonel J. Rufus Wallingford—since he had sold his right of way,
franchises, concessions and good will—and
every issue of the *Blade*, from news columns
to editorials, was a tribute to all that this
noble, high-spirited gentleman had done for
Battlesburg.

A score of impulsive women kissed Mrs. Wallingford good-by at the train, while the Honorable G. W. Battles strove against Billy Ricks and Judge Lampton and Clint Richards for the honor of the last handshake with her husband; and after Mrs. Wallingford had fluttered her handkerchief from the car window for the last time, she pressed it to her eyes.

"I'm going to keep my house there always," she said, when she had calmed, "and whenever we're tired of living at other places I want to come here—home! Why, just think, Jim, it's the only town you ever did business in that you can come back to!"

He agreed with her in this, but, by and by, she found his shoulders heaving with his usual elephantine mirth.

"What is it?" she asked him.

"The joke's on me," he laughed. "The biggest stunt I ever pulled off, and even the baa-baás satisfied. Why, Fanny," and the surprise in his face was almost ludicrous, "it turned out to be a legitimate deal, after all!"

That was the keynote of a startling new thought which came to him: that there might actually be more money in legitimate deals than in the dubious ones in which he had always engaged; and that thought he took to Europe with him It dwelt with him in the fogs of London

and the sunshine of Paris, at the roulette tables
of Monte Carlo and on the canals of Venice. It
was an ambition-rousing idea, and with perfect
confidence in his own powers he saw himself
rising to a commanding position in American
financial affairs. Why, he already owned a
round half million of dollars, and the mere
momentum of this huge amount caused quite
an alteration, not only in his mode of thought,
but of life. Heretofore he had looked upon such
gain as he wrested from his shady transactions
as a mere medium of quick exchange, which was
to be turned into pleasure and lavish display
as rapidly as possible. When he secured
money his only impulse had been to spend all
of it and then get more; but a half million! It
was a sum large enough to represent earning
capacity, and his always creative mind was
busy with the thought of how he might utilize
its power. After all, it was only another new
and expensive pleasure that he desired, the
pleasure of swaying big affairs, of enrolling
himself upon the roster of the pseudo-great,
and to that end, during his entire European
trip he devoured American newspapers wherever he could find them, seeking for means by
which he could increase his fortune to one of
truly commanding proportions. In the mean-

time he was as lavish as ever, scattering money with a prodigal hand; but now it was with a different motive. He used it freely to secure the best to be found in the way of luxury, but no longer spent it merely to get rid of it.

Mrs. Wallingford, content, viewed Europe with appreciative eyes, and no empress swathed in silk and diadem-crowned ever took more graciously to the pomp with which their royal progress was attended wherever they went. Wallingford's interest in foreign lands, however, had suddenly become a business one. Restless as ever, he moved from place to place with rapid speed, and covered in two months the ground that ordinary tourists above the financial standing of "trippers" would think they had slighted in six. Europe, as a matter of fact, did not please him at all. Its laws were too strict, and he found in nearly every country he visited, that a man, unless he happened to be an innkeeper, was expected to actually deliver value received for every coin that came into his possession! This was so vastly different from the financial and commercial system to which he had been used that he became eager to get back home, and finally, having been visited over night with the inspiration for a brilliant new enterprise, he cabled his bankers

to throw open a portion of his account to
Blackie Daw, and to the latter gentleman
cabled instructions to buy him a good farm in
the middle of the wheat belt and fit it for his
residence regardless of cost. Then he started
back for the land where the money grows.

The task he had set Blackie Daw was very
much to that gentleman's liking. There had
arisen a sudden crisis in his "business affairs,"
that very morning, which demanded his immediate absence, not only from his office, but from
any other spot in which the authorities might
be able to find him, and, relieved of his dilemma
in the nick of time by Wallingford's money, he
immediately put an enormous number of miles
between himself and New York. A week he
spent in search, and when he found the location which suited him, he set about his task
of constructing a Wallingford estate in great
glee. He built a big new barn, the finest in
the county; he put a new front to the house,
bigger than the house itself had been; he
brought on load after load of fine furniture; he
stocked the big cellar with beer and wines and
liquors of all kinds; he piped natural gas from
twelve miles away and installed a gas furnace
in the cellar and a gas engine in a workshop
near the barn; he had electricians wire the place

from cellar to attic, including the barn and the front porch and the trees in the front yard, and had a dynamo put in to be run by the gas engine and to illuminate the entire estate; he installed both line and house telephone systems, with extension phones wherever they would be handy, and, his work finished, surveyed it with much satisfaction. With the mail carrier stopping every day, with the traction line running right past the door, and with plenty of money, he decided that J. Rufus would be able to get along, through the winter, at least.

It was in the early part of September when J. Rufus, clad according to his notions of what a gentleman farmer should look like—a rich brown velvet corduroy suit with the trousers neatly tucked into an eighteen-dollar pair of seal leather boots; a twenty-dollar broad-brimmed felt hat upon his head; a brown silk negligé shirt and a scarf of a little deeper shade in the "V" of his broad vest; an immense diamond gleaming from the scarf—arrived at the Wallingford estate in a splendid equipage drawn by a pair of sleek bays.

Marching in time to the ringing "Soldiers' Chorus" from *Faust*, Blackie Daw came down the walk from the wide Colonial porch, carrying in his arms the huge phonograph from which the music proceeded, and greeted the laughing new master and mistress of the house with extravagant ceremony, while three country girls, a red-cheeked one, a thin one, and a mortally ugly one, stood giggling upon the porch.

"Welcome to Wallingford Villa!" exclaimed Blackie, setting the blaring phonograph on the gate post, and, with his left hand tucked into his coat bosom, extending his right hand dramatically toward the porch. "Welcome to your ancestral estates and adoring tenantry!"

"Fine business!" approved J. Rufus, shaking hands with Mr. Daw. "Invite the band in to have a drink, Blackie."

"Hush!" admonished Mr. Daw in a hoarse stage whisper. "*Not* Blackie. Here, in hiding from the minions of Uncle Sam, I am Horatio Raven. Remember the name."

"What's the matter?" asked Wallingford, detecting something real beneath all this absurdity. "I called at your place in Boston, and found a corn doctor's sign on the door. I didn't mean to plant you out here."

"Plant is the word," responded Mr. Daw, "and I've rooted fast in the soil. I'm going to take out naturalization papers and grow a chin beard. You're harboring a fugitive, Jim. The very day I got your letter from dear old

336

Lunnon, throwing open a section of your bank
account and telling me to buy a farm, the postal
authorities took it into their heads to stop all
traffic in the Yellow Streak gold mine; also
they wanted to mark one Horace G. Daw 'Ex-
hibit A,' and slam him in a cold cage for future
reference; so I put on my green whiskers and
snuck here to the far, far prairies."

A certain amount of reserve had been quite
noticeable in Mrs. Wallingford, and it was still
apparent as she asked courteously:

"Where is Mrs. Daw?"

"Raven, if you please," he corrected her, and,
in spite of his general air of flippancy, his face
lengthened a trifle. "Mrs. Violet Bonnie D.,"
he replied, "has returned to the original lemon
box of which she was so perfect a product, and
is now delighting a palpitating public in 'The
Jolly Divorcée,' with a string of waiting John-
nies from the stage door two blocks down
Broadway every night. Let us mention the
lady no more lest I use language."

"What a pretty place you have made of
this!" exclaimed Mrs. Wallingford, thawing
into instant amiability. She had her own reasons for being highly pleased with the absence
of Violet Bonnie Daw.

"Pretty good," agreed the pseudo Raven.

"Step inside and imagine you're in Peacock Alley at the Waldorf."

With considerable pride he led them inside. Knowing Wallingford as he did, he had spared no expense to make this house as luxurious as fine furnishings would render it, and, having considerable taste in Wallingford's own bizarre way, he had accomplished rather flaming results.

"And this," said he, throwing open a door upstairs, "is my own room; number twenty-three. Upon the walls you will observe the mournful relics of a glorious past."

The ceiling was papered with silver stock certificates of the late Los Pocos Lead Development Company, the walls with dark green shares of the late Mexican and Rio Grande Rubber Company, and dark red ones of the late St. John's Blood Orange Plantation Company, while walls and ceiling were divided by a frieze of the beautiful orange-colored stock certificates of the late Yellow Streak Gold Mining Company.

"My own little idea," he explained, as Mrs. Wallingford smiled her appreciation of the grim humor and went to her own dainty apartment to remove the stains of travel. "A reminder of the happy times that once were but that shall be no more. I have now to figure out another stunt for skinning the beloved public, and it's hard work. I wish I had your ability to dope up gaudy new boob-stringers. What are you going to do with the farm, anyhow?"

"Save the farmers," replied J. Rufus Wallingford solemnly. "The farmers of the United States are the most downtrodden people in the world. The real producers of the wealth of our great nation hold the bag, and the non-producers reap the golden riches of the soil. Who rises in his might and comes to their rescue? Who overturns the old order of things, puts the farmer upon a pinnacle of prosperity and places his well-deserved earnings beyond the reach of avarice and greed? Who, I ask? J. Rufus Wallingford, the friend of the oppressed and the protector of the poor!"

"Good!" responded Mr. Daw, "and the way you say it it's worse than ever. I'm in on the play, but please give me a tip before the blow-off comes so I can leave the county."

"The county is safe," responded Mr. Wallingford. "It's nailed down. You know me, Blackie. The law and I are old college chums and we never go back on each other. I'm going to lift my money out of the Chicago wheat pit, and when I get through that pit will be nothing but an empty hole. By this time next fall I'll have a clean, cool million, and then I can buy a stack of blue chips and sit in the big game. I'll never rest easy till I can hold a royal flush against Morgan and Rockefeller, and when I skin them all will be forgiven.''

"Jump right in, Jim; the water's fine for you just now. I'm not wised up yet to this new game of yours, but I've got a bet on you. Go to it and win.''

"It's my day to break the bank," asserted J. Rufus. "Your bet's safe. Go soak your watch and play me across the board.''

The telephone bell rang and Blackie answered it.

"Come right over," he told the man at the other end of the wire. "Mr. Wallingford has arrived.''

He hung up the receiver and conducted Wallingford downstairs into a well-lighted room that jutted out in an "L" from the house, with a separate outside entrance toward the rear.

"Observe the center of a modern agriculturist's web,'' he declaimed. "Sit at your desk, farmer, for your working superintendent is about to call on you.''

J. Rufus looked around him with vast appreciation.

"I thought I had my own ideas about looking the part," he observed, "but you have me skinned four ways from the Jack."

In the center of the room was a large, flat-top desk, and upon it was an extension 'phone from the country line. On the other side was the desk 'phone and call board of a private line which connected the house, the barn, the granary and a dozen fields throughout the farm. On one side was a roll-top desk, and this was Mr. Daw's. Opposite was another roll-top desk, for the "working superintendent."

"At least one real farmer will have to be on the job," Blackie explained, "and I nabbed Hamlet Tinkle, the prize of the neighborhood. He is a graduate of an agricultural college and all the farmers think he's a joke; but I have him doped out as being able to coax more fodder from unwilling mud than any soil tickler in these parts. He helped me select the farm library."

With a grin at his own completeness of detail, Mr. Daw indicated the sectional bookcases, where stood, in neat rows, the Government reports on everything agricultural, and treatises on every farm subject under the sun from the pip to the boll weevil. Filing cases there were, and card indexes, and every luxury that has been devised for modern office work. With an amused air the up-to-date farmer was leafing through one after the other of the conglomeration of strange books, when Hamlet Tinkle was ushered in by the ever-grinning Nellie. He was a tall, big-boned fellow, who had divided his time at the agricultural college between playing center rush and studying the chemical capabilities of various soils. Just now, though the weather was bracing, he wore a broad-brimmed straw hat with the front turned up, and a flannel shirt with no coat or vest; and he had walked two miles, from the place at which he had telephoned, in twenty-two minutes.

"Mr. Tinkle—Mr. Wallingford," said Mr. Daw. "Mr. Wallingford, this is the gentleman whom I recommend as your working superintendent."

Both Mr. Wallingford and Mr. Tinkle accepted this title with perfect gravity.

"Sit down," said Wallingford cordially, and himself took his place at the flat-top desk in the midst of the telephones and push buttons. Already he began to feel the exhilaration of his new *rôle* and loomed broadly above his desk, from the waist line up a most satisfying revelation to Mr. Tinkle of what the farmer of the future ought to be like. "Mr. Raven tells me," observed Wallingford, "that you are prepared to conduct this farm on scientific principles."

"Yes, sir," admitted Mr. Tinkle. "I shall be very glad to show to Truscot County what can be done with advanced methods. Father doesn't seem to care to have me try it on his farm. He says he made enough out of his own methods to send me to college, and I ought to be satisfied with that."

"Your father's all right, but maybe we can teach even him some new tricks. The first question, Mr. Tinkle, is how much money you want."

"Fifteen a week and board," responded Mr. Tinkle promptly. "The seasons through."

"Fine!" responded Wallingford with a wave of the hand which indicated that fifty a week and board would have been no bar, as, indeed, it would not have been. "Consider yourself engaged from the present moment. Now let's get down to brass tacks, Mr. Tinkle. I don't know enough about farming to stuff up the middle of a cipher; I don't know which end down you plant the grains of wheat; but wheat is what I want, and nothing but wheat!"

Mr. Tinkle shook his head.

"With Mr. Raven's permission I have been making tests of your soil," he observed. "Your northeast forty is still good for wheat and will make a good yield, possibly thirty bushels, but the southwest forty will do well if it gives you eight to ten bushels without thorough fertilization; and this will be much more expensive than planting it in some other crop for a couple of years."

"Jolly it any old way to get wheat," directed Wallingford. "Wheat is what I want; all you can get."

Mr. Tinkle hesitated. He made two or three false starts, during which his auditors waited with the patience born to those who lie in crouch for incautious money, and then displayed his altruistic youth.

"I have to tell you," he blurted. "You have here one hundred and sixty acres. Suppose that you could get the high average of thirty bushels per acre from it. Suppose you got a dollar a bushel for that wheat, your total income would still be less than five thousand dollars. You are hiring me as manager, and you will need other hands; you have a machinist, who is also to be your chauffeur, I understand; you have three house servants, and upon the scale you evidently intend to conduct this farm and your residence I judge that you cannot get along for less than eight to ten thousand a year. I am bound to tell you that I cannot see a profit for you."

"Which of these buttons calls one of the girls?" asked Wallingford.

"The third button is Nellie," replied Mr. Daw gravely, and touched it.

The rosy-cheeked girl appeared instantly, on the point of giggling, as she had been from the moment Mr. Daw first engaged her.

"Bring in my grip from the hall," Mr. Wallingford directed; "the one with the labels on it."

This brought in, Mr. Wallingford extracted from it a huge bundle of documents bound with rubber bands. Unfolded, they proved to be United States Government bonds, shares of railroad stocks and of particularly stable industrials, thousands of dollars worth of them. For Mr. Tinkle's inspection he passed over his bank book, showing a balance of one hundred and fifty thousand.

"Wheat," cheerfully lied Mr. Wallingford, with a wave of his hand; "all wheat! Half a million dollars!"

"Speculation?" charged Mr. Tinkle, a trace of sternness in his voice.

"Investment," protested Wallingford. "I never sold; I bought, operating always upon margin sufficient for ample protection, and always upon absolute information gathered directly from the centers of production. This farm is for the purpose of bringing me more thoroughly in touch with the actual conditions that make prices. So, as you see, Mr. Tinkle, the trifling profit or loss of this venture in a business way is a mere bagatelle."

Both Mr. Daw and Mr. Tinkle were regarding Mr. Wallingford with awe and admiration, but for somewhat different reasons. Mr. Tinkle, elated, went home to get his clothes and books, and on the way he put into breathless circulation the fact that the new proprietor of the old Spicer place was the greatest man on earth, with the possible exception of Theodore Roosevelt, and that he had already made half a million dollars in wheat! He had seen the money!

"I pass," observed Mr. Daw to Mr. Wallingford. "I'm in the kindergarten class, and I take off my lid to you as being the most valuable combination known to the history of plain or fancy robbery. You have them all beat twice around the track. You make an amateur of Ananias and a piker of Judas Iscariot."

CHAPTER XXIII

A CORNER IN FARMERS IS FORMED AND IT BEHOLDS
A MOST WONDERFUL VISION

IT was already high time for fall planting operations on the Wallingford estate, and Truscot County was a-quiver with what might be the result of the new-fangled test-tube farming that Ham Tinkle was to inaugurate. From the first moment of his hiring that young enthusiast plunged into his work with a fervor that left him a scant six hours of sleep a night.

In the meantime J. Rufus took a flying trip to Chicago, where he visited one broker's office after another. Those places with fine polished woodwork and brass trimmings and expensive leather furniture he left without even introducing himself — such stage settings were too much in his own line of business for him not to be suspicious of them—but, finally, he wandered into the office of Fox & Fleecer, a dingy, poorly lighted place, where gas was kept burning on old-fashioned fixtures all day long, where the woodwork was battered and blackened, where the furniture was scratched and hacked and bound together with wires to keep it intact, and where, on a cracked and splintered blackboard, one small and lazy boy posted, for a score or so of rusty men past middle age, the fluctuating figures of the Great Gamble. Mr. Fox, a slow-spoken and absolutely placid gentleman of benevolent appearance and silvery mutton-chop whiskers, delicately blended the impressions that while he was indeed flattered by this visit from so distinguished a gentleman, his habitual conservatism would not allow him to express his delight.

"How much money can you be trusted with?" asked Wallingford bluntly.

"I would not say, sir," rejoined Mr. Fox with no resentment whatever. "We have been thirty years in these same offices, and we never yet have had enough in our hands to make it worth while for us to quit business. Permit me to show you our books."

His ledger displayed accounts running as high as two hundred and fifty thousand dollars that had been intrusted to their care by single individuals. But thirty years in business at the same old stand! He insisted gently upon this point, and Wallingford nodded his head.

WALLINGFORD

"Before I'm through I'll make all these bets look like cigar money," he asserted, "but just now I'm going to put fifty thousand in your hands, and I want it placed in exactly this way: Monday morning, with ten thousand dollars buy me one hundred thousand bushels of December wheat on a ten-cent margin. No more money will be put up on this deal, so place a stop-loss order against it. If wheat drops enough to wipe out the ten thousand dollars, all right; say nothing and report the finish of the transaction to me. I'll do my own grinning. If wheat goes up enough to leave me five cents a bushel profit, clear of commissions, close the deal and remit. On the following Monday, if wheat has gone up from the quotations of to-day, sell one hundred thousand bushels more at ten cents margin and close at a sufficient drop to net me five cents clear. If it has gone down, buy. Do this on five successive Mondays and handle each deal separately. Get me one winning out of five. That's all I want."

Mr. Fox considered thoughtfully for a moment, carefully polishing his bald, pink scalp around and around with the palm of his hand. He gave the curious impression of being always engaged with some blandly interesting secret problem along with the business under consideration.

"Very well, sir," he observed. "Fox & Fleecer never makes any promises, but if you will put your instructions into writing I will place them in the hands of our Mr. Fleecer, who conducts our board operations. He will do the best he can for you."

Mr. Wallingford looked about him for a stenographer. There was none employed here, and, sitting down to the little writing table which was pointed out to him, he made out the instructions in long hand, while Mr. Fox polished away at his already glistening pate, still working at that blandly interesting secret problem.

Ten days later, at the test-tube farm, arrived a report from Messrs. Fox & Fleecer, inclosing their check for fifteen thousand dollars. Wheat, in the week following Wallingford's purchase, had fortunately gone up nearly six cents. This check, and the accompanying statement of the transaction which had brought it forth, Wallingford showed to Ham Tinkle, quite incidentally, of course, and Ham, in awe and enthusiasm, confided the five-thousand-dollar winning to Hiram Hines, who spread the report through Truscot County

that Judge Wallingford had already made fifteen thousand dollars in wheat since he had
come among them. The savings of an ordinary lifetime! The amount was fifty thousand
when it reached Mapes County. Two weeks
later Messrs. Fox & Fleecer reported on the
second of Wallingford's deals. Wheat sold at
ninety-four had dropped to eighty-eight. Luck
was distinctly with J. Rufus Wallingford.

"Why, oh, why, do cheap skates sell gold
bricks and good come-on men waste their tal-
ents on Broadway?" wailed Blackie Daw.
"But what's the joke, J. Rufus? I see your
luck, but where do the surrounding farmers get
in? Or where do you get in on the surrounding farmers? Show me. I'm an infant."

"You couldn't understand it, Blackie," said
J. Rufus with condescending kindness. "The
mere fact that you look on these pocket-change
winnings as real money lets you out. Wait till
I spring the big game. To-morrow night you
shall attend this winter's opening meeting of
the Philomathean Literary Society at the
Willow Creek schoolhouse, and observe the
methods of a real bread winner."

For the memorable occasion that he had
mentioned, Wallingford wore a fur-lined overcoat and quadruple-woven blue silk sweater,

and, being welcomed with great acclaim, proposed for debate that burning question: "Resolved: That the farmer is a failure as a business man."

With much stamping and pawing of the air that subject was thrashed out by Abe Johnson and Dan Price for the affirmative, and Cal Whorley and Ed Wiggin for the negative. The farmer as a gold-brick purchaser, as prey for every class of tradesmen, as a producer who received less net profit than any other from the capital and labor invested, was presented to himself by men who knew their own grievances well, and the affirmative was carried almost unanimously. Flushed with pleasure, beaming with gratification, the most advanced farmer of them all arose in his place and requested of the worthy chairman the privilege to address the meeting, a privilege that was granted with pleasure and delight.

It was an eventful moment when J. Rufus Wallingford stalked up the middle aisle, passed around the red-hot, cannon-ball stove and ascended the rostrum which had been the scene of so many impassioned addresses; and, as he turned to face them from that historic elevation, he seemed to fill the entire end of the schoolroom, to blot out not only the teacher's desk but the judges' seats, the blackboard and the four-colored map of the United States that hung upon the wall behind him. He was a fine-looking man, a solid-looking man, a gentleman of wealth and culture, who, unspoiled by good fortune, was still a brother to all men. Already he had gained that enviable reputation among them.

Friends and neighbors and fellow-farmers, it was startling to reflect that the agriculturist was the only producer in all the world who had no voice in the price which was put upon his product! The manufacturer turned out his goods and set a price upon them and the consumer had to pay that price. And how was this done? By the throttling of competition. And how had competition been throttled? By consolidation of all the interests in any particular line of trade. Iron and steel were all controlled by one mighty corporation against which could stand no competitor except by sufferance; petroleum and all its by-products were in the hands of another, and each charged what it liked. The farmer alone, after months of weary, unending toil, of exposure in all sorts of weather, of struggle against the whims of nature and against an appalling list of possible disasters, himself hauled his output to market and meekly accepted whatever was offered him. Prices on every product of the soil were dictated by a clique of gamblers who, in all probability, had never seen wheat growing nor cattle grazing. Friends and neighbors and fellow-farmers, this woeful condition must end! They must coöperate! Once compacted the farmers could stand together as firm as a rock, could demand a fair and reasonable and just price for their output, and get it. To-day wheat was quoted at ninety-four cents on the Chicago Board of Trade. If the farmer, however, secured eighty-two at his delivery point in actual cash he was doing well. There was no reason why the farmers should not agree to establish a standing price of a dollar and a half a bushel for wheat; and that must be their slogan. Wheat at a dollar and a half!

He was vitally interested in this project, and he was willing to spend his life and fortune for it; and, in the furtherance of it, he invited his friends and neighbors and fellow-farmers to assemble at his house on the following Saturday night and discuss ways and means to bring this enormous movement to a practical working basis. Incidentally he *might* find a bite and a sup and a whiff of smoke to offer them.

All those who would attend would please rise in their seats.

As one man they arose, and when J. Rufus Wallingford, glowing with the immensity of his noble project, stepped down from that platform, the walls of the Willow Creek schoolhouse echoed and reëchoed with the cheers which followed his speech.

The Farmers' Commercial Association! There had been farmers' affiliations without number, with motives political, economical, educational; alliances for the purchasing of supplies at wholesale and for every other purpose under the sun, but nothing like this, for, to begin with, the Farmers' Commercial Association had no initiation fee and no dues, and it had for its sole and only object the securing of a flat, uniform rate of a dollar and a half a bushel for wheat. The first meeting, attended by every able-bodied tiller of the soil in Truscot County and some even from Mapes County, was so large that there was no place in the Wallingford homestead to house it, and it had to be taken out to the great new barn, where, in the spacious aisle between stalls and mows, enthusiasm had plenty of room to soar to the rafters. One feature had stilled all doubts: J. Rufus Wallingford alone was to pay!

GET-RICH-QUICK

With a whoop the association was organized, Judge Wallingford was made its president, and with great enthusiasm was authorized to go ahead and spend all of his own money that he cared to lay out for the benefit of the association. Only one trifling duty was laid upon the members. President Wallingford introduced an endless chain letter. It was brief. It was concise. It told in the fewest possible words just why the Farmers' Commercial Association had been formed and what it was expected to do, laying especial stress upon the fact that there were to be no initiation fees and no dues, no money to be paid for anything! All that the members were to do was to join, and when enough were in, to demand one dollar and a half for their wheat. It was a glittering proposition, for there was no trouble and no expense and no risk, with much to gain. Every one of the ninety-odd who gathered that night in Wallingford's barn was to write three or more of these letters to wheat-growing acquaintances, and each recipient of a letter was told that the only thing which need be done to enroll himself as a member of the order was to write three more such letters and send in his name to Horatio Raven, Secretary.

Horatio Raven himself was there. There

was a barrel of good, hard cider on tap in the barn, and every few minutes Mr. Raven could be seen conducting one or two acquaintances quietly over to the cellar, where there were other things on tap. Cigars were passed around, and the good cheer which was provided became so inextricably mingled with the enthusiasm which had been aroused, that no farmer could tell which was which. It only sufficed that when they went away each one was profoundly convinced that J. Rufus Wallingford was the Moses who should lead the farmers of America out of their financial Wilderness.

During the next two or three days nearly three hundred letters left Truscot and Mapes counties, inviting nearly three hundred farmers in the great wheat belt, extending from the Rockies to the Appalachians, to take full sixty per cent. more for their produce than the average price they had always been receiving, to invite others to receive like benefits, and all to accept this boon without money and without price. It was personal solicitation from one man to another who knew him, and the first flood that went out reached every wheat-growing State in the Union. Within a week, names and requests for further information began pouring in upon Horatio Raven, Secretary, and the card index drawers in the filing cabinet, originally bought in jest, became of actual service. One, then two, then three girls were installed. A pamphlet was printed explaining the purpose of the Farmers' Commercial Association, and these were sent to all "members," J. Rufus Wallingford furnishing both the printing and the postage.

Through the long winter the president of that great association was constantly upon the road, always in his corduroy suit and his broad felt hat, with his trousers tucked neatly into his seal-leather boots. His range was from Pennsylvania to Nebraska and from Minnesota to Texas, and everywhere his destination was some branch nucleus of the Farmers' Commercial Association where meetings had been arranged for him. Each night he addressed some body of skeptical farmers who came wondering, who saw the impressive and instantly convincing "Judge" Wallingford; who, listening, caught a touch of that magnetic thrill with which he always imbued his auditors, and who went away enthusiastic to carry to still further reaches the great work that he had planned. By the holiday season he had visited a dozen States and had addressed nearly a

WALLINGFORD

hundred sub-organizations. In each of these he
gave the chain letters a new start, and the December meeting of the central organization of
the Farmers' Commercial Association was also
a Christmas celebration in the barn of that
progressive and self-sacrificing and noble
farmer, J. Rufus Wallingford.

It was a huge "family affair," held two
nights before Christmas so as not to interfere
with the Baptist Church at Three Roads or the
Presbyterian Church at Miller's Crossing, and
the great barn was trimmed with wreaths and
festoons of holly from floor to rafters. At one
end was a gigantic Christmas tree, from the
branches of which glowed a myriad of electric
lights and sparkled innumerable baubles of
vivid coloring and metallic luster. Handsome
presents had been provided for every man,
woman and child, and down the extent of the
wide center had been spread two enormous,
long tables upon which was placed food enough
to feed a small army; huge turkeys and all
that went with them. At the head of the
ladies' table sat Mrs. Wallingford, glittering
in her diamonds, the first time she had worn
them since coming into this environment, and
at the head of the men's table, resplendent in
a dinner coat and with huge diamond studs

flashing from his wide, white shirt bosom, sat
the giver of all these bounties, Judge J. Rufus
Wallingford, president of the vast Farmers'
Commercial Association. He was flushed with
triumph, and he told them so at the proper
moment. Beyond his most sanguine hopes the
Farmers' Commercial Association had spread
and flourished in every State, nay, in every
community where wheat was grown, and the
time was rapidly approaching when the farmer,
now turned business man, would be able to get
the full value of his investment of money, time
and toil. Moreover, they would destroy the
birds of prey, feathers, bones and beaks, fledge-
lings, eggs and nests.

Around the table, at this point, Horatio
Raven, Secretary, passed a sheaf of reports
upon the various successful deals that Wallingford had made, each one showing a profit
of five thousand dollars on a ten-thousand-dollar investment. The secret facts of the case
were that fortune had favored Wallingford
tremendously. By one of those strange runs
of luck which sometimes break the monotony
of persistent gambling disasters, he had won
not less than five out of every six of the continuous deals intrusted to Fox & Fleecer. The
failures he kept to himself, and Ham Tinkle

added to the furore that the proofs of this success created by rising in his place and advising them how, upon Wallingford's certain and sure advance information of the market, he himself had been able to turn his modest little two hundred dollars into seven hundred during the past three months, with the profits still piling up.

But J. Rufus Wallingford, resuming, saw such profits vanishing in the future, for by the aid of the Farmers' Commercial Association he intended to wipe out the iniquitous grain and produce exchange, and, in fact, all gambling in food products throughout the United States. The scope of the Farmers' Commercial Association was much broader, much more far-reaching than even he had imagined when he at first conceived it. When they were ready they would not only establish a firm cash basis for wheat, but they would wipe this festering mass of corruption, called the Board of Trade, off the face of the earth by the simple process of taking all its money away from it. With their certain knowledge of what the price of wheat would be, when the time was ripe they would go into the market and, themselves, by their aggregate profits, would break every man who was in the business of manipulating prices

on wheat, on oats and corn and live stock.
Why, nearly one million names were now enrolled in the membership of the association,
and to these million names circulars explaining in detail the plans of the organization had
been mailed at a cost in postage alone of nearly
ten thousand dollars. This expense he had
cheerfully borne himself, in his devotion to
the great work of reformation. Not one penny
had been paid by any other member of the
organization for the furtherance of this project. He had spent nearly twenty thousand
dollars in travel and other expenses, but the
market had paid for it, and he was not one
penny loser by his endeavors. Even if he
were, that would not stop him. He would sell
every government bond and every share of
industrial and railroad stock that he owned,
he would even mortgage his farm, if necessary, to complete this organization and make
it the powerful and impregnable factor in
agricultural commerce that he had intended it
to be. It was his dream, his ambition, nay,
his determined purpose, to leave behind him
this vast organization as an evidence that his
life had not been spent in vain; and if he
could only see the wheat gamblers put out of
that nefarious business, and the farmers of

the United States coming, after all these toiling generations, into their just and honest dues, he would die with peace in his heart and a smile upon his lips, even though he went to a pauper's grave!

There were actual tears in his eyes as he closed with these words, and his voice quivered. From the foot of the table Blackie Daw was watching with a curious smile that was almost a sardonic grin. From the head of the parallel table Mrs. Wallingford was watching him with a pallor that deepened as he went on, but no one noticed these significant indications, and as J. Rufus Wallingford sat down a mighty cheer went up that made every branch of the glittering Christmas tree dance and quiver.

He was a wonderful man, this Wallingford, a genius, a martyr, a being made in his entirety of the milk of human kindness and brotherly love; but this rapidly growing organization that he had formed was more wonderful still. They could see as plain as print what it would do for them; they could see even plainer than print how, with the certain knowledge of the price to which wheat would eventually rise, they could safely dabble in fictitious wheat themselves, and by their enormous aggregate winnings, obliterate all boards of trade. It was a conception

GET-RICH-QUICK

Titanic in its immensity, perfect in its detail, amazing in its flawlessness, and not one among them who listened but went home that night —J. Rufus Wallingford's seal-leather pocketbook in his pocket, J. Rufus Wallingford's box of lace handkerchiefs on his wife's lap, J. Rufus Wallingford's daintily dressed French doll in his little girl's arm, J. Rufus Wallingford's toy engine in his little boy's hands—but foresaw, not as in a dream but as in a concrete reality that needed only to be clutched, the future golden success of the Farmers' Commercial Association; and on the forehead of that success was emblazoned in letters of gold:

"$1.50 WHEAT!"

CHAPTER XXIV

THE holidays barely over, Wallingford was upon the road again, and until the first of May he spent his time organizing new branches, keeping the endless chain letters booming and taking subscriptions for his new journal, the *Commercial Farmer*, a device by which he had solved the grave problem of postage. The *Commercial Farmer* was issued every two weeks. It was printed on four small pages of thin paper, and to make it second-class postal matter a real subscription price was charged—five cents a year! For this he paid postage of one cent a pound, and there were eighty copies to the pound. He could convey his semi-monthly message to a million people at a cost of one hundred and twenty-five dollars, as against the ten thousand dollars it would cost him to mail a million letters with a one-cent stamp upon them. And five cents a year was enough to pay expenses. On the first of May, the enterprising promoter, who seriously aspired now to become a financial star of the first magnitude, took a swift thousand-mile journey to the offices of Fox & Fleecer, where Mr. Fox, polishing, as always, at his glazed scalp, was still intent upon that bland but perplexing secret problem. Mr. Wallingford, as a prelim· inary to conversation, drew his chair up to the opposite side of the desk and laid upon it a check book and a package of documents with a rubber band around them. "Four hundred and twenty-five thousand dollars in cash and negotiable securities," he stated, "and all to buy September wheat."

Mr. Fox said nothing, but unconsciously his palm went to the top of his head.

"The September option is at this moment quoted at eighty-seven and one-eighth cents," went on Mr. Wallingford. "Could it possibly go lower than sixty-two?"

"It is the invariable rule of Fox & Fleecer," said Mr. Fox slowly, "never to give advice nor to predict any future performances of wheat. Wheat can go to any price, up or down. I may add, however, that it has been several years since the September option has touched the low level you name."

"Well, I'm going to bet this four hundred and twenty-five thousand dollars that it don't

go as low as sixty-two," retorted Wallingford
stiffening. "I want you to take this wad and
invest it in September wheat right off the bat,
at the market, on a twenty-five cent margin,
which covers one million, seven hundred thousand bushels."

Mr. Fox, his eyes hypnotically glued upon the
little stack of securities which represented four
hundred and twenty-five thousand dollars, and
a larger commission than his firm had ever in
all its existence received in one deal, filled his
lungs with a long, slow intake of air which he
strove to make as noiseless as possible.

"You must understand, Mr. Wallingford,"
he finally observed, "that it will be impossible
to buy an approximate two million bushels of
the September option at this time without dis-
turbing the market and running up the price
on yourself, and it may take us a little time to
get this trade launched. Probably five hundred
thousand bushels can be placed at near the
market, and then we will have to wait until a
favorable moment to place another section.
Our Mr. Fleecer, however, is very skillful in
such matters and will no doubt get a good price
for you."

"I understand about that," said Wallingford, "and I understand about the other end of

it, too. I want to turn this four hundred and twenty-five thousand dollars into a clean million or I don't want a cent. September wheat will go to one dollar and a quarter."

Mr. Fox reserved his smile until Mr. Wallingford should be gone. At present he only polished his pate.

"That's when you would probably fall down," continued Wallingford; "when September wheat reaches a dollar and a quarter. If you try to throw this seventeen hundred thousand bushels on the market you will break the price, unless on the same day that you sell it you can buy the same amount for somebody else. Will that let you get the price without dropping it off ten or fifteen cents?"

"Fox & Fleecer never predict," said Mr. Fox slowly, "but in a general way I should say that if we were to buy in as much as we sold, the market would probably be strengthened rather than depressed."

"All right," said Wallingford. "Now I have another little matter to present to you." From his pocket he drew a copy of the *Commercial Farmer*, the pages scarcely larger than a sheet of business letter paper. "I want an advertisement from you for the back page of this. Just a mere card, with your name and address

A Larger Commission than Fox and Fleecer Had Ever
Received in One Deal

and the fact that you have been in business at the same location for thirty years; and at the bottom I want to put: 'We handle all the wheat transactions of J. Rufus Wallingford.' "

Of course in a matter so trifling Mr. Fox could not refuse so good a customer, and J. Rufus departed, well satisfied, to work and wait while Nature helped his plans.

Across a thousand miles of fertile land the spring rains fell and the life-giving sun shone down; from the warm earth sprang up green blades and tall shoots that through their hollow stems sucked the life of the soil, and by a transformation more wonderful than ever conceived by any magician, upon the stalks there swelled heads of grain that nodded and yellowed and ripened with the advancing summer. From the windows of Pullman cars, as he rode hither and yonder throughout this rich territory in the utmost luxury that travelers may have, J. Rufus Wallingford, the great liberator of farmers, watched all this magic of the Almighty with but the one thought of what it might mean to him. Back on the Wallingford farm, Blackie Daw and his staff of assistants, now half-a-dozen girls, kept up an ever-increasing correspondence. Ham Tinkle was jealous of the very night that hid his handiwork for a space out of each twenty-four hours, and begrudged the time that he spent in sleep. During every waking moment, almost, he was abroad in his fields, and led his neighbors, when he could, to see his triumph, for never had the old Spicer farm brought forth such a yield, and nowhere in Truscot County or in Mapes County could such fields be shown. Upon these broad acres the wheat was thicker and sturdier, the heads longer and larger and fuller of fine, fat grain than anywhere in all the region round.

The Farmers' Commercial Association, a "combination in restraint of trade" which was well protected by the fear-inspiring farmer vote, met monthly, and Wallingford ran in to the meetings as often as he could, though there was no need to sustain their enthusiasm; for not only was the plan one of such tremendous scope as to compel admiration, but Nature and circumstances both were kind. There came the usual early rumors of a drought in Kansas, of over-much rotting rain in the Dakotas, of the green bug in Oklahoma, of foreign wars and domestic disturbances, and these things were good for the price of wheat, as they were exaggerated upon the floors of the great boards of trade in Chicago and New York. Through these causes alone September wheat climbed from eighty-seven to ninety, to ninety-five, to a dollar, to a dollar-five; but in the latter part of July there came a new and an unexpected factor. Dollar-and-a-half wheat had been the continuous slogan of the Farmers' Commercial Association, and every issue of the *Commercial Farmer* had dwelt upon the glorious day when that should be made the standard price. Now, in the mid-July issue, the idea was driven home and the entire first page was given up to a great, flaming advertisement:

HOLD YOUR WHEAT!
SEPTEMBER WHEAT WILL GO TO
$1.50!
DON'T SELL A BUSHEL OF IT FOR LESS!

The result was widespread and instantaneous. In Oklahoma a small farmer drove up to the elevator and asked:

"What's wheat worth to-day?"

"A dollar, even," was the answer.

"This is all you get from me at that price," said the farmer, "and you wouldn't get this if I didn't need fifty dollars to-day. Take it in."

"Think wheat's going higher?" asked the buyer.

"Higher! It's going to a dollar and a half," boasted the farmer. "I got twelve hundred bushels at home, and nobody gets it for a cent less than eighteen hundred dollars."

"You'd better see a doctor before you drive back," advised the elevator man, laughing.

Over in Kansas at one of the big collecting centers the telephone bell rang.

"What's cash wheat worth to-day?"

"Dollar-one."

"A dollar-one! I'll hold mine a while."

"Better take this price while you can get it," advised the shipper. "Big crop this year."

"A dollar and a half's the price," responded the farmer on the other end of the wire.

"Who is this?" asked the shipper.

"J. W. Harkness."

The man rubbed his chin. Harkness owned five hundred acres of the best wheat land in Kansas.

In South Dakota, on the same day, two farmers who had brought in their wheat drove home with it, refusing the price offered with scorn. In Pennsylvania not one-tenth of the grain was delivered as on the same date a year before, and the crop was much larger. In Ohio, in Indiana, in Illinois, in Iowa, in Nebraska, all through the wheat belt began these significant incidents, and to brokers in Chicago and New York were wired startling reports from a hundred centers: farmers were delivering no wheat and were holding out for a dollar and a half!

"You can scare the entire Board of Trade black in the face with a Hallowe'en pumpkin," Wallingford had declared to Blackie Daw. "Say 'Boo!' and they drop dead. Step on a parlor match and every trader jumps straight up into the gallery. Four snowflakes make a blizzard, and a frost on State Street kills all the crops in Texas."

Results seemed to justify his summing up. On that day wheat jumped ten cents within the last hour before closing, and ten thousand small speculators who had been bearing the market, since they could see no good reason for the already high price, were wiped out before they had a chance to protect their margins. On the following day a special edition of the *Commercial Farmer* was issued. It exulted, it gloated, it fairly shrieked over the triumph that had already been accomplished by the Farmers' Commercial Association. The first minute that it had shown its teeth it had made for the farmers of the United States ten cents a bushel on four hundred million bushels of wheat! It had made for them in one hour forty million dollars net profit, and this was but the beginning. The farmers themselves, by standing together, had already raised the price of wheat to a dollar-fifteen, and dollar-and-a-half wheat was but a matter of a few days. On the boards of trade it would go even higher. There would be no stopping it. It would soar to a dollar and a half, to a dollar-seventy-five, to two dollars! Speculation was a thing ordinarily to be discouraged, yet under these circumstances the farmers themselves should reap the wealth that was now ripe. They should take out of "Wall Street" and La Salle Street their share of the money that these iniquitous centers of financial jugglery had taken from the agricultural interests of the country for these many years. They themselves knew now, by the events of one day, that the Farmers' Commercial Association was strong enough to accomplish what it had meant to accomplish, and now was the time to get into the market. It should be not only the pleasure and profit of every farmer, but the duty of every farmer, to hit the gamblers a fatal blow by investing every loose dollar, on safe and conservative margins, in this certain advance of wheat. On the last page of this issue of the *Commercial Farmer* appeared for the first time the advertisement of Fox & Fleecer, and copies went to a million wheat growers.

The response was many-phased. Farmers who were convinced of this logic, and those who were not, rushed their wheat to market at the then prevailing price, not waiting for the dollar and a half, but turning their produce into cash at once. To offset this sudden release of grain, buying orders poured into the markets, the same cash that had been received from the sale of actual wheat being put into margins upon fictitious wheat. Prices fluctuated in leaps of five and ten cents, and the pit went crazy. It was a seething, howling mob, tossing frenzied trades back and forth until faces were red and voices were hoarse; and the firm of Fox & Fleecer, long noted for its conservative dealing and almost passed by in the course of events, suddenly became the most important factor on the floor.

On the ticker that on the first of May he had installed in his now mortgaged house upon his mortgaged farm, Wallingford saw the price mount to a dollar and a quarter, drop to a dollar-eighteen, jump to a dollar-twenty-two, back to twenty, up to twenty-five, back to twenty-two, up to twenty-eight. This last quotation he came back into the room to see after he had on his hat and ulster, and while his automobile, carrying Blackie Daw and Mrs. Wallingford, was spluttering and quivering at the door. Then he started for Chicago, leaving his neighbors back home to keep his telephone in a continuous jingle.

Hiram Hines met Len Miller in the road, for example. Both were beaming.

"What's the latest about wheat?" asked Len.

"A dollar twenty-eight and seven-eighths," replied Hiram; "at least it was about an hour ago when I telephoned to Judge Wallingford's house. Suppose its climbing for a dollar-thirty by now. How much you got, Len?"

"Twenty thousand bushels," answered Len jubilantly. "Bought it at a dollar twenty-four on a five-cent margin, and got that much profits already, nearly. Raised a thousand dollars on my sixty acres and have made nearly a thousand on it in two weeks; with Judge Wallingford's own brokers, too."

"So's mine," exulted Hiram. "Paid a dollar-twenty-six, but I'm satisfied. When it reaches a dollar-forty I'll quit."

Ezekiel Tinkle walked six miles to see his son Ham at the Wallingford place.

"Jonas Whetmore's bragging about two thousand dollars he's made in a few days in this wheat business," he stated. "I don't

rightly understand it, Hamlet. How about it?
I don't believe in speculating, but Jonas says
this ain't speculating, and if there's such a lot
of money to be made I want some."

"We all do," laughed Ham Tinkle, who,
since he had "made good" with his new-
fangled farming, was accepted as an equal by
his father. "I had two hundred when I started.
It's a thousand now, and will be five thousand
before I quit. Bring your money to me, father,
and I'll show you how to get in on the profits.
But hurry. How much can you spare?"

"Well," figured Ezekiel, "there's that fifteen hundred I've saved up for Bobbie's school-
ing; then when I sell my wheat ——"

"Don't do that!" interposed his son quickly.
"Wheat is going up so rapidly because the
growers are holding it for a dollar and a half.
Every man who sells his now, weakens the price
that much."

"Is *that* the way of it!" exclaimed the old
man, enlightened at last, and he kicked reflectively at a piece of turf. "To make money
out of this all the farmers must hold their wheat
for a dollar and a half! Say, Hamlet; Charlie
Granice sold his wheat at a dollar-six to go into
this thing. Adam Spooner and Burt Powers
and Charlie Dorsett all sold theirs, and they're

all members of this association. Ham, I'm going right home to sell my wheat."

"They are traitors!" charged Hamlet angrily. "I won't send that money away for you."

"Send it away!" retorted the old man. "Not by a danged sight you won't! I'll sell my wheat right now while it's high, and put my money in the bank along with the fifteen hundred I've got there; and you go ahead and be your own fool. I know advice from your old daddy won't stop you."

Not many, however, were like old man Tinkle, and J. Rufus Wallingford, as he sped toward Chicago, was more self-congratulatory than he had ever been in all his life. A million dollars! A real million! Why, dignity could now attach to the same sort of dealing that had made him forever avoid the cities where he had "done business." Heretofore his operations had been on such a small scale that they could be called "common grafting," but now, with a larger scope, they would be termed "shrewd financiering." It was entirely a matter of proportion. A million! Well, he deserved a million, and the other millions that would follow. Didn't he look the part? Didn't he act it? Didn't he live it?

"Me for the big game!" he exulted. "Watch

me take my little old cast-iron dollars into Wall Street and keep six corporations rotating in the air at one and the same time. Who's the real Napoleon of Finance? Me; Judge Wallingford, Esquire!"

"Pull the safety-rope and let out a little gas, J. Rufus," advised Blackie Daw dryly. "Your balloon will rip a seam. The boys on Wall Street were born with their eye-teeth cut, and eat marks like you before breakfast for appetizers."

J. Rufus only laughed.

"They'd be going some," he declared. "Any wise Willie who can make a million farmers jump in to help him up into the class of purely legitimate theft, like railroad mergers and industrial holding companies, ought to be able to stay there. The manipulator that swallows me will have a horrible stomachache."

Mrs. Wallingford had listened with a puzzled expression.

"But I don't understand it, Jim," she said. "I can see why you got the farmers together to raise the price of wheat. It does them good as well as you. But why have you worked so hard to make them speculate?"

J. Rufus looked at her with an amused expression.

"My dear infant," he observed; "when Fox & Fleecer got ready to sell my near-two-million bushels of wheat this morning, somebody had to be ready to buy them. I provided the buyers. That's all."

"Oh!" exclaimed Mrs. Wallingford, and pondered the matter slowly. "I see. But, Jim! Mr. Hines, Mr. Evans, Mr. Whetmore, Mr. Granice, and the others—to whom do they sell after they have bought your wheat?"

"The sheriff," interposed Blackie with a grin.

"Not necessarily," Wallingford hastened to contradict him in answer to the troubled frown upon his wife's brow. "My deal don't disturb the market, and I expect wheat to go on up to at least a dollar and a half. If these farmers get out on the way up they make money. But the boobs who buy from them ——"

"Ain't it funny?" inquired Blackie plaintively. "There's always a herd of 'em just crazy eager to grab the hot end."

A boy came on the train with evening papers containing the closing market quotations. Wheat had touched thirty-four, but a quick break had come at the close, back to twenty-six! Another column told why. Every cent of advance in the actual grain had brought out cash wheat in floods. Members of the great Farmers' Commercial Association had hurried their holdings to market, trusting to the great body of the loosely bound organizations to keep up the price—and the great body of the organization was doing precisely the same thing. At bottom they had, in fact, small faith in it, and the Board of Trade, sensitive as a barometer, was quick to feel this psychological change in the situation. Wallingford said nothing of this to his wife. He had begun to fear her. Always she had set herself against actual dishonesty, and more so than ever of late as he had begun to pride himself upon being a great financier. In the smoking compartment, however, he handed the paper to Blackie Daw, with his thumb upon the quotations.

"There's the answer," he said. "The Rubes have cut their own throats, as I figured they would, and you'll see wheat tumble to lower than it was when this raise began. Hines and Evans and Granice and the rest of them will hold the bag on this deal, and they needn't blame it to me. They can only blame it to the fact that farmers won't stick. I'm lucky that they hung together long enough to reach my price of a dollar and a quarter."

"How do you know you got out?" asked

Blackie, passing over as a matter of no moment whatever the fact that all their neighbors of Truscot and Mapes Counties, who had followed "Judge" Wallingford's lead and urging in the matter of speculation, would lose their all; as would hundreds if not thousands of other "members" who had been led through the deftly worded columns of the *Commercial Farmer* to gamble in their own grain.

"Easy," explained J. Rufus. "The quotations themselves tell it. Fox & Fleecer had instructions to unload at a dollar twenty-five, and they follow such instructions absolutely. They began unloading at that price, buying in at the same time for my farmers, and, in spite of the fact that they were pitching nearly two million bushels of wheat on the market after it hit the twenty-five mark, it went on up to thirty-four before it broke, showing that the buying orders until that time were in excess of selling orders. The farmers throughout the country simply ate up my two million bushels of wheat."

"Then it's their money you got, after all," observed Blackie.

"It's mine now," responded J. Rufus with a chuckle. "I saw it first."

CHAPTER XXV

MR. FOX SOLVES HIS GREAT PROBLEM, AND MR. WALLINGFORD FALLS WITH A THUD

THEY arrived in Chicago late and they arose late. At breakfast, with languid interest, Wallingford picked up the paper that lay beside his plate, and the first item upon which his eyes rested was a sensational article headed: "BROKER SUICIDES." Even then he was scarcely interested until his eye caught the name of Edwin H. Fox.

"What is the matter?" asked his wife anxiously, as, with a startled exclamation, he hastily pushed back his chair and arose. It was the first time that she had ever in any emergency seen his florid face turn ghastly pale. Dilemmas, reverses and even absolute defeats he had always accepted with a gambler's coolness, but now, since his vanity had let him dignify his pursuit of other people's money by the name of financiering, the blow came with crushing force; for it maimed not only his pocketbook but his pride as it swept

383

away the glittering air castles that he had been building for the past year.

"Matter!" he spluttered, half choking. "We are broke!" And leaving his breakfast untasted he hastily ordered a cab and drove to the office of Fox & Fleecer, devouring the details of the tragedy as he went. The philanthropic Mr. Fox, he of the glistening bald pate and the air of cold probity, the man who had been for thirty years in business at the old stand, who had seemed as firm as a rock and as unsusceptible as a quart of clams, had been leading not only a double but a sextuple life, for half a dozen pseudo-widows mourned his demise and the loss of a generous banker. To support all these expensive establishments, which, once set up, firmly declined to ever go out of existence, Mr. Fox had been juggling with the money of his customers; robbing Peter to pay Paul, until the time had come when Paul could be no longer paid and there was only one debt left that he could by any possibility wipe out—the debt he owed to Nature. That he had paid with a forty-four caliber bullet through the temple. At last he had solved that perplexing problem which had bothered him all these years.

Wallingford had expected to find the office

of Fox & Fleecer closed, but the door stood wide open and the dingy apartment was filled with a crowd of men, all equally nervous but violently contrasted as to complexion, some of them being extremely pale and some extremely flushed, according to their temperaments. Mr. Fleecer, one of those strangest of all anomalies, a nervous fat man, stood behind Mr. Fox's desk, his collar wilted with perspiration and the flabby pouches under his eyes black from his vigil of the night. He was almost as large as Wallingford himself, but a careless dresser, and a pitiable object as he started back on hearing Wallingford's name, tossing up his right hand with a curious involuntary motion as if to ward off a blow. His crisp, quick voice, however, did not fit at all with his appearance of crushed indecision.

"I might as well tell you the blunt truth at first, Mr. Wallingford," he said. "You haven't a cent, so far as Fox & Fleecer is concerned. Nobody has. I haven't a dollar in the world and Fox was head over heels in debt, I find. How that sanctimonious old hypocrite ever got away with it all these years is the limit. I looked after the buying and selling orders as he gave them to me, and never had anything to do with the books. I never knew when a deal was in the office until I received market orders. I have spent all night on Fox's private accounts, however, and since yours was the largest item, I naturally went into it as deeply as I could. If they had telephones in Hell I could give you more accurate information, but the way I figure it is this: when he got hold of your four hundred and twenty-five thousand dollars with instructions to buy and not to close until it reached a dollar and a quarter, he evidently classed your proposition as absurd. There was absolutely nothing to make wheat go to that price, and, with the big margin you had put up, he figured that the account would drag along at least until September, without being touched; so he used what he had to have of the money to cover up his other steals, expecting to juggle the market with the rest of it on his own judgment, and expecting, in the end, to have it back to hand to you when you got tired. When he understood this upward movement, however, and saw the big thing you had done, he jumped into the market with what was left, something less than three hundred thousand dollars. The only way to make that up to the amount you should have by the time it reached a dollar and a quarter was to pyramid it, and this he did.

He bought on short margin, closed when he had a good profit, and spread the total amount over other short margin purchases. He did this three times. On the last deal he had upward of five million bushels bought to your account, and it was this strong buying, coupled with the other buying orders which came in at about the dollar-and-a-quarter mark, that sent the market up to a dollar thirty-four. If the market could have held half an hour he would have gotten out all right and turned over to you a million dollars, after using two hundred and fifty thousand for his own purposes, but when he attempted to unload the market broke; and by —— we're all broke!''

Mr. Wallingford laughed, quite mechanically, and from his pocket drew two huge black cigars with gold bands around them.

"Have a smoke," he said to Mr. Fleecer.

Lighting his own Havana he turned and elbowed his way out of the room. One of the men who had stood near him exchanged a wondering stare with his neighbor.

"That's the limit of gameness," he observed.

But he was mistaken. It was not gameness. Wallingford was merely dazed. He could find no words to express the bitter depth to which he had fallen. As he passed out through the ticker-room he glanced at the blackboard. The boy was just chalking up the latest morning quotation on September wheat—a dollar twelve.

In the cab he opened his pocketbook and counted the money in it. Before he had started on this trip he had scarcely thought of money, except that at Fox & Fleecer's there would be waiting for him a cool, clean million. Instead of that he found himself with exactly fifty-four dollars.

Mrs. Wallingford was in her room, pale to the lips.

"How much money have you?" he asked her.

Without a word she handed him her purse. A few small bills were in it. She handed him another small black leather case which he took slowly. He opened it, and from the velvet depths there gleamed up at him the old standby—her diamonds. He could get a couple of thousand dollars on these at any time. He put the case in his pocket, but without any gleam of satisfaction, and sat down heavily in one of the huge leather-padded chairs.

"Fanny," said he savagely, "never preach to me again! I have tried a straight-out legitimate deal and it dumped me. Hereafter, be satisfied with whatever way I make money, just so long as I have the law on my side.

Why," and his indignation over this last reflection was beyond expression, "I've coaxed
a carload of money out of the farmers of this
country, and I don't get away with a cent of
it! A thief got it! *A thief and a grafter!*"

Mrs. Wallingford did not answer him. She
was crying. It was not so much that they had
lost all of this money, it was not that he had
spoken harshly to her for almost the first time
since he had come into her life, but the shat-
tering once more of certain hopeful dreams
that had grown up within her since their so-
journ in Battlesburg. Of course, he was instantly regretful and made such clumsy amends
as he could, but the sting, not of bitterness but
of sorrow, was there, and it remained for long
after; until, in fact, she came to realize how
much to heart her husband had taken his only
real defeat. For the first time in his life he
became despondent. The height to which he
had aspired and had almost reached, looked
now so utterly unattainable that the contem-
plation of it took out of him all ambition, all
initiative, all life. He seemed to have lost his
creative faculty. Where his fertile brain had
heretofore teemed with plans and projects,
crowding upon each other, clamoring for ful-
filment, now he seemed incapable of thought,

and fell into an apathy from which he could not arouse himself no matter how hard he tried. Parting company with Blackie Daw, who seemed equally rudderless, they moved aimlessly about from city to city, pawning Mrs. Wallingford's diamonds as they needed the money, but the man's spirit was gone, and no matter how often he changed his environment or brought himself into contact with new fields and new opportunities, no plan for getting back upon his feet seemed to offer itself. He was too much disheartened, in fact, even to try. To husband their fast waning resources they even descended to living in boarding houses, where the brief gratification of exciting awe among the less impressive boarders was but small compensation for the loss of the luxury to which they had been used.

It was the sight of a miserable dinner in one of these boarding houses that proved the turning point for him. His chair was drawn back from the table for him when he suddenly shoved it to its place again, and with a darkening brow stalked out of the dining room, followed by the bewildered Mrs. Wallingford.

"I can't stand this thing, Fanny," he declared. "I've insulted my stomach with that sort of fodder until it's too late for an apology."

"What are you going to do?" she asked in concern.

"Go where the good steaks grow," he answered emphatically. "We're going to pack up and move to the best hotel in town and eat ourselves blue in the face, and to-morrow J. Rufus is going to go back on the job. I haven't the money in my pocket to pay for it, and we haven't another thing we can soak, but if I run up a hotel bill I'll have to get out and dig to pay it, and that's what I need. I'm lazy."

It was a positive elation to him to dash up in a cab to a palatial hotel, to walk into its gilded and marble corridors with a deferential porter carrying his luggage, to loom up before a suave clerk in his impressive immensity and sign his name with a flourish, to demand the best accommodations they had in the house and to be shown into apartments that bathed him once more in a garish atmosphere where everything tasted and felt and smelled of money. It was like the prodigal son coming home again, and instantly his spirits arose with a bound. He began as of old to live like a lord, and though the long sought idea did not come to him for almost two weeks, he held to

the untroubled tenor of his way with all his
old arrogance, blessed with a cheerful belief
that some lucky solution of his difficulties
would be found.

One thing alone bothered him toward the
last, and that was the rapid disappearance of
such little ready money as he needed for tips
when he was in the hotel, and for drinks and
cigars when he found himself away from it.
He was sensitive about ordering inferior goods
in good places, and when away from his source
of credit supplies, took to turning in at obscure cigar stores, preferring to buy the best
they had rather than to taking a second grade
in a better place. It was in one of these obscure little establishments that the elusive inspiration at last came to him.

"The government is rotten!" the stoop-
shouldered cigar maker had complained just a
moment before, rasping the air of his dingy
little store with a high-pitched voice that
was almost a whine. "It fosters consoli-
dations. Big profits for rich men and bank-
ruptcy for poor men, that's what we have
come to!"

The stoop-shouldered cigar maker had no
chin worth mentioning, and grew a thin, down-
pointed mustache which accentuated that lack.

He wore a green eye-shade and an apron of bed ticking, and he held in his hand a split mold, gripping the two parts together while he feebly and hopelessly groped for an inspiration in the mending line. The flabby man in the greasy vest, who was playing solitaire with a pack of cards so grimy that it took an experienced eye to tell whether the backs or the faces were up, did not raise his head, nor did the apathetic young man with the chronic dent in his time-yellowed Derby, who, sitting motionless with his crossed arms resting on his knees, had been making a business of watching the solitaire game in silence.

"That's right," agreed the flabby man, laying the trey of diamonds carefully upon the four of clubs and peeping to see what the next card would have been; "all the laws are against the poor man, and we're ground right down."

A pimple-faced youngster, clearly below the legal age, came in and bought two cigarettes for a cent, and the cigar maker waited upon him in sour-visaged nonchalance; neither the solitaire expert nor his interested watcher raised his eyes; a young man with a flashy tie and a soiled collar bought three stogies for a nickel and still apathy reigned; then Wal-

lingford's huge bulk darkened the open doorway and everybody woke up.

Wallingford was so large that he seemed to
crowd the little shop and absorb all its light,
and he approached the cigar case doubtingly,
surveying its contents with the eye of a *con-
noisseur*. A brand or two that he knew quite
well he passed over, for the boxes were nearly
empty and no doubt had been reeking for a
long time in that sponge-moistened assort-
ment of flavors, but finally he settled upon a
newly opened box from which but two cigars
had been sold, and tapped his finger on the
glass above it. The cigar maker reached in
for that box with alacrity, for they were two-
for-a-quarter goods, and as he brought them
forth he gave to the buyer the appreciative
scrutiny due one of so impressive appearance.
He did not know that under his inspection the
big man winced. In the fine scarf there should
have glowed a huge diamond; the scarf itself
had two or three frayed threads; the binding
of the hat brim was somewhat worn; the cuffs
were a little ragged. Wallingford felt that all
the world saw this unwonted condition, but still
he smiled richly; and the cigar dealer saw
only richness. Probably the imposing customer would have left the store in the same

silence in which he had made his purchase, but, as he stopped to fastidiously cut the tip from one of his cigars, an undersized but pompous young collector bustled in and threw down a bill.

"Hundred Blue Rings," he announced curtly. With a mechanical curiosity, Wallingford glanced into the case where a box of cigars with cheap blue bands was displayed. The cigar maker opened his money drawer and slowly counted out a pile of small silver.

"Three fifty," he lifelessly whined as he shoved it over, and the collector receipted the bill, dashing out with the same absurd self assertiveness with which he had come in.

"Thirty-five a thousand," observed Wallingford incredulously. "That price is claimed for every nickel cigar on earth, but I always thought it was phoney. It's a stiff rate, isn't it?"

"It's a hold up," snarled the other, "but I got to keep 'em. I make a better cigar myself but people don't know anything about tobacco. They only smoke advertising. Here's my cigar," and he set a box on the case; "Ed Nickel's Nickelfine. There's a piece of real goods."

The big man picked one out of the box, and

twirled it in his deft fingers with a scrutiny that betokened keen judgment of all small articles of manufacture.

"It's well made," he admitted; "but what's the use? I could deliver your week's output in my pocket, and on the way back could spend the money getting my shoes shined; all because you haven't the wherewith to advertise."

"I got a little money," insisted the other aggressively, touched on a point of pride; "money I saved and pinched and scraped together; but it ain't enough to push a cigar. Some of these big manufacturers spread around a fortune on a new brand before they sell a single box. There's John Crewly & Company. They spent a hundred thousand dollars advertising Blue Rings."

"And you small dealers have handed it back to them," laughed Wallingford. "You pay that advertising difference above what the cigar is worth."

"Ten times over!" exploded Mr. Nickel. "The houses that buy in big quantities get them for below twenty-eight, I've heard. But that's where the government is rotten! It's fixed so the little man always gets it in the neck. Combines and trusts eat us up. Every man that joins a consolidation ought to get ten years at hard labor."

"Don't grouch," advised Wallingford, grinning; "consolidate. If all the small dealers in this town formed a consolidation, they could buy their supplies in quantity for spot cash and get the lowest price going."

Ed Nickel looked out of the window at the clanging street cars and digested this palatable new idea.

"I reckon they could," he mused, "if there was any way to work it so they wouldn't all spike each other trying to get the best of it," and J. Rufus chuckled as he recognized this business anarchist's willingness to undergo an instant change of opinion about consolidation.

The door opened, and a tall, thin man, with curly gray hair and a little gray goatee, strode nervously in and threw a half dollar on the case.

"Two packs of Kiosks," he demanded.

Almost in the same breath he saw Wallingford, whose face was at that moment illuminated by the lighter to which he held his cigar.

"J. Rufus, by Heck!" he exclaimed.

Before Wallingford could give voice to his amazement the strangely altered Blackie Daw was shaking hands eagerly with him.

"You probably don't remember me," went

on Blackie with an expansive grin. "Rush is the name. I. B. Rush, and I never was so bug-house glad to see anybody in my life!"

The eyes of Wallingford twinkled.

"Well, well, well, Mr. Rush! How you have changed!" he declared.

Blackie shook his head warningly.

"Nix on the advertisement," he cautioned. "Wallingford, you're the long-sought message from home! Feel in your vest pocket and see if there isn't an overlooked hundred or two down in the corner."

J. Rufus was cheerful, nay, happy, complaisance itself.

"Certainly, Mr. Rush," he said heartily; "a thousand if you want it. Just step over to the bank with me till I draw the money," and they walked out of the door.

With a sigh the flabby man laid the long-suspended jack of hearts upon the queen of spades.

"Hear the big guy tossin' over a thousand like it was car fare," he observed. "If I had a piece of lead pipe I'd follow him."

"What do you suppose his graft is?" queried the watcher at the game.

"He's made his money off poor people; that's what!" announced Ed Nickel. "How else does a man get rich?"

CHAPTER XXVI

J. RUFUS SCENTS A FORTUNE IN SMOKE AND LETS
MR. NICKEL SEE THE FLAMES

WALLINGFORD had good cause to survey his friend with amused wonder.

"How you have aged, Blackie," he chuckled. "What has turned you gray in a single month?"

"Beating it," replied Blackie, hoarsely. "Did you see that guy just now look around and give me the X-ray stare?"

"He was only admiring your handsome make-up," retorted J. Rufus. "What's got your nerve all of a sudden?"

"Nerve!" scorned the other. "Say, J. Rufus, when I cut my finger I bleed yellow, and the mere sight of a brass button gives me hydrophobia. They're after me, dear friend of my childhood days, for going into the oil-well industry without any oil wells, and you're the first human being I've seen in three weeks that didn't look like he had the iron bracelets in his pocket. Even you're a living frost. For a minute you gave me that glad feeling, but when you said to come around to the bank and I could have a thousand, I knew it was all off. If you'd had it, nothing but paralysis would have stopped you from putting your hand in your pocket and making a flash with the two hundred I wanted. I have to make a quick get-away from this town or have the door of a nice steel bedroom locked from the outside!"

Solemnly J. Rufus drew from his pocket his total supply of earthly wealth, a ten-dollar bill and the change he had received at the cigar store.

"I'll give you the ten," he offered, "although I'm glued to the floor myself."

"I can see it, for your sparks are gone," said Mr. Daw, glumly looking his friend over from head to foot as he pocketed the ten. "How did the beans get spilled? I thought there was a fresh crop of your particular breed of come-ons every morning."

"I'm overtrained," explained J. Rufus with cheerful resignation. "I used to be able to jump into a town with ten dollars in my pocket, and have to lock myself in my room to keep 'em from forcing money on me faster than I could take it; but I've lost my winning ways, I guess. The fact of the matter is, Blackie, I

400

need an oculist. I can't see small enough since the big blow-up. I had climbed too high, and when I tumbled off the perch I fell so hard I couldn't see anything but stars. A dollar is small as a pea now, and perfectly silent, and it takes at least a thousand to emit even a faint click. I can't learn to pike again.''

"I wish I could learn anything else," complained Mr. Daw in disgust. "Why, blind-men's tincups look like fat picking to me, and my yellow streak shows through so strong that I cross the street every time I see a push cart; I'm afraid the banana men will make a mistake and pull my fingers off. Say! See that mug over there on the corner with his back to us? Well, that's a plain-clothes man. I know him all right and he knows me. It's Jimmy Rogers and I can't hand him a sou to plug his memory!''

Blackie was visibly distressed and edged around the corner.

"I should say you had developed a saffron streak," observed J. Rufus, eying him with a trace of contempt. "I wouldn't have known you till you spoke. Come on and we'll go right straight past Jimmy Rogers.''

He put his hand behind Blackie's elbow to take him in that direction, but to his surprise Daw shrank back.

"Not for mine!" he declared. "I know I'm due, but I won't go till they come after me. Why, J. Rufus, do you know we're all that's left of the old bunch? Billy Riggs, Tommy Rance, Dick Logan, Pit Hardesty— all put away, for stretches of from five to twenty years! And Jim, mind what I say; our turn's next! There, he's turning this way! I'm on the lope. Me for the first train out of town. Good-by, old man."

He shook hands hastily and, drawn-chested, plunged down the side street at a swift pace. Wallingford looked after him and involuntarily expanded his own broad chest as he turned in the direction of his hotel. He looked back at Ed Nickel's cigar store after a few steps, and hesitated as if he might return, but he did not. On the way he counted five such establishments, and he peered keenly into each one of them. They were all of a little better grade than the one he had visited, but none of them was stocked in such manner as to tell of wholesale purchases and cash discounts. Suddenly he chuckled. At last he had the detail for his heretofore vague idea, and it was a draught of strong wine to him. He had been the high jester of finance, always, and once more the bells upon his cap jingled merrily. Inspired, he walked into his hotel with a swaggering assurance entirely out of keeping with the lonely two dollars in his pocket. The clerk had been instructed to look after Wallingford, for though he had been an extravagant guest for within a day of two weeks, no one but the bellboys and waiters had seen a penny of his money—and his bill was nearly two hundred dollars. The clerk firmly intended to call to him if he strode past on the far side of the lobby, as had been his custom in the past two or three days; but he did not need to call, for J. Rufus approached the desk without invitation, beaming as he turned toward it, but growing stern as he neared it.

"The wine I had served in my rooms last night was vile," he charged. "If I cannot get the brand of champagne I want, have it perfectly frappé when it gets to my apartments, and secure better service all around, I shall pay my bill and leave!"

The clerk touched a bell instantly.

"Very sorry, Mr. Wallingford," said he. "I shall speak to the wine steward about the matter at once."

J. Rufus grunted in acknowledgment of this apology, and with a feeling of relief the clerk surveyed that broad back as it retreated in immeasurable dignity. There was no need to worry about the money of a man who took that attitude. On the way to his suite, however, J. Rufus, as he handed the elevator boy a quarter with one hand, drew down his cuff furtively with the other, under the impulse of a sudden idea, and, grinning, looked at his cuff button. It was diamond studded, and he ought to be able to raise at least twenty-five apiece on the pair.

Mrs. Wallingford was sewing when her capable husband came in. Something in the very movement of the door caused her to look up with an instant knowledge that he brought good news, and a sight of his face confirmed the impression. She smiled at him brightly, and yet with a trace of apprehension. There had come over her a curious change of late. Her color was as clear as ever, even clearer, for it seemed to have attained a certain pure transparency, but there seemed, too, a slight pallor beneath it, and her eyes were strangely luminous.

"I got the fog out of my conk to-day, Fanny," he said exultantly. "It seemed as if I never would be able to frame up a good business stunt again, but it hit me at last. How do you like this place?"

"I can't tell," she slowly returned. "I haven't seen much of it, you know."

"You will," he laughed. "You may pick out any part of it you like, because I think I'll settle down here for good."

She looked up with a little gasp.

"Then you're going into a—a *real* business?" she faltered.

"A hundred of them," he boasted. "I've just decided to rake off half the profits of all this town's cigar stores, except a few of the best ones, and stay right here to collect. The hundred or more ought to yield me one or two dollars a day apiece. Looks good, don't it?"

"I'm so glad," she said simply. It never occurred to either of them to doubt that he could do what he had planned, and just now she was less inclined than ever to inquire into details. She sat, her hands folded in the fluffy white goods upon her lap, with a deepening color in her cheeks.

"I'll tell you why I'm glad we are to settle down at last and have a real home," she said suddenly, and, arising, advanced to him and shook out the dainty article upon which she had been sewing, holding it outstretched before him so that he could gather its full import.

"What?" he gasped.

She nodded her head, half crying and half laughing, and suddenly buried her head upon his shoulder, sobbing. He clasped her in his arms, tiny white garment and all, and looked on over her head, out of the window at the gathering dusk in the sky where it stretched down between the tall buildings. For just one fleeting second a trace of the Eternal Mystery came to awe him, but it passed and left him grinning.

"I'd just been figuring on a new house," he observed, "but I guess I'll have to plan it all over now."

He led her to a chair presently, and went back to the window, where he stood until the darkness warned him that it was time to dress for dinner. The meal finished, he sat down to write, tearing up sheet after sheet of paper and crumpling it into the waste basket until far into the night, and later he sent down for a city directory, making out a list of cigar stores, dropping out those that were printed in black-face type; but whatever he did he paused once in a while to turn toward that tiny white garment upon the table and survey it with smiling wonder.

In the morning he called upon a job printer of reputation, and then he went again to Ed

Nickel's cigar store; but this time he dashed up to the door in a showy carriage drawn by two good horses. The same flabby man sat in the corner playing solitaire as if he had never left off, and the same apathetic young man with the dent in his hat was watching him. The split cigar mold had not yet grown together, though Ed Nickel still held its two parts matched tightly in his left hand. Upon the entrance of Wallingford the magnificent, however, the three graven figures, glancing first upon him and then upon the carriage, inhaled the breath of life. The solitaire player suddenly pushed his cards together and began shuffling them over and over and over and over, though he had not yet exhausted the possibilities of the previous game. The apathetic young man stood up to yawn but changed his mind after he had his mouth open. Ed Nickel bowed, smiled and hurried behind his counter.

"What will you take for your business, Mr. Nickel?" asked J. Rufus, throwing a coin on the case and tapping his finger over the box from which he had purchased the cigars the night before. Freshly shaven, he wore a new collar, a new shirt with fine, crisp cuffs, and a new silk lavender tie—also plain new cuff buttons.

Ed Nickel's ears heard the astounding question, but Ed Nickel's mind did not grasp it, for Ed Nickel's hand went on mechanically into the case after the designated cigars. It secured the box, it brought it partly out—and then dropped it just inside the sliding door. The hand came out and its fingers twined with those of the other hand.

"What did you say?" asked Mr. Nickel's mouth.

"How much will you take for your business?" repeated J. Rufus.

Mr. Nickel looked slowly around his walls, past the dust-hung wire screen to the dingy back room, under the counter, into the case, over the sparsely filled shelves.

"I don't know," he said, his eyes roving back to those of J. Rufus. "Besides the stock and fixtures, there's the good will, the trade I've worked up, and the call for my Nickelfine and the Double Nickel, my leading ten-cent cigar. I'd have to take an invoice to set a price on this business."

"I know," laughed J. Rufus with a wink, "but you can invoice it with your eyes shut and we can lump the rest of it. Say five hundred for the stock and fixtures and three hundred for the good will, which is crowding it some."

Ed Nickel's cupidity gave a thump. Eight hundred was a good price for his business, especially in this location. He had often thought of moving. In a better location he would do a better business; he was sure of that, like every other unsuccessful merchant; but of course he objected.

"Make it a thousand and I'll listen," he proposed.

J. Rufus looked about the place coldly.

"No," he decided. "I'd be cheating the consolidation."

Mr. Nickel immediately woke up another notch.

"What consolidation?" he wanted to know.

"The one I spoke to you about yesterday," said the prospective buyer, and picking up the coin he had tossed down he tapped with it on the glass.

Thus reminded, the benumbed one brought out the delayed box and Mr. Wallingford lit one of the cigars.

"I'm going to finance a consolidation of all the smaller cigar stores in the city," he then explained. "I expect to buy several for spot cash and put in charge of them managers who know their business. The rest I am going to allow to purchase shares in the consolidation, with the value of their stock and good will, so that altogether we shall have a quarter-of-a-million-dollar corporation. With this enormous buying power I intend to get the lowest spot-cash discount on all goods, manufacture a few good brands, cut rates and control the cigar business of this town. But I'm going to be fair to every man. I'll give you eight hundred dollars for your business, in cold coin."

The day before, had any providentially sent stranger offered Ed Nickel eight hundred dollars in real money for his store, he would have jumped at the chance, and with the purchase price would have opened a better one in some other part of the town. Now it suddenly occurred to him ——

"And if I don't sell or come in I get froze out, I suppose," he gloomily opined. "That's the regulation poor man's chance. But how are you going to work this consolidation, anyhow?"

"The same plan upon which all successful organizations are put together," patiently explained the eminent financier whose resplendent carriage was waiting outside. "For instance, five of us organize a holding company. Having incorporated for, say, two hundred and fifty thousand dollars, I buy your business for eight

410

hundred dollars in stock of the new corporation, fit it up new till it glitters, and put you in charge of it. A hundred other stores go in on the same proposition, their valuations varying according to their location, their stock, and the volume of business their books can show. You get a salary of just as much as you can prove you're making now, and every three months the business is footed up and a dividend is paid. The difference is just this. The cigars for which you now pay thirty-five dollars a thousand, you will get for twenty-eight and less, and so on down the line. Your profits will be increased nearly a hundred per cent., and all financial worry will be lifted off your shoulders."

Ed Nickel suddenly awoke to the fact that the flabby solitaire player was pressed closely upon one side of the eminent financier, and the apathetic young man upon the other, both drinking in every word, and quivering.

"Come in the back room," invited Mr. Nickel, and on two reeking stools, with tobacco scraps strewn all about them, they sat down to really "get together." Patiently the energetic man of wealth went over the proposition again, point by point, and the cigar maker enumerated these upon his fingers until he got it quite clear in his mind that his business was not to pass out of his hands at all. If it was put in at a valuation of eight hundred dollars, he received a salary equal to his present earnings for taking care of it, and also the net profits on eight hundred dollars worth of stock. It was a great scheme! It would put all the goods he wanted upon his shelves. It would brighten up his place of business and he would no longer have the aggravation of knowing that rich dealers, just because they were rich, could buy cigars a shameful per cent. cheaper than he could. Moreover, there sat Wallingford, a wonderful argument in himself! When he had fully grasped the idea Mr. Nickel was enthusiastic.

"Of course I'll come in!" said he. "Surest thing, you know!"

"Suit yourself," said J. Rufus, with vast indifference. "I have a little agreement that I'll bring around in a couple of days to let you see, and then you may finally decide. By the way, Mr. Nickel, I may need you for one of the original five incorporators, and as a director for the first year."

Mr. Nickel hesitated.

"That'll cost me something, won't it?" he wanted to know.

Mr. Wallingford laughed.

"A little bit," he admitted. "But there are ways to get it back. For instance, as one of the directors I do not suppose there would be any particular harm in selling your business to the consolidation for a thousand in place of eight hundred."

The first stock subscriber to the Retail Cigar Dealers' Consolidation became as knowingly jovial as the genial promoter.

"It listens good to me," he declared, and shook hands.

The big man got up to go, but turned and came back.

"By the way," said he, "I don't know the cigar men in this town, and if you have a couple of friends in the business who would like to help form this incorporation with the same advantages you have, let's go see them."

Mr. Nickel was already throwing off his apron and eye shade, and now he took his coat and hat from their hook.

"I've got two of them, and they ain't too darned smart, either," he stated, showing wise forethought in that last remark; then, putting the flabby man in charge of the store, he went out and *rode in that carriage!*

CHAPTER XXVII

IN the smart carriage Mr. Wallingford took
Mr. Nickel and his two friends down to
his hotel for lunch to talk over the final
steps in the great consolidation. The
chief thing the three remembered when they
left the hotel was that they had been most liberally treated in the matter of extravagant food
and drink, and that the lunch had cost over
twenty dollars! Also they recalled that the dis-
tinguished-looking head waiter had come over
to their table half a dozen times to see that
everything was served at the proper minute
and in the pink of condition. Nobody but
a rich man could command that sort of attention, and they left the table not only
willing but thankful to take any business
tonic this commercial genius should pre-
scribed. As they passed the desk, the manager called Mr. Wallingford to him, and
the great promoter, instantly bidding his
friends good-by, promised to see them

to-morrow. Then he walked back to the manager.

"Good morning, Senator," said that official, shaking hands. "How are they treating you? Nicely?"

"Very well, indeed," replied Wallingford, "except I'd like to have corner rooms if I could get them."

"I know; you spoke of that last week. I've been trying to secure them for you, but those apartments are always dated so far ahead. I think the corner suite on the second floor will be vacant in a day or so, though, and I'll let you know. By the way, Mr. Wallingford"— this in the most pleasantly confidential tone imaginable—"I'm afraid I'll have to draw on you. The proprietor is a little strict about his rules, and you have been here two weeks to-day."

"Is that so?" exclaimed Wallingford, very much surprised. "I'll have to look after that," and he reached out his hand with courteous alacrity for the bill which the manager was handing to him. Without the quiver of an eye-lash he glanced over the items and stuck the bill in his pocket. "I'm glad you spoke of it. I'm rather careless about such matters," and he walked away in perfect nonchalance.

The telegraph desk mocked him. There was not a soul he knew to whom he could wire with a certainty of getting money, and if he pretended to wire he must certainly produce quick results. Instead of making that error he walked out upon the street briskly. Half way to Ed Nickel's cigar store he paused. Mr. Nickel was not yet ripe, and it would be folly to waste his chances. Thinking most deeply indeed, he strolled into a cigar store of far better appearance than any he had yet visited. The place was a-quiver with life; there was much glitter of beveled plate mirrors; there were expensive light fixtures; the shelves were crowded with rows upon rows of cigar boxes, and at a most ornate case stood three rather strikingly dressed men, playing "ping pong" on a mahogany edged board that was covered with green baize. He had seen these boards before, but they were all set away behind counters, for this game—of dice, not of balls and paddles — was strictly taboo. A moral wave had swept over the town and had made dice shaking for cigars, as well as every other form of gambling, next door to a hanging offense. A heavy-set young fellow, with a red face and a red tie and red stripes in the thread of his broad-checked clothing, was at the end of the counter, half behind it, scoring the game. He was evidently the proprietor, though he had his hat on, and he asked Wallingford what he wanted.

"I don't know your brands, so I'll leave it to you," said the large man, with a pleasant smile. "I want a nice three for a half, rather heavy, but not too tightly rolled."

The proprietor gave his customer a shrewd "sizing-up," as he promptly set out three boxes of different brands. Evidently the general appearance of Wallingford satisfied him that the man asked for this grade of cigars because he liked them and could afford them, for after the selection had been made the salesman observed that it was quite pleasant weather, looking Wallingford squarely in the eyes and smiling in sheer goodfellowship with all the world. He then renewed his attention to the "ping pong" game, and Wallingford, aimless for the time and occupied with that tremendous puzzle of the hotel bill, stood by and watched. A policeman came through, but no one paid any attention.

"Hello, Joe!" he said affably to the man in charge, and passed on into the back room. As the door of this was opened the sharp click of ivory chips came through, and Wallingford heard one strident voice say, "I'll raise you ten." A brisk and gimlet-eyed young man came out a moment later with a fifty-dollar bill, for which he got change.

"How you making it, Tommy?" he asked perfunctorily of one of the men who were shaking dice.

"Rotten!" said the dice shaker. "I've won ten two-for-a-quarter cigars that have cost me four dollars."

"I'd blow the game," advised the young man with a bantering laugh. "Shoot somebody for the four and quit double or even."

"I'll do it," said the man addressed as Tommy. "Fade me, Joe?"

"Any amount, old man," said the proprietor nonchalantly, and taking four dollars from the cash register he left the drawer open. "How do you want to be skinned?"

"First-flop poker dice," said Tommy, picking up the leather box which Joe had slammed upon the board, and rattling the five dice in it.

One turn apiece and the proprietor picked up the money. Tommy silently threw a five on the case.

"You other fellows want in on this?" he asked.

J. Rufus suddenly felt that mysterious thing called a "hunch" prickling in his wrist.

"How about letting a stranger in?" he observed, considering himself far enough west for this forwardness.

With a smile he made ready for that lightning glance of judgment which he knew would be leveled at him from three pairs of eyes at least.

"I'd rather anybody would have my money than Joe," said the man next to him, after that brief but pleased inspection and after an almost imperceptible nod from the proprietor. "Joe's a robber and we none of us like him."

"I don't think I like him very well myself," laughed Wallingford, throwing down his money, and, having accepted him, they judged him again from this new angle. He was a most likeable man, this big fellow, and an open-handed sport. Anybody could see that. It would make no difference to him whether he won or lost. All he wanted was to be in on the game. Rich as the mint, no doubt.

In reality J. Rufus had but three five dollar bills in his pocket, but desperate needs require desperate remedies, and, in view of those vast needs, if he lost he would be but little worse off than he was now. Twice he staked his last five, and then luck steadily alternated between him and the proprietor. One at a time the three others dropped out, and the two winners were left confronting each other.

"Well, old man," said the proprietor to Wallingford, shaking the box up and down while he talked, and smiling his challenge, "we split 'em about even. Shall we quit satisfied, or shoot it off to see who owns the best rabbit's foot?"

Wallingford glanced down at the crumpled pile of greenbacks in front of him and made a hasty computation. He was sure that he had fully two hundred dollars, but he could not in decency quit now.

"I never saw a finer afternoon for a murder in my life," he declared.

"Shoot you fifty," said Joe.

In for it, Wallingford covered the bet, and by this time a throng of interested spectators was at his elbows. It was Wallingford's first throw, and four aces tumbled up. His opponent followed him with fours, but they were four sixes.

"Cover the hundred and be a real sport," advised Wallingford with a grin.

Joe counted the money in front of him. There was enough to cover the bet, with a ten-dollar bill left over. He threw down the pile.

"I'll press it ten," said he, and Wallingford promptly added a ten from his own stack.

Four aces again. Again the man who was called Joe threw four sixes.

"I'll just leave that bundle of lettuce once more," observed J. Rufus. "I've a hunch that you'll be sorry you saw me."

"I'm sorry now," admitted the other, "but I'll skin the money drawer rather than have you go away dissatisfied," and from the cash register he took two hundred and twenty dollars. "Now shoot your head off," he advised.

Wallingford, in perfect confidence, rattled the box high in the air and tossed the five little ivory cubes upon the baize; and a dash of cold water fell on his confidence. A single, small, lonely, ashamed-looking pair of deuces confronted him.

"Here's where we get it all-l-l-l-l back again," laughed Joe in much joy. "Somebody call the porter to throw this stranger out when I get through," and with a crash he dumped the box upside down, lifting it with a sweep. The dice rattled about the board, and when they had all settled down he leaned over to count them. There was a moment of silence and then everybody laughed. There was not even a pair. Wallingford's miserable two deuces had won a two-hundred-and-forty-dollar pot. Gently he leaned over.

"How much of this spinach would you like to cover now?" he asked in soothing tones.

"Wait till I ask the safe," replied his antagonist, but at that moment the telephone bell just behind him rang and he turned to answer it. With almost the first words that he heard he looked at his watch and swore, and when he had hung up the receiver he turned to Wallingford briskly.

"Afraid I'll have to let you carry that bundle of kale for a while," he grudgingly admitted, "for I have to hurry over to the court or lose more than there is in sight right here. But for heaven's sake, man, remember the number and bring that back to me. I want it."

"Thanks," said J. Rufus. "If there's any left after I get through with it I'll bring it back," and he walked out, the admired of all beholders.

He headed straight for a bank, where he exchanged his crumpled money into nice, crisp, fifty-dollar bills, and then with profound satisfaction he strolled into his hotel and threw two hundred dollars in front of the manager. The circumstance, however, was worth more

than money to him. It meant a renewal of
his confidence. The world was once more his
oyster.

That evening, just as he had finished a late
dinner, a boy brought a card to him in the
dining room; "Mr. Joseph O. Meers."

"Meers!" read Wallingford to his wife.
"That isn't one of the men I had to lunch,
and besides, none of that bunch would have
an engraved card. Where is he?" he asked
the boy.

"Out in the lobby, sir."

Wallingford arose and went with the boy.
Sitting in one of the big chairs was the "Joe"
from whom he had won the money that afternoon, and the man began to laugh as soon as
he saw J. Rufus.

"So *you're* Wallingford!" he said, extending his hand. "No wonder I wanted to hunt
you up."

"Yes?" laughed Wallingford, entirely at
ease. "I had been expecting either you or a
warrant."

"You can square that with a bottle of
wine," offered the caller, and together they
trailed in to the bar, where, in a snug little
corner, they sat down. "What I came to see
you about," began Meers, while they waited

for the wine to be made cold, "is this cigar dealers' association that I hear you're doping up."

"Who told you?" asked Wallingford.

Mr. Meers winked.

"Never mind about that," he said. "I get it before the newspapers, and if there's a good game going count little Joseph in."

Wallingford studied this over a bit before answering. That afternoon he had decided not to invite Mr. Meers into the combination at all. He had not seemed likely material.

"I want to give you a little tip," added Mr. Meers, observing this hesitation. "No matter what the game is you need me. If I see my bit in it it goes through, but if I don't I'll bet you lose."

"The thing isn't a game at all," Wallingford soberly insisted. "It is a much needed commercial development that lets the cigar store be a real business in place of a peanut stand. What I'm going to do is to consolidate all the small shops in the city, for the purpose of buying at large-lot prices and taking cash discounts."

"That's a good play, too," agreed Meers; "but how about the details of it? How do you organize?"

"Make it a stock company," explained Wallingford, expanding largely; "incorporate as the Retail Cigar Dealers' Consolidation and issue each man stock to the value of his present business; leave each man in charge of his own shop and pay him a salary equal to his present proved clear earnings; split up the surplus profits every three months and declare dividends."

"That's the outside," commented Mr. Meers, nodding his head wisely; "but what's the inside? Show me. Understand, Mr. Wallingford, except for a little friendly gamble like we had this afternoon, I only run a game from behind the table. I do the dealing. I'm not what they call rich back in the *effete* East, but I'm getting along pretty well on one proposition: *I always bet they don't!*"

"It's a good healthy bet," admitted Wallingford; "but you want to copper it on this deal. This is a straight, legitimate proposition."

"Sure; sure," assented the other soothingly. "But where do you get in?"

"Well, I'm going to finance it. I'm going to take up some of the stock and get my quarterly dividends. I'll probably buy a few stores and put them in, and I hope to be made manager at a pretty good salary."

"I see but I don't," insisted the seeker after intimate knowledge. "That all sounds good, but it don't look fancy enough for a man that's down on the register of this hotel for suite D. If you come in to get my store in the consolidation—"

"Which I don't know whether I'll do or not," interrupted Wallingford.

"Wait and you will, though," retorted the other. "If you come into my place of business to get my store into the consolidation, I say, how do you close the deal? I suppose I sign an agreement of some sort, don't I?"

"Well, naturally, to have a safe understanding you'd have to," admitted the promoter.

"Let me see the agreement."

J. Rufus drew a long breath and chuckled.

"You're a regular insister, ain't you?" he said as he drew a carbon copy of the agreement from his pocket.

Mr. Meers read the paper over twice. The wine was brought to their table and served, but he paid no attention to the filled glass at his elbow. He was reading a certain portion of that agreement for the third and fourth time, but at last he laid it down on the chair beside him and solemnly tilted his hat to Mr. Wallingford.

"You're an honor to your family," he announced. "I didn't suppose there were any more games left, but you've sprung a new one and it's a peach!"

Wallingford strove to look magnificently unaware of what he meant, but the attempt was a failure.

"The scheme is so smooth," went on Mr. Meers with a heartfelt appreciation, "that it strained my eyesight to find the little joker; but now I can tell you all about it. It's in the transfer of the stock, and here's what you do. The consolidation buys my place for, say, five thousand dollars, and gives me five thousand dollars' worth of stock in the consolidation for it. That's what this paper seems to say, but that's not what happens. It's *you* that buys my place for five thousand dollars and gives me five thousand dollars' worth of stock in the consolidation for it, and *you*, being then the temporary owner through a fake trusteeship, turn around and sell my business to the consolidation, the management of which is in your flipper through a board of dummy directors, for *ten* thousand dollars; and you

427

have our iron-clad contract to let you do this, though it don't say so! When you get through you have consolidated a hundred and twenty-five thousand dollars' worth of business into a two-hundred-and-fifty-thousand-dollar stock company, and you have a hundred and twenty-five thousand dollars' worth of stock which didn't cost you a cent! Say! Have this wine on me. I insist! I want to buy you something!"

Slowly Mr. Wallingford's shoulders began to heave and his face to turn red, and presently he broke into a series of chuckles that expanded to a guffaw.

"I don't see how I ever won that five hundred from you this afternoon," he observed, and shook again.

"The pleasure is all mine," said the loser politely. "Now I'm sorry it wasn't a thousand. You're worth the money and I'm glad I came to see you. Count me in on the Retail Cigar Dealers' Consolidation."

"All right, sign the paper," said Wallingford with another chuckle.

"Watch me sign it not," said Meers. "I'm too patriotic. I'm so patriotic that I hate to see all this good money go to a stranger, so I'm going to take sixty-two and one half thousand dollars' worth of that free stock myself. I declare myself in. You hear me?"

By the time Mr. Meers was through talking Wallingford was delighted so far as surface went, though he was already doing some intense figuring.

"I don't know but that it's a good thing you came to see me," he admitted. "However, I hope it don't strike you that I intend to give you half a nice ripe peach without a good reason for it. What do I get for letting you in?"

"That's a fair question. I guess you noticed that if we want to cut a melon or open a keg of nails over in my place we don't go down in the cellar?"

"I certainly did," admitted the big man with a grin.

"Well, that's it. I'm permanent alderman from the fifth ward, and every time they hold an election they come and ask me whether I want it served with mushrooms or tomato sauce. The job has belonged to me ever since I was old enough to lie about my age. What I say goes in the privilege line, and I guess a mere child could figure out what that privilege would be worth to the Retail Cigar Dealers' Consolidation; the dice box privilege; the back room privilege with a nice little poker game going on twenty-four hours a day; faro if I want it. Besides, I'm coming in just because. Why, I'm the man that stopped the ping pong game in this town so I could have a monopoly of it!"

"How soon can you be ready to incorporate?" asked Wallingford, satisfied to all external appearances; for this man could stop him. "To-morrow?"

"To-night, if you say so."

Wallingford laughed.

"It won't spoil over night," he said; "but there's just one thing I want to know. Is there anybody else to cut in on this?"

In reply, Mr. Meers slowly drew down the under lid of his right eye to show that there was no green in it, and when they parted an hour or so later it was with mutual, even hilarious expressions of good will. Immediately thereafter, however, Wallingford retired within himself and spent long, long hours in thought.

CHAPTER XXVIII

THE name of Meers was magic. It is
quite probable that the magnetic Wallingford would have been able to
carry through his proposed consolidation alone; but with the fifth ward alderman
to back him his work was easy. A few of the
small dealers were afraid of Meers, but they
were also afraid to stay out; for the most part,
however, they were glad to enter into any combination with him, particularly since it was
tacitly understood that this would open up to
them the much coveted "ping pong" privilege,
an attraction which not only increased the sale
of goods but gave an additional hundred per
cent. of profit.

The first steps in the incorporation were
taken the next day after the interview of Wallingford and Meers, and within a few days the
Retail Cigar Dealers' Consolidation was for-
mally effected, even to the trifling little mum-
meries which covered the state's requirement

431

of a certain percentage of "fully paid up stock." Wallingford's share of the initial expense was one hundred dollars, but he had no mind to give up any of his precious pocket money at this time.

"Suppose you just pay the whole bill yourself, and let us pay you," he suggested in an offhand way to Meers. "It looks so much better all in one lump."

Of course, Mr. Meers was agreeable to this eminently respectable suggestion; but when Wallingford handed over his own check it was dated a week ahead.

"If this won't do you I'll have to give up some cash," he explained with an easy laugh. "I'm having some securities negotiated back East to open an account here, and it may take three or four days to have it arranged."

Meers heard him with a curious smile.

"I beat a pleasant stranger's head off once for putting up a line of talk like that," he commented; "but, of course, this is different," and he took the check.

He had become an enthusiastic admirer of Wallingford's undoubted genius, and at nothing was he more amused than by the caliber of the three other incorporators who had been chosen. Stock valuations were at once made

"Your Fine Little Wife Here Swears that It Will."

for these three, at an exaggerated estimate of the value of their concerns, and when they came to Meers himself the same plan was followed.

"For," said Wallingford, "to make this strong you have to come in just like the rest, and I have to take up the balance of the stock right now as trustee."

Meers balked a trifle at that.

"I never feel so cheerful as when I'm my own stakeholder," he stated frankly. "When I hold all the coin it's a cinch I'll get mine, but when somebody else holds it I keep trained down for a foot race."

"Fix it any way to suit yourself," offered Wallingford with a carelessness that he was far from feeling. "If you can figure out a better stunt, show it to me."

Mr. Meers tried earnestly to think of a better plan but was forced to concede that there was none.

"Oh, well," he gave in at last, "it don't matter. It's only for a week or so I'll have to rub salve on my fingers to cure that itch."

"Certainly," Wallingford assured him. "It won't take more than a week, after we get the stock certificates from the printers, to make all the transfers, and then we'll have from a hundred and twenty to a hundred and forty thousand dollars' worth to split up. If we can't make that yield us five or six thousand a year apiece, aside from salaries, the buying and manufacturing grafts and other rake-offs, we ought to have guardians appointed.''

"Fine business," agreed Meers complacently.

That complacency, which meant forgetfulness of the fact that all the stock would be temporarily in Wallingford's hands and under his absolute legal mastery, was what J. Rufus wished to encourage, and to that end he arranged for "secret" meetings of the Retail Cigar Dealers during the constructive period. Here the promoter was at his best. Singly, his big impressiveness dominated men; in masses, he swayed them. Enthusiasm was raised to fever heat. Even the smallest among these men grew large. Individually they were poor; collectively they were rich. Outside the consolidation not one of them amounted to much; inside it each one was a part of a millionaire! In the business of cigar selling a new era had come, and its name was Wallingford! By the close of the second meeting, scarcely a small dealer in the town but had signed the cleverly worded agreement.

It was while the stock certificates were being

printed that Wallingford, who almost lived in the resplendent carriage these days, drove up to Ed Nickel's place of business, at a time when both the flabby solitaire player and the apathetic watcher had gone out to whatever mysterious place it was that they secured food.

"I say, Mr. Vice President," asked Wallingford, addressing the amazingly spruced up Mr. Nickel quite as an equal, "do you know where I could buy a nice house? One for about fifteen thousand?"

"I don't know, I'm sure," regretted Nickel, pleased to be taken thus into the great Wallingford's intimacy, "but there ought to be plenty of them. I wish I could figure on a house like that."

"Stick to me and see what happens to you," advised Wallingford with no thought of the joke he was uttering. "There's no reason you shouldn't have anything you want if you just go after the big game. Watch me."

"But you've got money," protested the Vice President.

"Did I always have it?" demanded the eminent financier. "Every cent I have, Mr. Nickel, I made myself; and you can do the same. The trouble is, you don't go in big enough. You have only a thousand dollars worth of stock in our consolidation, for instance. You ought to have at least ten thousand."

"I haven't the money," said Nickel.

"How much have you?"

"Just a shade over five thousand. Say, man, I'm forty-six years old and I been slavin' like a dog ever since I was sixteen. Thirty years it took me to scrape that five thousand together."

"Saved it!" snorted Wallingford. "No wonder you haven't but five thousand. You can't make money that way. You have to invest. Do you suppose Rockefeller *saved* his first million? Tell you what I'll do, Nickel. Can you keep a secret?"

"Sure," asserted Mr. Nickel, with the eagerness of one who has never been entrusted with a secret of consequence.

"If you want it and will pay for it on delivery next Saturday, I can scheme it for you to take up an extra five thousand dollars' worth of stock in the consolidation; but if I do you must not say one word about it to any one until after everything is settled, or some of these other fellows will be jealous. There's Meers, for instance. He's crazy right now to take over every share of the surplus, but, between you and I, we don't want him to have such a big finger in the pie."

"I should say not," agreed Mr. Nickel emphatically. "He's too big as it is. Why, he pretty near runs this town."

"He can't run the consolidation; I'll tell him that!" declared Mr. Wallingford with much apparent heat. "It's *my* project and I'll favor whoever I want to. But about this stock, old man. You think it over, and if you want it let me know by not later than to-day noon. If it isn't spoken for by that time I'll take it myself; but remember, not one word!"

Mr. Nickel promised, on his honor as a man and his self-interest as a favored stockholder, to say nothing, and Wallingford started out. At the door he turned back, however.

"By the way," said he, "when we get going I've made up my mind to push the Nickelfine and the Double Nickel brands. I've been trying those two boxes you gave me and they're great. But don't say anything. Jealousy, you know!"

Mr. Nickel put his finger to his lips and smiled and bowed significantly. Fine man, that Wallingford! Knew a good thing when he saw it, and easy as an old shoe in spite of all his money. Regular howling swell, too.

GET-RICH-QUICK

The regular howling swell was at that very
moment on his rubber-tired way to the shop of
Alfred Norton, where he made a similar proposition to the one he had made Nickel. In all
his manipulating he had kept careful track of
the gentlemen who had or who might have
money, and now he made it his business to visit
each of them in turn, to talk additional stock
with them and bind them to inviolate secrecy.
For three days he kept this up, and on Friday
evening was able to mop his brow in content.

"Fanny," he opined, "you have a smart husband."

"That's the only fault I have to find with
you, Jim," she retorted smiling. "What have
you done this time?"

"I've just tapped Mr. Joseph O. Meers on
the solar plexus," he exulted. "I'll show that
gentleman how to horn into my game and take
the rake-off that's coming to a real artist! He's
dreaming happy dreams just now, but when I
leave town with the mezuma he'll wake up."

"I thought you were going to stay here," she
objected with a troubled frown.

He understood her at once, and reached over
to stroke her hair.

"Never mind, girl," he said. "I'm as anxious now as you are to settle down," and he

glanced at the fluffy white sewing in her lap; "but this isn't the town. I had a nice clean business planned here, but the village grafter tried to jiu-jitsu me, so I just naturally had to jolt him one. I'll clean up about a hundred thousand to-morrow, and with that I'll go anywhere you say and into any business you pick out. Suppose we go back to Battlesburg, clear off that mortgage on your house and settle down there?"

"Oh, will you?" she asked eagerly. "But who loses this money, Jim?" she suddenly wanted to know. "I'm more particular than ever about it just now. I don't want to take a dollar that isn't right."

Again he understood.

"Don't worry about that," he replied seriously. "This money is legitimate water that I am sopping up out of a reorganization, just like a Harriman or a Morgan. The drag-down I get is simply my pay as promoter and organizer, and is no bigger percentage than other promoters take when they get a chance."

He had never taken so much pains to justify himself in her eyes, and she felt that this was due to a new tenderness. What if the wonderful influence that was dawning upon their lives should make a permanent change in him?

There came a knock at the door. Wallingford opened it and was confronted by a tall and stoutly built gentleman, who wore a blue helmet and numerous brass buttons upon his clothes.

"Mr. Wallingford," said the caller, with a laborious wink and a broad brogue, "could ye step across to the Court House wid me a few minutes and sign them papers?" and when Wallingford had stepped outside, he added: " 'Twas on account of the lady I told ye that, but on the level, I'm after arrestin' yez!"

"What's the charge?" asked Wallingford with a tolerant smile, knowing his entire innocence of wrong.

"Obtainin' money under false pretenses."

Wallingford whistled, and, still unworried, excused himself for a moment. His statement to his wife was characteristic.

"I'll be back in about an hour," he said, "but I don't feel safe with so much wealth in my clothes when I'm out with a policeman," and with a laugh he tossed into her lap practically all the money that he had—an even fifty dollars.

Of course Wallingford sent immediately for Joseph O. Meers, and that gentleman came at once.

WALLINGFORD

"Lovely place to find your old college chum," the prisoner cheerfully remarked. "I wish you'd go find out what this charge is all about and get me out of this, Meers. It might hurt the consolidation if it becomes known. There's a mistake some place."

"Oh, is there?" Mr. Meers wanted to know. "I'll bet there ain't a mistake, because I'm the baby that secured the warrant, and I'm going to send you over. Tried to double cross me, didn't you?" he asked pleasantly. "Well, it can't be done. Any grafter that tries to hand me the worst of it is going to find himself sucking at the sour end of a lemon, —— quick. So I was to be the mark, eh? Just because there wasn't a paper signed between us to show that I was entitled to half that surplus stock, you was going to sell the bunch of it and make a quick get-away. I was to be the fall guy for that nice little futurity check, too! You remember that little old hundred, don't you? Well, it got you. I was hep to you day before yesterday, but your date didn't run out on that check till to-day, so I waited; and I'm going to send you over the road for as long a stretch as a good lawyer can hand you. Now stay here and rot!" and Joseph O. Meers, highly pleased with himself, walked out.

GET-RICH-QUICK

Jail! Mr. J. Rufus Wallingford, to whom tufted carpets and soft leather chairs were not luxuries but necessities, looked around him with the nearest substitute for a "game" grin that he could muster, and the prophetic words of Blackie Daw occurred to him:

"Our turn's next!"

"It's a fine joke I played on myself," he mused. "Me that a few weeks ago had a million in sight and that two hours ago had a hundred thousand cinched for to-morrow, to lose out like this; *and for a hundred dollars!*"

That was the rub! To think that after all these years, during which he had conducted his pleasant and legally safe financial recreations with other people's money upon a scale large enough to live like a gentleman, his first introduction to a jail should be because of a miserable, contemptible hundred dollars! *Why* had he forgotten that check? *Why* had he been fool enough to think he could swear a lot of spineless jelly fish to secrecy? *Why* hadn't he been content with half? It served him right, he admitted, and unless Meers relented, the penitentiary yawned its ugly mouth very close to him. At any rate, he was now a full-fledged member of the largest organization in the world —the Down and Out Club. It was queer that

442

in all this thought there came no trace of regret for what he had done; there came only regret for the consequences, only self-revilement
that he had "overlooked a bet." His "conscience" did not reproach him at all, except for
failure; for, monstrous as it may seem, to his
own mind he had done no wrong! Nor had he
meant any wrong! With no sense of moral ob-
ligation whatever—and no more to be blamed
for that than another man is for being born
hunchbacked—he merely looked upon himself
as smarter than most men, doing just what they
would have done had they been blessed with
the ability. Only at last he had been unfortunate! Well, the joke was on him, and he must
be a good loser.

The humor of the situation rather wore off
when, after a night upon a hard pallet and a
breakfast of dry bread and weak coffee, he sent
a message to Ed Nickel and learned from that
indignantly virtuous citizen that he would have
nothing to do with swindlers! Then he sent
word to his wife and the answer he got to that
message was the last straw. Mrs. Wallingford
had quitted the hotel early that morning! He
was sure of her, however. She would turn up
again in her own good time, but what could she
do? Nothing! For the first time in his life,

the man who had never thought to have need
of a friend outside a few moral defectives of
his own class, realized what it is to be absolutely friendless. There was no one left in all
this wide world upon whom he could make any
demand of loyalty. Blackie Daw a fugitive,
Billy Riggs a convict, all the old clan scattered
far and wide, either paying their penalty, or,
having transgressed the law, fleeing from it, the
universe had come to an end.

Hour after hour he spent in trying to think
of some one to whom he could appeal, and the
conviction gradually burned itself in upon him
that at last he was "up against it." It was
a bad mess. He had made no deposit whatever
in the local bank upon which he had drawn that
check, though he had intended to do so. Moreover, Meers, to prove fraudulent intent, could
show his intended bad faith in the other matter
between them; and besides all that the alderman cigar dealer had a "pull" of no mean proportions. It had seemed impossible, the night
before, that he who had dealt only in thousands
and hundreds of thousands should be made a
felon for a paltry hundred. It had seemed too
absurd to be true, an anomalous situation that
a day would clear up and at which he could
afterwards laugh. Even now he joked with the

turnkey, and that guardian of social recalcitrants was profoundly convinced that in J. Rufus Wallingford he had the swellest prisoner upon whom he had ever slid a bolt. The policeman who arrested him and the judge who next morning remanded him for trial shared that opinion, but it was a very melancholy satisfaction. After his preliminary hearing he went from the city prison to a more "comfortable" cell in the county jail, to think a number of very deep thoughts. Not a friendly eye had been turned on him but that of Joseph O. Meers, who had come around to see the fun. Mr. Meers had been quite jovial with him, had handed him a good cigar and told him the latest developments in the Retail Cigar Dealers' Consolidation. He was reorganizing it himself. It was really a good "stunt," and he thanked J. Rufus most effusively for having started it. This was "kidding" of a broad-gauge type that Wallingford, for the same reason that a gambler tries to look pleased when he loses his money, was bound to enjoy very much, and with right good wit he replied in kind; but in this exchange of humor he was very much handicapped, for really Meers had all the joke on his side.

Another restless night and another dreary

day, and then, just as he had begun to sincerely pity himself as a forlorn castaway upon the barrenest shore of all living things, there came visitors for him, and the turnkey with much deference threw open his cell and led him out to the visitor's cage. His wife! Well, he had expected her, and he had expected, too, since this great new tenderness had come upon her, to find her eyes suffused with bravely suppressed tears as they now were; but he had never expected to see again the man who was with her. E. B. Lott! the man to whom he had once sold rights of way to a traction line which he had never intended to build! one of his most profitable victims!

"So they got you at last, did they, Wallingford?" said Lott briskly, and shook hands with him, positive pleasure in the meeting beaming from his grizzled countenance. "I expected they would. A nice little game you played on me up in Battlesburg, wasn't it? Well, my boy, it was worth the money. You really had a valuable right of way, with valuable franchises and concessions, and the Lewisville, Battlesburg and Elliston Traction Line is doing a ripping business; so I'll forgive you, especially since you're not an individual criminal at all. You're only the logical development of the American tendency to 'get there' no matter how. It is the national weakness, the national menace, and you're only an exaggerated molecule of it. You think that so long as you stay inside the *law* you're all right, even morally; but a man who habitually shaves so close to the narrow edge is going to slip off some time. Now you've had your dose and I shouldn't wonder but it *might* make a man of you. Your fine little wife here, who hunted me up the minute she found out your real predicament, swears that it will, but I'm not sure. You're too valuable, though, to coop up in a penitentiary, and I'm going to buy you off. I can use you. I've been in the traction business ever since the first trolley touched a wire, and I never yet have seen a man who could go out and get a right of way for nothing, as you did, nor get it in so short a space of time, even for money. We expect to open up two thousand miles of lines this coming year and I'm going to put you on the job. I can't fix it to make you such quick riches as you can rake in on crooked deals, but I'll guarantee you will have more in the end. It's a great chance for you, my boy, and just to protect you against yourself I'm going to hire a good man to watch you."

GET-RICH-QUICK

Wallingford had already regained his breadth of chest, and now he began to laugh. His shoulders heaved and the hundred jovial wrinkles about his eyes creased with the humor of the thought that had come to him.

"You'd better hire three," he suggested, "and work them in eight-hour shifts."

Nevertheless there was a bit of moisture in his eyes, and his hand, dropping down, sought his wife's. Perhaps in that moment he vaguely promised himself some effort toward a higher ideal, but the woman at his side, though knowing what she knew, though herself renewed and made over wholly with that great new reason, though detecting the presence of the crippled moral sense that was falling back baffled from its feeble assault upon his soul, pressed her other palm over his hand protectingly and shook her head—for at last she understood!

Upon thistles grow no roses.

THE END

448